JO DERESKE

MISS ZUKAS SHELVES THE EVIDENCE

AVON BOOKS
An Imprint of HarperCollins*Publishers*

This is a work of fiction. Names, characters, places, and incidents are products of the author's imagination or are used fictitiously and are not to be construed as real. Any resemblance to actual events, locales, organizations, or persons, living or dead, is entirely coincidental.

AVON BOOKS
An Imprint of HarperCollins*Publishers*
10 East 53rd Street
New York, New York 10022-5299

Copyright © 2001 by Jo Dereske
ISBN: 0-380-80474-3
www.avonbooks.com

First Avon Books paperback printing: February 2001

Avon Trademark Reg. U.S. Pat. Off. and in Other Countries, Marca Registrada, Hecho en U.S.A.
HarperCollins® is a trademark of HarperCollins Publishers Inc.

Printed in the U.S.A.

10 9 8 7 6 5 4 3 2 1

For K., my light

And with gratitude to
Ruth Baacke

CONTENTS

❄ *chapter one* ❄

THE
UNCLOUDED BROW

On Sunday afternoon Miss Helma Zukas dressed for an event she'd never experienced, surprisingly enough, in all her thirty-nine years. She stood before the full-length mirror in her bedroom, briefly clad, holding first a light blue button-up blouse on a hanger in front of her and then a green long-sleeved cotton pullover. Behind her, spread neatly and wrinkle-free on her bed, lay a khaki skirt.

Indecisiveness was not a state of mind Helma Zukas was accustomed to, and frankly, she was puzzled by her rising frustration. In fact, she routinely made more critical decisions with less consternation than it was now taking to select her attire.

"Just choose one," she whispered aloud to her reflection, which held a crisply pressed garment in each hand, then closed her lips tightly. Talking to herself was another habit she'd never acquired, even though it was what George Melville, the cataloger at Bellehaven Public Library, called an occupational hazard of working in a library. "An affliction that overtakes the sanest of us," he pronounced.

She caught a glimpse of black low in her mirror, reflecting from the floor of the open doorway of her bedroom, but when she spun around, holding the two garments strategically in front of her, the doorway was empty; Boy Cat Zukas had disappeared. The black former alley cat was allowed inside her apartment as far as the wicker basket Helma had placed near her balcony door, no farther. But she'd found evidence Boy Cat Zukas had no patience for her rules and stretched his boundaries when she wasn't looking: cat hair on the bathroom rug, a depression on a chair cushion, and once, even a tuft of feathers in her hallway.

The blue blouse was more attractive—she knew it emphasized the Baltic blue of her eyes—but the green pullover wouldn't wrinkle as easily. Helma didn't even know where they were going; maybe they wouldn't go anywhere at all, only sit on her balcony and gaze out at Washington Bay, talking companionably. It was warm enough, the sun still high in the sky so it wouldn't shine in their eyes, and today the air was clear, cleanly washed by last night's rain. Summer had slid into autumn, bright clear days that remained overwarm for the Pacific Northwest, similar to the Indian summers from Helma's Michigan childhood. Beyond the blue waters of Washington Bay, the near and distant islands followed one after the other to the horizon, green treed humps fading to mounds of blue.

Helma was prepared either way: to go or to stay. Freshly cut carrot and celery sticks, radishes and jicama slices, were arranged on a plastic-covered platter on the top shelf of her refrigerator next to a selection of diet and regular soda pop, bottled water, and white wine. Pretzels, corn chips, and a bright red box of cheese crackers sat on her counter. Matching bowls, one containing mints and the other mixed nuts—without peanuts—sat on the coffee table in her living room, along with white paper napkins and cloth coasters. A Vivaldi CD her cousin Ruby had sent her issued cheery notes of "Summer" through her apartment.

The doorbell pealed and Helma gasped, glancing at the red digital numbers on the clock radio beside her bed: 1:41. Chief of Police Wayne Gallant and his two children weren't due until two o'clock. This was surprising; he knew she was as annoyed by guests arriving too early as she was by people who were tardy.

But the children. Children were an unknown factor, mysteries Helma unintentionally encountered in stores and parks or when they wandered into the adult area of the library. Aside from her nephews, she didn't know any on a personal basis. The children might have thrown off Wayne Gallant's schedule or even been impatient to meet her. Whatever, it couldn't be helped now.

The doorbell rang again, and Helma opted for the green pullover so she didn't have to waste time buttoning, and pulled on her khaki skirt, zipping and tucking as she slipped her feet into a new pair of brown loafers, stopping once to straighten the leather that was curling beneath her left heel.

She smoothed her hand across her hair, tucking down the stubborn curl on the left side of her head as she hurried down the hallway and through her living room, casting a glance at the casually aligned pillows, the fanned magazines, stopping once to nudge the coffee table square on the carpet. The bay shimmered; happy voices rose from Boardwalk Park at the edge of the water and through the open door onto her balcony. The bell was rudely rung again. Wayne Gallant was seldom so impatient.

But when Helma opened her apartment door, it wasn't Bellehaven's chief of police and his two children who stood on her doormat, it was the new neighbor who'd moved into Mrs. Whitney's old apartment next door.

"Mr. Stone," Helma said, peering behind him to the third floor landing, still somehow expecting to see

Wayne Gallant and the two children she'd only seen in photographs.

Mr. Stone was agitated. He rubbed his jaw, pulling at his grizzled skin, then wiped his thick hand over his brush cut. Gray hair sprang up behind his hand like newly cut grass. His mouth worked, lips pursing, then sucked between his teeth. He'd moved into 3E the week before, bounding again and again up the three flights of outside stairs of the Bayside Arms despite there being an elevator, whistling, his arms full of cardboard boxes. Again and again.

That first day, he'd stopped Helma as she left her apartment. Balancing a box of kitchenware in one arm, he thrust a large hand toward her. "I'm your new neighbor," he told her. "TNT."

"Tiente?" Helma asked, watching her hand disappear into his.

"Nah, like the dynamite." He dropped her hand and made single-handed explosion motions. "TNT." He leaned toward her. "You know, TNT Stone." He was barrel chested, lumpy-faced, thick-necked. Gray hair curled over the neck of his gray sweatshirt. *Love a fighter* and a pair of boxing gloves decorated the chest of his sweatshirt. Helma guessed him to be in his early sixties.

"Are you a pugilist?" she'd asked diplomatically, phrasing the question in the present tense.

For a moment he frowned, then shrugged almost apologetically, as if he were embarrassed for her that she didn't know. He laughed a deep-voiced gurgle that came from the depths of his chest. "Not anymore. But I can't expect you to know who's dropped in and out of the ring." He grinned modestly. "I spar now and then. The Golden Gloves days are behind me."

"You won a Golden Gloves award?" Helma asked.

He pinched thumb and forefinger a quarter inch apart. "That close. Now I just fight to stay ahead of the big guy with the scythe."

Helma had heard rhythmic bumping each morning and evening coming from TNT Stone's apartment and had once seen, and felt the vibration of, TNT jumping rope on his tiny balcony before Walter David, the manager, had politely requested that he stop.

She'd seen TNT jogging in the park, a towel wrapped around his neck and earphones over his head, perspiration staining his sweats. He jogged up and down the steps of the Bayside Arms punching the air, and within two days was calling out to apartment dwellers by name. Mrs. Dayton, who was widowed and lived beneath TNT Stone in 2E, had taken to leisurely sweeping her landing whenever he "did" the steps. Helma had overheard Mr. Ritter in 1C ask Walter David, "How do I disconnect that guy's battery?"

But now the customary smile was gone. TNT Stone pulled his hand away from his hair and exhaled a deep breath. He looked beseechingly at Helma and said, "I need a woman."

Helma took a step backward, her hand searching behind her for her doorknob. "I beg your pardon?"

TNT raised his wiry eyebrows. "I said I need—" He stopped and lightly punched his own chin, tipping his head to the side as if he'd just delivered a powerful smack to himself. "Not like that, honey. Not that way. Nope. It's my daughter—my stepdaughter, if you want to know the truth, but I love that little girl like she sprang from my own . . ." He made a gesture downward, then raised his hand to his chest. ". . . you know."

"She's hurt?" Helma asked, glancing down toward the parking lot, not seeing or hearing an injured girl.

He shook his head. "She's crying. I can't stand it when a woman cries, you know what I mean? What's a guy supposed to do? You can't just fix everything and turn it off like that." TNT snapped his fingers and then punched his right fist into his left palm. "I mean, how do you stop it? She needs to talk to a woman. Come over, would you?

She's in my apartment." He pointed toward the next door on the landing, using his whole arm like a figure of doom.

Again Helma glanced down toward the parking lot, then at her watch. The chief and his children should arrive in fourteen minutes. "I'm expecting company at two o'clock," she told TNT.

"Plenty of time, then," he said, his craggy face brightening, already turning toward his apartment. "All you have to do is tell her to stop crying. She'll listen to you. It'll just take a jiffy. Turn off the waterworks; that's it, and I'll take it from there. I can't reason with somebody who's bawling like her heart's broke."

"Is it?" Helma asked, not moving to follow.

"Is what?" TNT asked, stepping impatiently back to Helma. "Oh, you mean her heart? Broken? Maybe, but I don't see why. The guy was almost as old as me."

"Mr. Stone," Helma said, enunciating clearly, her voice edging toward the silver-dime timbre she used on out-of-control library patrons, "I'm expecting company any minute. Besides, I can't leave my apartment unlocked."

"You go in," he said, bowing toward his apartment door. "I'll stay out here and guard your apartment and wait for your company, okay?"

"But—" Helma began.

His craggy face softened to pleading. "Ah, it'll just take a minute. I'll owe you. She's a good kid."

"But her romance ended?" Helma asked, taking a small step onto her plastic doormat.

"Permanently," he said. "The guy's dead."

"What?" she exclaimed. "Her boyfriend died?"

"Her husband."

"Her husband," Helma repeated, staring down the walkway toward his open apartment door. "Mr. Stone. I can't just intrude on her grief. She doesn't even know me."

"Please. I need your help. I don't know what else to do."

Helma stepped tentatively past TNT, checking the left pocket of her khaki skirt for a tissue.

"I'm watching your apartment. You go ahead now." TNT assumed a vigilant pose between their apartments, crossing his arms over his thick chest. "Let me know when it's safe to come back."

✤ chapter two ✤

SHADOW OF A SIGH

The door of TNT Stone's apartment stood
ajar about twelve inches. Helma glanced back at the ex-
boxer and he nodded encouragement, a smile on his face
that was half grimace. Soft sobbing came from inside,
and Helma took a deep breath before tapping lightly on
the wooden door, realizing she didn't even know TNT's
stepdaughter's name. It was too late now because the sobbing abruptly halted, followed by a sniff, then a hesitant,
"Who is it?"

"My name is Miss Wilhelmina Zukas," Helma said,
still outside the door. She couldn't see the woman but
the voice sounded young. "I live in the next apartment.
Your stepfather asked me to speak to you." Helma
waited for a moment, but there was no response. TNT
again nodded encouragement. "May I come in?" she
asked.

The reply was muffled. "I don't care."

Helma pushed open the door and entered TNT's apartment. It was the first time she'd been inside since he
moved into the Bayside Arms, and in the living room
where Mrs. Whitney had sat crocheting and knitting in
her flowered chair, surrounded by bright crafts and her
collections of dolls, stood a large screen television. Opposite it sat an oversized brown leather recliner. Domi-
nating the remaining space was a metal contraption that

at first glance resembled a complicated cage but which after a moment Helma recognized as expensive exercise equipment she'd seen advertised on television. A stack of folded white towels sat on the floor beside the equipment, two more draped across a metal crosspiece. Instead of a dining table and chairs, a single tall stool was pushed beneath the kitchen counter. There were no pictures on the walls, no rugs on the floors, not a book or magazine in sight.

TNT's stepdaughter sat hunched on the edge of the leather recliner, one of the white towels held close to her face, covering her mouth.

She was slender, dressed in white shorts and a blue scoop-necked cotton shirt that was a size tighter than Helma Zukas liked to wear her shirts. Her dark hair tangled around her face, strands sticking against her teary cheeks. Remnants of her makeup stained the towel. After glancing once at Helma, she rocked back and forth, then moaned into her towel and squeezed her eyes closed.

Helma knelt beside the chair, "I'm so sorry about your husband."

The young woman nodded. Tears squeezed from the corners of her closed eyes. They remained in that pose for a few minutes until Helma placed her hand on the woman's shoulder then gradually, slowly, the crying subsided. "Would you like to talk about what happened?" she asked.

The young woman pulled the towel away from her face, and Helma recognized her as a frequent patron of the Bellehaven Public Library. She didn't know her name but she recalled the woman's interest: British literature, nineteenth century specifically, and even more specifically, George Eliot and her literary views of rural society. Helma remembered because the subject was so incongruous with her appearance as . . . well, as a carefree young woman.

The woman hiccuped and studied Helma's face as she

twisted the towel in her hands. "Oh," she said. "you're that librarian. You found the Spencer quote for me. Why did TNT ask you to come talk to me?"

"I live in the next apartment," Helma repeated. She shifted on her knees. "He was worried about you."

"You mean he panicked because I was crying." A brief expression, almost a smile, crossed her face.

"Naturally he's upset," Helma told her. "I'm sorry but I don't recall your name, only your reading tastes."

"Mary Lynn," she answered, her voice catching on another hiccup. "Mary Lynn Dixon. My husband, Lewis . . ." For proof and explanation, she held up her left hand where a gem-encrusted gold band intricately encircled a second ring: a diamond that Helma's friend Ruth would have pronounced "a godawful boulder."

Mary Lynn was quite beautiful, fragile-appearing, with fair skin contrasting against her dark curling hair, the kind of woman who reminded Helma of fairy tales and stories of consumptive women. Her blue eyes held a curious watery light. She might have been thirty but Helma doubted it. More likely in her mid- to late twenties. And had TNT said she married a man as old as he was?

Helma rose and said, "I'll make you a cup of tea," then remembering she was in TNT's apartment, not her own, she amended, "or find you something to drink." Mary Lynn nodded.

In TNT's kitchen, which was in the reverse order of her own, she opened the cupboard where Mrs. Whitney had kept her tea and found it completely bare. In the next cupboard one shelf was laden with bottles of vitamins and supplements and the other with three different brands of powdered protein drinks.

She couldn't find a teakettle or a coffee maker. A heavy-looking white machine called a Juice-o-matic sat on the counter next to a microwave and a large box of straws. There were juices in the refrigerator but none with straightforward names she recognized. Finally she found a shelf of dishware: three mismatched plates, four mugs, and three glasses. She chose a glass and rinsed it before filling it with water and taking it to Mary Lynn, who drank half of it immediately.

"When did your husband die?" Helma gently asked.

"This morning." Mary Lynn dabbed at her eyes with the towel, "I still can't believe it. I couldn't find the newspaper. I like to sleep in and he was an early riser; he usually left the paper beside my coffee cup. After he read it, he always put it back in order, each section inside the next, you'd never know it had been touched." She wiped at her cheek, smearing a black stream of mascara, speaking disjointedly, delaying the heart of her story. "But it wasn't there. I like to read the news every morning. Does that make me anachronistic? Most of the news is on the twenty-four-hour TV channel. The top stories, I mean. Anytime you care to watch it. But I'd rather not have to be so attentive; you can interrupt a newspaper." Mary Lynn drank the remaining water and lowered her voice. "He was on the ground beside his tomatoes, already . . . I was too late." She gazed at the floor in the same horror as if she were reliving the scene in her husband's garden, then she turned to Helma beseechingly. "I called an ambulance anyway, but . . . if I hadn't slept in . . . or if I'd gone looking for him right away . . ." She peered wildly around the room.

"That probably wouldn't have changed the outcome," Helma assured her. And she added, thinking sadly how trite but true it was, "These things happen so quickly." She patted Mary Lynn's arm and Mary Lynn grasped her hand.

"That's what the ambulance driver told me, too. He said it was probably a heart attack. Lewis exercised and he ate right, but he took medication for arrhythmia—an irregular heartbeat. Mother said I shouldn't have married a man so old but I never thought of him that way. Not *old*." She clung to Helma's hand, squeezing it so tightly that Helma's knuckles pinched.

"You were happy," Helma said.

A slight smile crossed Mary Lynn's blotched face. "Very. I didn't expect to be. Lewis was funny, too. A lot of people didn't see that because his humor was so quiet. He had a way of waiting until just the right moment. . . ." The smile faded and Mary Lynn's lip began to quiver.

"Would you like me to call your mother?" Helma asked as she gently disentangled her hand from Mary Lynn's.

"She was already there," Mary Lynn said. She jiggled her leg the way Helma had seen restless young children in the library do. "She's always there. And besides, she'd never come here. She hates TNT because I decided to live with him instead of her when they divorced. They don't speak to each other anymore, only *about* each other."

This was more than Helma felt she was privileged to hear. Under the stress of losing her husband, Mary Lynn was relating personal information she might regret later. Helma politely stopped listening and surreptitiously glanced at her watch.

Four minutes until two o'clock. Any minute now the chief and his two children would arrive. Joseph was fourteen, Cynthia—Cindy, the chief said she liked to be called—had just turned thirteen. Over the past four years, Helma had watched them grow up through the photos on the chief of police's desk. They lived with their mother in Oregon, and Wayne Gallant visited them or arranged for them to visit him as often as possible. But never had he introduced them to Helma.

Ruth called it a "major move," the equivalent to being

taken home to meet mother. Helma wasn't so sure. She and the chief weren't exactly participating in a serious romance, but they *were* close, she'd admit that.

In preparation for meeting his children, Helma had read a book titled *Raising a Happy Teenager*, and attempted to watch music videos on television but surrendered after ten minutes. She supposed being a teenager today wasn't that much different from when she was young, and that had only been twenty years ago.

"Will the hospital call me after it's finished?" Mary Lynn asked, and Helma jerked in surprise, horrified that her mind had spun off on its own while poor Mary Lynn Dixon struggled with the reality of her husband's death. After what was finished? An autopsy?

"I'm sure you'll be kept apprised of every aspect that you're entitled to," Helma assured her.

Mary Lynn nodded, blotting her forehead, then her neck. "Thank you. I'm grateful TNT asked you to come in."

"I hope—" Helma began. Voices from the landing brought her to her feet, unconsciously smoothing down the front of her skirt and checking to be sure the back of her pullover was tucked in.

It was exactly two o'clock according to her watch, which she'd set to match the Official U.S. Time on the National Institute of Standards and Technology website.

"Who is it?" Mary Lynn asked, standing too, following Helma.

Helma stepped onto the landing of TNT Stone's apartment, her lips parted to explain to Mary Lynn it was the chief of police here for his afternoon with her, when she was stopped dead by the sight of the two young people standing, no, slouching, behind Wayne Gallant.

The boy, his hands stuffed in his pockets, his shoulders rounded, gazed above their heads as if none of them existed. He was handsome, she suspected, but his expression was so blank as to be anonymous, the planes of his face still emerging from childhood softness. His jeans were several sizes too large, draping over his feet so that only the toes of his black sneakers showed. His black t-shirt hung nearly to his knees. He might have been as tall as Wayne Gallant; Helma couldn't tell by the way he slumped against the railing. His hair was honey blond and looked like it had been whirled through a blender.

The girl, in tight red shorts and an equally tight top that exposed her navel, had darker hair, more like her father's; in fact it was so dark and unreflective Helma suspected it had been dyed. It was cut in a style that would have been becoming on her brother. The same shade of inexpertly applied black makeup rimmed her eyes and lips. She would be attractive but she wasn't yet, still awkwardly prepubescent while rushing toward her teenage self. There was no mistaking the expression on her face. Helma didn't need a book on teenage temperament to decipher it. She glared at Helma as if Helma were trying to swipe her most cherished possession.

To the side, TNT watched them, scratching his shoulder, curiosity plain on his face. "I told him where you were," he said to Helma.

Wayne Gallant half turned toward his children, raising his hand, a frown on his face. He was a big man, broad-shouldered, the kind of man who would develop a stomach if he didn't remain active, which he did. Mostly Helma saw him in more formal clothes but today he wore khakis and a cotton shirt. She'd heard women refer to him as handsome, but the feature she had first noticed was his eyes: intense, quick to change from piercing policeman's eyes to a softer gaze, even a humorous twinkle. Today his eyes appeared perplexed. "These are my—" he began.

Behind Helma, Mary Lynn Dixon gasped a breath that issued forth as a small scream. "The chief of police," she cried, pointing to Wayne Gallant. "Are you here be- cause— Was Lewis *murdered*?"

❧ *chapter three* ❧

ALONG THE BRINY BEACH

The two young people didn't move, but the chief of police, TNT Stone, and Helma all reached out to steady Mary Lynn Dixon, who'd turned ashen and begun to sway precariously. TNT pulled her upright with such ease that Mary Lynn's feet lifted two inches above the landing floor.

"Breathe," Helma ordered Mary Lynn as she gripped her arm. "In for a count of four," she coached. "One. Two. Three. Four. Hold for four. Now exhale for a count of eight." Three times Mary Lynn dutifully followed Helma's instruction, until she stood upright and steady, blinking her eyes as if she'd just awakened. Helma nodded in approval. It worked for her every time, although she would have required at least four breaths to regain her composure. "But why are you . . ." Mary Lynn began, pointing to Wayne Gallant.

"Let's go back inside," Helma suggested, holding TNT Stone's apartment door open for Mary Lynn. "We can sit down and discuss this."

But of course, the only furniture in TNT's living room was the leather recliner where Mary Lynn sat

16

while the others, even the children, stood in a semicircle around her.

"Was he?" Mary Lynn asked the chief in a quavering voice, reaching for one of the towels lying on the arm of the chair; then, seeing TNT's stricken face, she dropped it and said, "I'm not going to cry again. I don't have any tears left."

"This is Mary Lynn Dixon," Helma told the chief. "Her husband died this morning." Behind him, the chief's son was sidling toward TNT's exercise apparatus, a spark of interest on his sullen face.

"Lewis," the chief said, nodding and briefly taking Mary Lynn's hand. "I was sorry to hear about his death but I understood from the first reports that it was a probable heart attack. I'm actually here to visit Helma."

"Oh," Mary Lynn said. "I jumped to conclusions. Seeing the chief of police at the door . . ."

"I have that effect on a lot of people," the chief told her.

"Will you be all right with your stepfather now?" Helma asked her.

TNT nervously stepped forward. "I'll call one of your friends, okay? Who do you want to talk to? Ginny? Sara Hill? She's a bright girl."

Mary Lynn shook her head and TNT's voice cracked in desperation. He rose up and down on his toes as if he were performing warm-up exercises. "Okay, what about that kid you used to bring to all my fights? The one who sparred with us sometimes. What was his name? Jiffy?"

"Skippy," Mary Lynn corrected. "Skip. Never mind. I'm fine."

TNT ran both hands across his head, one after the other. "But he's a nice kid. You used to talk about all those dead writers remember? You had a great time. And you two do that tutoring together; he'd be good for you, wouldn't he?" TNT urged.

"You can call him, I guess," Mary Lynn finally agreed as she blotted her eyes with the towel.

TNT joined his hands in a winner's clasp and glanced around the room. "Okay, that's what we're going to do. We have a plan. Where'd I put the phone book? Hey, kid, don't touch those weights."

Joseph looked up, his hand still hovering over a stack of weights shaped like bars that were attached to the machine.

"Joseph," the chief told his son. "You and your sister wait outside. We'll be right out."

Joseph shrugged and pulled his hand away from the exercise machine. He walked toward the door, elbowing his sister as he passed her. She muttered too softly for Helma to hear, then followed her brother onto the third floor landing. Neither looked back at the adults.

"That age, eh?" TNT said when the two teenagers had departed. "I remember . . . whoa, don't get me started." He pulled the phone book from under a gym bag sitting on his kitchen counter. "Here it is. What's Jiffy's last name again, honey?"

"Skip," Mary Lynn reminded him again. "It's Skip Riems and you don't have to call him. We're not that close . . ."

"Then how about your mother?"

"No. Definitely not."

Helma saw the brief look of satisfaction that crossed TNT's face. "Okay. Skip it is," he said, already punching out numbers on his red telephone, one finger on a page of the directory. "You need somebody your own age, not an old f— I mean, goat like me. Just be a minute."

Mary Lynn stood and pressed her palms to her face. When she took away her hands, white marks remained on her cheeks for a few seconds. "I'll be all right now, really," she told Helma and the chief. "It was the shock. Lewis and I . . . Some people didn't think it would work but we were very happy. I loved him."

Her lips trembled, and behind her, TNT, with the phone to his ear, said, "Now now."

"I'm okay," Mary Lynn assured him. TNT looked doubtful.

"I'll be home later this evening," Helma told her. "Please call me or come over if you'd like to talk."

TNT flashed Helma a grateful smile and a thumbs-up sign.

The chief's two children leaned against the third floor railing outside TNT's apartment, both wearing earphones, their eyes half closed, oblivious to their father and Helma's approach.

Helma took the moment to marvel how photographs only caught one instant, one minuscule segment, of a person's life, only an instantaneous likeness out of years of living. Until today, that was all she'd seen of the chief's two children: posed moments that had nothing to do with their personalities and lives. From their photos, she'd expected adolescents, naturally, but now she searched for a resemblance to their father in more than physical characteristics.

The chief tapped his son's shoulder and pantomimed removing the headset. Both did, leaving them around their necks like necklaces, and Helma heard rock music buzzing from the earphones as if from a great distance.

"Helma, this is my son, Joseph, and my daughter, Syndi," Wayne Gallant told her, briefly touching each child's shoulder firmly enough to pull them away from the railing toward Helma.

"Hello, Joseph," Helma said. She lifted her hand to shake his, but Joseph didn't even glance toward her offered hand, instead saluting her with two fingers to his forehead, catching his fingers in his tangled blond hair. "Yeah," he said. He mumbled syllables that sounded like, "Goodtameetya."

Helma turned to his daughter, who was the same

height as she, perhaps even an inch taller. "Hello, Cindy."

Syndi, whose short haircut exposed the same widow's peak her father kept covered, gazed at Helma without smiling. "You're saying my name wrong," she said.

"Cindy?" Helma repeated, puzzled. She was sure that was what the chief had said.

"Dad, you should have told her." She rolled her eyes and with exaggerated patience explained, "It's S-Y-N-D-I. I can tell by the way you're saying it that you think it's spelled C-I-N-D-Y. Well, it's not."

"All right," Helma told her, enunciating her name and imagining the unusual spelling hanging in the air above Syndi's head. "Syndi. Is that better?"

Syndi shrugged. "It's okay, I guess."

"Some guy got popped?" Joseph asked his father, nodding toward TNT's apartment. His voice rose a hopeful notch. "You've got to work? We can skip this afternoon."

His sister, Syndi, took a step toward the staircase, already raising her headphones. "Yeah. Okay, let's go."

The chief held up his hand, on his face a mixture of sternness and bewilderment as his gaze moved between his two children. "No, I don't have to work. Nobody got 'popped,' and no, we're not canceling this afternoon. We'll go to the park like we discussed. It's low tide."

Syndi heaved a sigh and leaned against the railing again, rubbing her bare midriff. Helma glimpsed the tattooed wings of a monarch butterfly just above the waistband of her red shorts. "Dad, puh-lease. Low tide? I'm not a kid anymore."

"We could stay here," Helma offered. "I've prepared snacks. It's a beautiful day and the view of the bay is gorgeous from my balcony. We could sit—"

"Okay, we can go to the park," Syndi said without looking at Helma.

"If we have to," Joseph added.

"I'll get my purse and keys," Helma told them.

"Purse?" Syndi drawled in a soft voice from behind Helma. "Cute."

Helma turned. "Excuse me, Syndi. Did you say something?"

Syndi's black-rimmed eyes flashed. "Just talking to myself, that's all."

As Helma entered the sanctuary of her apartment she heard the low rumble of the chief's voice as he spoke to his children. She didn't hear any sound from either Syndi or Joseph.

🌿 chapter four 🌿

THE RAVING BLAST

"**Y**ou already knew Lewis Dixon was dead?" Helma asked Wayne Gallant as they drove the short distance to Boardwalk Park. Helma frequently walked to the park after work for exercise, and had thought she and the chief and his two children would do the same. But both Syndi and Joseph declined the invitation and now sat in the backseat, leaning against their respective doors, their eyes unfocused as they listened to music through their headphones.

They rode in Wayne Gallant's personal car, a four-door Ford, and as if he wanted to remove himself as far from police and official vehicles as possible, his car was the color of a candy apple, including the deep shine.

"I stopped by the office this morning." The chief shook his head with regret. "Lewis was three months into an early retirement."

"You knew him?" Helma asked. She felt a rhythmic thumping against the back of her seat and turned around, but Joseph was gazing out the window, his head bobbing in time with the bumping against her seat.

"Not well," Wayne Gallant said, turning into the park that edged Washington Bay. "We worked out together a few times at the gym. Nice guy." Since it was a sunny day, still warm for September, the park was bustling: cars filled the parking spaces, families ate at picnic tables, a group of young men tossed a Frisbee, and two unleashed dogs ran beneath each toss, barking and leaping.

"What did he do?" Helma asked.

"Taught at the college. English, I think. Fished during the summers, too, back when there were still enough fish. Gardened, and I saw him once playing classical guitar at Carl's coffee shop. You forgot where you were, he was that good. Rode a bicycle to work."

"You're saying he was youthful?" Helma asked, picturing one of the typical Bellehavenites of a certain age: graying hair, clear-eyed from healthful diets and exercise, defiantly active, youthful clothes. Always curious, always learning. The library received its share. "Autodidactics," George Melville called them. "Death will never catch them sitting in a rocking chair."

"I guess so," Wayne Gallant told her. A parked van's back-up lights flashed white and he stopped, waiting for it to pull out so he could take their space. "But don't think he ditched a middle-aged wife to marry . . ." He frowned as if searching for a name. ". . . Mary Lynn. It was his first marriage, and a surprise, I think."

"To whom?"

"Everybody." The chief laughed as he pulled into the space. "Probably even to Lewis." His face went solemn. "It's a shame, though. It was thoughtful of you to comfort his widow."

"TNT asked me to," Helma explained. "He was uncomfortable with her crying."

"What man isn't?" the chief asked, then raised his hand as if he expected her to take offense. "I get rattled when *anybody* cries."

"Not when Mom cried," Syndi's voice accused from the backseat. She'd removed her headset and glared at the back of her father's head.

As if he hadn't heard her, the chief turned off the engine and said, "Well, here we are. Low tide, just like I promised. Maybe you two can find some starfish."

Syndi jammed her earphones back on her head and jumped out of the car, slamming the door behind her.

Helma climbed out of her side and stood, meeting the chief's troubled eyes over the car roof. "No matter what I do . . ." he said, shaking his head.

"The teenage years are confusing," Helma said, quoting from *Raising a Happy Teenager.* "Her mood will pass."

"Yeah, in seven years," Joseph said, raising one side of his mouth in a grin that was identical to his father's. Then he followed his sister across the park.

The chief looked after them: Syndi stomping in quick, angry steps; Joseph lazily ambling behind. "Six months ago, I knew these kids inside out. Now I swear they're alien beings."

Like a curious anthropological ritual, Syndi and Joseph, without speaking, stayed within ten feet of each other, walking along the rocky shore. Occasionally one would toe a rock or pick up a purple starfish or prod barnacles with a stick. Whenever Helma and the chief ventured within twenty feet of them, both teenagers immediately moved farther away. A yellow dog ran up to Joseph, and just as he was reaching to pet it, a man across the park whistled and the dog raced away. Seagulls flew overhead, then dropped low, screeching, checking for unattended food.

A paved walk edged the bay the length of the long narrow park, and the view shifted from the city to the islands toward the ferry docks. It was Bellehaven's most popular park, and whenever the sun shone, it became crowded.

Helma and the chief's conversation was stilted and formal; they spoke in low tones, as if every word were being broadcast across the grassy park to the water. Wayne Gallant continually turned toward his children, distracted each time one of them took a step or leaned over to pick up an object from the rocky shore.

"I had plans," he said once. "Camping, hiking, even some horseback riding. Now I think I'd better start from scratch." He grinned at Helma. "Know of any good rock concerts?"

A toddler separated itself from its parents who were picnicking on a blanket and ran straight for Wayne Gallant. Helma stepped aside so the chief could shake the tiny boy's hand and keep him occupied until his mother laughingly scooped him up in her arms and carried him back to the blanket.

They'd followed or led Syndi and Joseph from one parameter of the park to the opposite and were on their return trip when Helma spotted two women leaving a bench. "Let's sit down for a while," she suggested.

"Good idea."

The bench faced the opposite side of Washington Bay, a long low sweep of purplish land. Fishing boats and a few pleasure boats crisscrossed the calm bay. On the wide grassy lawn to their left, five young men without shirts tossed a Frisbee back and forth, shouting to each other. The two dogs lay stretched in the grass, panting and idly watching each sweeping curve of the plastic disk.

Now, as if the unspoken rules of the dance had suddenly changed, Syndi and Joseph remained within thirty feet of the bench where Helma and the chief sat. As if a string led from his foot to their wrists, they gradually circled the bench, just within the sound of Helma's and the chief's voices.

"And this is only the third day," the chief said, as if he were continuing a conversation. "Twenty-seven more to go."

"They haven't settled in yet," Helma said, hoping her words were true. "It may take a few more days."

"As long as it doesn't take the whole twenty-seven," he said, and laughed without much humor.

Joseph and Syndi attended a private "year-round" school with briefer holidays that didn't match the public school holidays. Their month with their father fell when their public school peers were just growing accustomed to their new academic year.

Around them, Helma suddenly grew aware of the way people in the park were lifting their heads and gazing behind her and Wayne Gallant, back toward the parked cars. The young men tossing their Frisbee faltered, the orange disk tumbling across the grass, and turned as one, grins on their faces.

Helma had seen that reaction before and wasn't at all surprised when she turned around and spotted her friend Ruth striding across the park.

Ruth Winthrop had never been bothered by subtleties or convention, not even when she was a child. Helma had known Ruth since they were nine years old, when Ruth's parents, in desperation, had enrolled her in St. Alphonse, the Catholic school Helma attended. That had been in Michigan. In the beginning they'd been enemies, quarreling over which of them had first laid claim to the blue paint box. But they'd each made their separate ways to Bellehaven, Washington, where they continued their bewildering friendship.

Ruth was a little over six feet tall, a height she emphasized with tall heels, bushy hair, and clothing in colors that were never intended to lie down together.

Despite Helma's gentle—and frequent—suggestions that perhaps Ruth's makeup was overemphasized, her face was as bright as ever, her eyes in black à la Colette, her lipstick in various shades of blood.

Ruth arced her arm, waving to Helma and Wayne Gallant. The young men dropped all pretense and stood watching Ruth cross the park. She wore a pale orange dress that fell to her calves and wrists and even covered the hollow of her throat, but it was the way the dress clung and allowed the sunlight to pass through the fabric that made it far more than it was. Her dark hair with its Bride of Frankenstein streak of white was pulled behind her head.

A wolf whistle crossed the park and Ruth raised her chin and squared her shoulders. "Never forget," she'd defiantly misquoted at age eleven when she hit her growth spurt and towered over everyone, including Sister Mary Martin, who taught fifth grade, "you can pull off anything with good posture."

"Hey, kids," Ruth said as she reached the bench. "You out here keeping the park safe for all Bellehaven?"

"Bellehaven is momentarily crime free," the chief said, rising from the bench and offering Ruth his seat.

"No thanks," Ruth told him, shaking her head, dislodging the loose knot that tied her hair off her neck, half of it fanning at the left side of her head. "I lose my impact when I sit." And she laughed her big laugh, which turned even more heads.

Because Ruth and the chief were standing, Helma rose, and an elderly couple immediately slipped behind them and sat down on the bench, smiling the victor's smile.

"Stopped by your apartment," Ruth told Helma, her eyes on one of the taller young men still watching her. "I left that book on your doormat."

"Did you read it?" Helma asked. Ruth was banned— again—from checking out books at the Bellehaven Public Library because she owed over fifty dollars in overdue fines. Occasionally, if Helma saw a book she thought Ruth might enjoy, she borrowed it for her. The book had been a biography of a well-known Northwest artist.

"I looked at the pictures," Ruth told her. "Isn't that what

you intended? Pretty tame stuff. I recognized a couple from greeting cards. Are you trying to send me a message?"

Actually, the idea that more, well, "realistic" art might influence Ruth's own art, which was anything but tame. *had* occurred to Helma. "I just thought you might like it."

"Mmm," Ruth said. "TNT told me you were down here. I caught him cowering on the landing outside his door. Trying to keep out of his stepdaughter's way, I gathered. The old softie. He said you soothed poor Mary Lynn in her grief." A tiny light of eagerness glittered in Ruth's eyes. "Now *there's* a rat's nest."

"Do you know Mary Lynn?" Helma asked, hoping to deflect any looming gossip.

"A little. Lewis, the deceased, was a local eligible bachelor. What a surprise when those two formed a permanent union."

The chief, who had been politely listening, now leaned toward Ruth, an answering glint of interest in his own eyes. "Were they happily married?" he asked.

Ruth held two fingers together and crossed them. "Disgustingly so, as far as I know."

"Then why did you call it a 'rat's nest'?" he asked. He still smiled, still stood casually, but Helma heard that policeman's edge in his voice. She supposed it was second nature, the same way a librarian's interest was piqued by the mention of a newly published book.

Ruth licked her lips, then smoothed the skirt of her dress, and her voice dropped to conspiratorial levels. "Forget the fact that Lewis was almost thirty years older than Mary Lynn. I believe a girl owes it to herself to nail down true love wherever she finds it. It's no secret that Mary Lynn doesn't get along with her mother; the girl chose to live with TNT, her stepfather, rather than her own mother. Anyway, Mama is closer to Lewis's age and lives in the apartment above the happy couple's garage. Can you picture it?" Ruth shuddered. "Nasty woman. I met her once in a bar with, guess who, Lewis."

Helma caught movement at the corner of her vision and saw Syndi and Joseph edging up to them, their eyes intent on Ruth.

"I bet Mama killed Lewis," Ruth finished.

"I believe it was a heart attack," the chief told her.

"Have they performed an autopsy yet?" Ruth asked.

Wayne Gallant glanced at his watch. "One was scheduled for this afternoon."

"Hah. So you have your doubts, too."

"No. That's standard procedure."

Ruth raised her chin. "You just wait and see."

The chief laughed. "Maybe." He pointed to his children. "These are my children, Syndi and Joseph."

Ruth thrust her hand at Joseph, surprising him enough that he took it in a limp handshake. "So you two really are really real. I thought the man was joking." She studied Joseph's tangle of hair. "Nice dreadlocks. Not easy for a kid with your kind of hair."

Joseph nearly smiled. Ruth didn't even try to take Syndi's hand but merely said, "That's a good shade of lip gloss," without sounding sarcastic.

Syndi raised a finger toward her lips, then pulled it away, looking quizzically at Ruth.

"Well, carry on. Just thought I'd say hi. I'm on my way to a barbecue or some eating event like that." She held out her hand as if testing for rain. "Can't expect this stuff to last forever."

Even Syndi mumbled "Seeya" as Ruth walked away. The two teenagers moved away from Helma and the chief as if they were about to follow Ruth themselves.

"It doesn't take long for the gossip to begin," the chief said, looking after Ruth.

"And Ruth will nudge it along in whatever way she can," Helma added.

"Well, at least this death appears pretty straightforward. Sad, but no mystery."

The next time Joseph and Syndi drifted within speaking distance, the chief clapped his hands together and said, "Say, I'm hungry. How would you two like to get something to eat? It's been a long time since breakfast."

"The Bay Café has a nice salad bar," Helma offered.

Syndi and Joseph stared at her, lips identically curled, as if she'd suggested eating worms.

"Bobby Lee's has good hamburgers *and* a salad bar," the chief offered.

Syndi shrugged and Joseph mumbled, "I guess."

"Okay, then," Wayne Gallant said, as if they'd shouted out in enthusiasm. "Let's go."

Nearly to the chief's car, with Syndi and Joseph straggling behind them, the chief's cell phone rang. Helma hadn't realized he was carrying it and she jumped.

"Easier than a radio," he said, shrugging in apology as he removed the tiny phone from his pants pocket and said, "Gallant."

He stood in the middle of the sidewalk, listening intently as people passed by, swerving around him and casting impatient looks his way. Syndi and Joseph paused fifteen feet behind, looking in every direction except at Helma and their father, as if they'd never seen the two adults in all their lives.

Wayne Gallant brushed his free hand through his hair and spoke tersely, too low for Helma to hear, then he flipped the phone closed and stood staring at nothing.

"Is everything all right?" Helma asked.

"Your friend Ruth was right."

"What do you mean?"

"Lewis Dixon was murdered."

❧ chapter five ❧

A DISMAL THING

Syndi and Joseph waited in the car while Wayne Gallant walked Helma up to her third floor apartment. All of Helma's Bellehaven years had been spent in apartment 3F in the Bayside Arms. The building was now surrounded by larger, pricier, more upscale condominiums that crowded closer, but long ago the builder had situated the Bayside Arms too close to the shore, assuring that there'd be no development in front of the building to block the view. On the street side, outside landings edged each floor like a motel, and on the water side, balconies jutted off each apartment.

The complex was quiet for a Sunday afternoon, as if the inhabitants were all away or inside taking naps. Even Walter David's first floor apartment door was closed. If it wasn't raining, the manager usually kept his door open, and he often sat on the small brick patio he'd created beside his door, Moggy, his cat, on his lap, ever vigilant for the unexpected in "his" apartments. Wayne Gallant was distracted, and when they reached 3E, TNT Stone's apartment, the chief raised his hand and rang the doorbell. The curtains were drawn and there was no answer.

"Maybe they're already at the police station," Helma suggested.

"Maybe."

"Was Lewis Dixon poisoned?" she asked, finally able

31

to talk about the murder now that his children couldn't hear. "Mary Lynn said Lewis had arrhythmia, and even the EMTs thought it was a heart attack."

"It *was* a heart attack," the chief told her. He raised his fist toward TNT's door, then dropped it and followed Helma the few feet to her own apartment. "But insulin was involved. It's likely that insulin triggered his death." He took the keys from Helma's hand and inserted one in the lock. "It doesn't leave much trace in the body."

"Insulin," Helma pondered. "How did the coroner discover it, then?"

"After a certain high-profile case, it became routine to search for an injection site: between the toes, behind the ears . . . other discreet places. A massive overdose of insulin sends the body into hypoglycemia, not enough glucose to run the brain. Confusion, convulsions, coma. Add to that a heart problem and you can see the probable results."

"And Lewis wasn't a diabetic?" Helma asked.

"No. Aside from the arrhythmia, he was healthy as any guy his age, probably more so."

Helma looked back at TNT's door, thinking of the fragile and distraught young woman. "Poor Mary Lynn."

The chief didn't answer, and Helma remembered how he'd once told her that spouses were the first suspects in a murder and it bore out too often to ignore. "Mary Lynn was genuinely upset," Helma told him. "You can't believe she was involved in her husband's death."

Wayne Gallant pulled the key from her lock and opened her apartment door, glancing inside in that unconscious habit of the always-observant. His jaw had tightened, and Helma said no more about Mary Lynn, recognizing that he'd donned his policeman's guise and undoubtedly regretted what little he'd said, even though rumors were probably already racing through Bellehaven.

"Thanks for the afternoon," he told her, stepping inside

her apartment and giving her a casual hug. "Sorry it didn't turn out the way I'd hoped."

"Murder investigations naturally take precedence," Helma told him. "I understand."

The chief looked briefly into her eyes then down at the floor. If he'd been holding a hat, he'd probably be turning it in his hands, Helma thought, not used to seeing Wayne Gallant exhibit embarrassment. "I didn't mean the murder." He waved his hand toward the parking lot. "I meant Syndi and Joseph."

As if on cue, a car horn sounded: an impatient dum da da dum dum—dum dum. The chief's lips tightened.

"This is a confusing and rebellious time in their lives," Helma said, again remembering the soothing platitudes of the book she'd read. "They're trying to establish their independence. They grow out of it," she added, trying not to think of how the adolescent years lasted nearly a decade.

"Maybe next time everybody will be more relaxed," he said, sounding hopeful. "I'll call you. I'd better get to the office."

She stood in her doorway and watched Wayne Gallant hurry down the steps, hearing as he reached the bottom a youthful voice call out in exaggerated syllables, "Fi-nal-ly."

Helma closed her door and locked both locks. On the opposite side of the sliding doors onto her balcony, Boy Cat Zukas pressed against the glass, hunkered down and staring in at her as if she'd shut him out in a storm. She doubted it was any healthier for an animal than a human to spend all day inside, so she left him glaring at her and began putting away the snacks she'd prepared for Wayne Gallant and his children.

Syndi and Joseph were a surprise, she admitted, and not at all what she'd been led to expect from their photos and the chief's description: "Sunny," he'd called them. "Polite and creative." Creative, maybe, judging from their clothes and hair and Syndi's makeup. Perhaps, as the book had described, the teenage years *were* only a phase, but she didn't recall her own as being a time of rebellion and experimentation. Now, Ruth, on the other hand . . . Stories still circulated around Scoop River.

Helma's doorbell rang, and she closed the cupboard door on the box of cheese crackers before she answered. On her doormat stood a muscular young man in his late twenties, his dark brown hair matted close to his head and his face shiny with perspiration. He wore tight bicycling pants and a blue windbreaker with strips of glow-in-the-dark tape on the sleeves.

"TNT left a message on my answering machine," he said the moment Helma opened her door, before she could say a word. His round face was creased by a frown. "But nobody's home. I got here as fast as I could but my car battery's dead and I couldn't get a jump so I rode my bike. The chain . . ." He pointed to his inside calf, which was smeared with grease. "Do you know where they are?"

"And you are?" Helma asked.

"Sorry. Skip Riems." He held out his hand, then glanced down at the grease that blackened it and pulled it back. "I'm a friend of Mary Lynn's. Sorry. Grease. The chain—"

"I just returned home," Helma told him, keeping the rest of the story to herself, "so I don't know where they've gone."

Skip nodded and shifted from foot to foot, glancing again at TNT's door as if it should open on its own. "Maybe I'll wait around awhile. TNT said Lewis died."

"That's what I understand."

"What happened?" He rubbed his nose with the back of his wrist.

"I don't believe it's been determined yet."

Skip nodded again and started to wipe his hands on his legs, then jerked them away.

"Would you like a paper towel?" Helma asked.

"For what? Oh yeah. The grease. Sure. Thanks."

Helma Zukas was not a woman who foolishly left her door open to a stranger while she retreated deeper into her apartment, so she closed the door, letting it automatically lock itself, and left Skip to wait on the landing while she retrieved several sheets of paper towel.

"Thanks. Great. My chain . . ." he said as he vigorously wiped at his hands.

"You mentioned that," Helma reminded him.

She did not meddle; she was not a "nosy" woman, but there were opportunities that sometimes presented themselves and shouldn't be ignored. "Have you and Mary Lynn been friends a long time?" she asked.

"A few years. We took Victorian Literary Devices together. With Professor Dixon."

"Her husband, Lewis, taught the course?"

He spit on the paper towel and vigorously rubbed his left knuckle. "The husband part came later. She was dating a friend of mine at the time. He was doing Wilkie Collins and she was into Eliot. I did Swinburne, ' . . . the weariest river winds somewhere safe to the sea,' and Jan, my date, did Dickens. See? A lot of good conversation."

"Naturally," Helma agreed. "If occasionally depressing. Do you still do Swinburne?"

"Only recreationally. But Mary Lynn and I still talk now and then. We both do volunteer tutoring in the Y's youth program."

"And the others?"

"Who? You mean Jan and Dean? Jan moved to London to study Dickens on site and Dean's a manager at Hugie's."

"Hugie's?" Helma asked. Hugie's was a local upscale grocery store, with upscale aspirations, featuring soft music, decorative forest-green paint wherever possible, and displays of exotic imported food and drink.

Skip shrugged and said, "Not much call for a Wilkie

Collins scholar around here. Maybe if he'd studied Shakespeare or Poe—they're hot. But you hear Collins and what do you think of? Mysteries. Fun maybe but not scholarly." He glanced around the landing, holding the used paper towels in his hand, and Helma held out a plastic bag to drop them into.

"And is there call for a Swinburne scholar?" Helma asked him.

Skip actually blushed and shifted his feet. "I teach a poetry class for community education sometimes. TNT used to tell me I'd have had better luck as a boxer. He may have been right."

"So you became friends with TNT through Mary Lynn?"

"Yeah. He's a great guy, isn't he? He took me to a couple of boxing matches in Seattle. He had a kind of sparring club for a while. Not that I'm that interested in boxing, but, you know . . ." He made imaginary feints in the air between them.

"The concept of physical strength and confrontation is appealing?"

"Something like that." He took a step toward TNT's door. "Wonder what I ought to do now. I mean, he *called* me to come. They could have gone to the funeral home. I wouldn't feel right going there. I'm not exactly family."

A car backfired in the parking lot and Helma looked over the railing to see Ruth's aging Saab pull crookedly into the parking area, blocking two spaces. The engine was barely turned off before the driver's door was thrown open with a rusty squeal and Ruth leaped out. She still wore the same orange dress, and Skip watched her, his mouth slightly open.

"Hey, Helm," Ruth called, waving toward Helma and Skip.

"Helma," Helma automatically corrected, too softly for Ruth to hear.

Ruth cupped her hands around her mouth like a yodeler and shouted up at Helma. "I was right. Did you hear? Mary Lynn Dixon's husband was *murdered*. And I bet you Wayne Gallant is rounding up suspects even as we speak."

Mrs. Beardman from 1B, who was outside watering her flowers, gasped, and beside Helma, Skip stiffened. "Oh damn it to hell," he said in a trancelike voice. "Can that be true? I have to find Mary Lynn."

𐫱 chapter six 𐫱

AFTER THE
DAY WAS DONE

"**W**ho's this?' Ruth asked as she reached Skip and Helma. Skip was under six feet tall but his athletic body caught Ruth's attention.

Skip still seemed to be in a daze, so Helma answered for him. "Skip Riems. He's a friend of Mary Lynn's. She and TNT were gone when Skip arrived."

"My chain," Skip said vaguely.

Ruth squinted at him and said, "Oh. Whoops. You didn't know about Lewis? Am I the bearer of unexpected news?"

"It is to me," Skip told her, shaking his head as if recovering from a punch. A strand of sweaty hair stood straight out from his head. "Was he shot? Who did it? Did they arrest him?"

Ruth shrugged. "Couldn't say. I heard that our local chief of police," she raised her eyebrows at Helma, "was hot on it. Stay tuned; details to follow. A surprise to one and all, except to me of course. I told you so."

"Mary Lynn must be at the police station," Skip said. "Isn't that where they take people to discuss murder? They don't do it in their homes, do they?"

"Depends on why they're talking to you," Ruth told

him. She patted his arm. "She'll be okay. TNT's a good guy to be with in a tough time."

"He might have driven her home," Helma offered. "Would you like to use my telephone?"

Skip patted his pocket. "Thanks but I have my cell." He glanced from Ruth to Helma, not really seeing them. "I guess I'll get going. If you see Mary Lynn before I do, tell her . . . No, never mind. I'll do it."

Skip raced down the steps, soundless in his soft-soled biking shoes, and climbed onto his bicycle. Helma noted with approval that he wore a helmet.

"Scattered little fella," Ruth said as Skip pedaled onto the street, barely glancing around for traffic. "What was he doing here?"

"You could have broken the news more gently," Helma told her. "TNT phoned him to keep Mary Lynn company. He was uncomfortable with her grief."

"Those outwardly tough guys are mush balls when a woman cries," Ruth said authoritatively. "Imagine what TNT's going through *now*. Poor Mary Lynn. Her husband was *murdered*. Geesh. Let's go inside and find something to drink."

"I thought you were on your way to a barbecue."

"I was, but when I found out it was murder I came right over so I could gloat." She frowned. "Not because Lewis was murdered—no way would I gloat over that, but I do enjoy hearing people admit I'm right."

"You were right," Helma acknowledged as she pulled a pitcher of iced tea from her refrigerator. "Where did you hear that Lewis had been murdered?"

"I'll tell you later, but what did our chief of law and order say?"

"He didn't mention you."

Ruth extended her lower lip and blew upward. "Funny. I mean about Lewis Dixon's murder. The details, puh-lease." Boy Cat Zukas meowed from the balcony, and Ruth opened the sliding glass doors, picking him up and lifting him to her shoulder where he sprawled as if his bones had melted.

"He received a phone call saying the autopsy indicated there'd been foul play in Lewis's death. He left immediately for the station."

"You know more than that, Helma Zukas," Ruth accused.

"I'm sure the details will be released to the public soon." The chief *hadn't* sworn her to secrecy, but then, he didn't have to. She understood that whatever he told her was in confidence.

Ruth's expectant face relaxed. "Okay, I surrender. Torture probably wouldn't make you divulge his secrets. So where are those two adolescent nightmares?"

"With him." Helma handed her a tall glass of iced tea. Ruth dropped Boy Cat Zukas to the floor and he wound once around Ruth's legs before strolling back through the open glass door onto the balcony. "Why did you call his children 'nightmares'? You seemed to like them."

"Let's just say I'm not blind to their little black hearts. The daughter wishes you'd die because you're stealing her father, and the son prefers that you turn invisible. Anybody over twenty-two is abysmally stupid and useless, and *such* an embarrassment. Don't you remember how you felt at that age? I swore I'd drown myself in Scoop River before I reached the advanced and decrepit age of thirty."

Helma couldn't remember wishing the loud and boisterous adults in her family would disappear, only that she could find herself a permanent distance away from them, a feat she'd accomplished by moving two thousand miles across the country from Scoop River, only to be followed in a few years by her mother after her father's death, and this year by Aunt Em. But somehow, having them close by didn't seem as embarrassing as it once had, and there were even moments when she wished she could transplant a few more family members to Bellehaven.

"I'm not trying to steal Syndi's father," Helma said. She wiped the moisture from her iced tea glass with a napkin.

"Tell her that."

"I will," Helma agreed, "the next time I see her."

"No!" Ruth held up her hand. "That was sarcasm, not advice. Never tell a kid that age *anything*, not even that the sky is blue."

"Well, actually," Helma explained, "they'd be correct arguing that point. Sunlight is white, a mixture of all the colors in the rainbow, but the molecules in the atmosphere scatter the blue wavelength, so that's the color our eyes pick up."

"Spare me. If it appears blue, it *is* blue. So he took the little darlings to the police station with him?" Ruth asked. "Tut tut. Those two impressionable kids are down there poking around in the coroner's office? You didn't offer to baby-sit?" Helma followed Ruth onto her balcony, where fall flowers bloomed in pots and a sisal rug softened the balcony floor. Two wicker chairs faced Washington Bay, with a wicker table between them.

"No," Helma said as she sat down, startled at the idea of being left alone with Syndi and Joseph, then she amended, "That is, he didn't ask me to look after them."

"Smart guy." Ruth gazed upward toward the sky, which at the moment *did* appear blue. More than blue, azure. But to the southwest a thickening bank of gray clouds was edging into view, clustering behind the islands. It had been a dry and sunny autumn, unusual for Bellehaven, and to be honest, tiresome. A little rain would be welcome.

"Knowing you plan for every contingency, I bet you

bought food for this get-together with the little police family, didn't you?" Ruth asked, still standing.

"Are you hungry?"

Ruth shrugged. "Well, since you're inviting, I wouldn't mind eating an early dinner with you. Thanks." Her prodigious appetite was a shock to anyone eating a first meal with Ruth, but Helma was long used to Ruth's eyes lighting up at the sight of food, meals three times as large as Helma's and five times as caloric. Still, her weight never fluctuated more than three to four pounds in either direction. "She burns it off with that smart mouth of hers," Helma's mother had once claimed.

"There's a plate of vegetables and dip in the refrigerator, and crackers in the cupboard," Helma told her.

"Sure thing."

Ruth returned to the kitchen and a noise on the roof caught Helma's attention. Boy Cat Zukas sat on the edge of the building roof, gazing down at her. "Shoo," she said, and he yawned but didn't move.

Ruth returned with the plate of sliced vegetables and spinach dip and set them on the wicker table. She picked up two carrots and held them next to each other. They were of identical size. "Do you still have that weird cutting board, the one with the ruler built into it?"

"Yes. Why?"

"Just wondered."

They each held a plate, gazing out toward the water. "Now tell me where you heard about Lewis's murder," Helma said.

Ruth swallowed a mouthful of carrot. "I didn't."

"You tricked me into telling you?" Helma accused her.

"Definitely not. Call it skilled deductive reasoning. I passed the police station on the way to my barbecue and what did I spy but an unusual amount of commotion for a lazy Sunday afternoon in Bellehaven."

"And from that you guessed Lewis Dixon had been murdered?" Helma asked doubtfully. "And that Wayne Gallant was working on the case?" A red and gold kite of several levels floated into their view of Washington Bay. It luffed, then caught a fresh breeze.

"It was on my mind. Well, actually, I recognized the chief's car and figured only one thing could drag him away from you: murder."

"So you returned here on a guess?"

"On the basis of a *deduction*," Ruth corrected, pointing a dip-laden stick of celery at her.

Helma's doorbell rang. "Maybe he's brought the kiddies back," Ruth suggested.

But it was TNT, appearing exhausted. His shoulders were slumped, and he rubbed at his left eye. He'd changed from his sweats into a button-up shirt and slacks for his meeting with the police. "I thought you'd want to know what happened since you were there from the beginning, I mean almost the beginning."

Ruth entered from the balcony, carrying her plate of food. "Hey, TNT," she said, raising her free hand and waving it toward him as if she'd blown him a kiss.

"Ruthie," TNT acknowledged, fatigue easing from his face as he squared his shoulders and pulled in his stomach, seeming to grow inches taller before Helma's very eyes.

"I'm sorry to hear about Lewis's death," Ruth told him. "Are there any leads?"

"You already know?"

Ruth nodded toward Helma. "We have inside connections." Before Helma could deny any duplicity, Ruth went on, "Have they arrested anybody?"

TNT shook his head and his face turned blotchy red. "No, but the damn cops grilled poor Mary Lynn until she almost fainted. I had to knock them back."

Helma couldn't help defending the policemen, at least the police *she* knew. "I believe that's standard procedure, to question the person who found the body or was closest to the deceased. Mary Lynn may have information that will lead to a quick arrest."

"They'd better hope so," TNT grumbled. "The poor kid was hanging on the ropes."

Ruth offered TNT her plate of vegetables. "Was the chief of police in on the questioning?"

TNT took a handful of carrots, crunching them distractedly as he spoke. "Yeah, for a while. Then something happened."

"What happened?" Helma asked, her hands involuntarily tightening around her glass of iced tea.

TNT shrugged. "Don't know. There were three cops, including Gallant, leaning on my little girl. I stayed with her, you bet. Then another cop interrupted and they all climbed into a huddle outside the door. The chief left and the questioning was different after that."

"Like how?" Ruth asked, making pulling motions with her hands.

"Like another fighter had snuck into the ring."

"I beg your pardon?" Helma asked.

"He means they were distracted," Ruth translated. "I bet one of his kids tried to burn down the station."

"I don't think so, but I saw a couple of kids when we left, sitting out front with a cop. Boy and girl. Wearing headsets." He made ear muff shapes over his ears with his hands.

"They're the ones."

"Those were the chief's kids?" He frowned. "Funny. You don't think of a cop having kids. But I guess they do. Hell of a life." He shook his head. "But, nah, they didn't look like they were in trouble, more like the cop was keeping an eye on them. All three of them looked bored."

"Did the chief return while you were there?" Helma

asked, wondering what was so pressing that Wayne Gallant had abandoned not only a murder investigation but his two children.

"Nope. After a while they ran out of questions. Mary Lynn was down for the count so I took her back to her house."

"To her mother?" Ruth asked.

"She wasn't there. Just as well. Beatrice doesn't pack a lot of comfort."

"You didn't leave her home alone after a blow like this?" Helma asked. "After discovering that her husband not only died but was *murdered*? She could have come here."

"I stayed awhile." He grinned sheepishly. "Outside. Puttered around."

"Sensitive, big guy," Ruth said.

"Hey, that's not fair. Besides, I hung around till that kid showed up. On a bike. Twenty-eight years old and the kid's riding a bicycle. Grease all over him."

"He said he was having trouble with his chain," Helma offered.

"I wonder if his horn worked," Ruth pondered.

Both Helma and TNT looked at Ruth and she shrugged.

"So you left when Skip arrived?" Helma asked.

"I did exactly that," TNT said with a touch of defiance. "Besides, I saw Beatrice's car heading back when I left, too."

"What comfort," Ruth said. "An old classmate who can't keep his car running and Mama Spider. Poor Mary Lynn."

"Would you like a glass of iced tea?" Helma asked, seeing the gleam in Ruth's eye and intending to break the thread of conversation before it devolved into gossip about Mary Lynn's mother.

"No thanks," TNT told her. He cleared his throat and cracked a knuckle joint. Helma winced.

"Sorry. I was just wondering. You're a good friend of the chief of police, right?"

"We're friends, yes," Helma confirmed.

"Maybe you could help him out a little on this case."

"What kind of help?" Helma asked warily.

"Don't tease the guy," Ruth said. She turned to TNT. "You're asking Helma to find Lewis's killer?"

TNT rubbed his hand across his chin. "Not exactly. But I heard you're real sharp." He licked his lips. "Just clear Mary Lynn, that's all."

"*Clear* her?" Helma asked. "She's not a suspect. Or is she?"

"Those cops sure acted like it. I can pay you."

"How much?" Ruth asked.

"*No*," Helma interrupted. "That's ridiculous. You're not paying me and I'm not a detective; I'm a librarian."

"Just ask a few questions, what would a few questions matter?" TNT pleaded. "Mary Lynn wouldn't hurt—"

"A fly," Ruth finished.

TNT nodded. "That's exactly right. She wouldn't." He patted Helma's shoulder. "Just think on this, would you? I'm bushed and I'm going home."

In imitation of his usual farewell, he wearily punched the air between them and left for his apartment.

"So do you think Mary Lynn murdered her husband?" Ruth asked Helma.

"TNT isn't aware it's police procedure to question the spouse first. Mary Lynn's not a suspect, I'm sure."

"Whatever you say." Ruth cupped her hand over her wristwatch. "Whoops. Gotta get home to catch a call. If Mary Lynn comes back, tell her she can call me. Keep me posted. That means if the main cop passes along any information, too."

"I doubt I'll know any sooner than the rest of Belle-haven," Helma told her.

"Yeah right. That's not the way it looks from here. And if you need advice on winning the hearts of reluctant teenagers, I'm the woman to ask."

"Why? You don't have children."

"Yeah, but *I* remember what it's like," Ruth told her, waggling her fingers as she left.

There wasn't any reason to expect Wayne Gallant to phone her, yet Helma spent the remainder of the evening sitting in her living room, in a subtle state of expectation, with her television turned low, her balcony doors closed to evening sounds. She even left the plastic bag filled with the day's trash beside her front door rather than leave her apartment long enough to take it down to the Dumpster at the end of the parking lot.

But no one, not even her mother, telephoned.

At exactly midnight, the phone beside Helma's bed jangled her awake. She checked the clock radio and the red numbers read 12:00. They changed to 12:01 as she picked up the receiver, thinking of all the bad news that awakened people in the middle of the night. Midnight. Deaths and accidents and broken hearts. Rarely was good news communicated at midnight.

"Let me talk to my dad," a young voice demanded.

"I'm sorry. You have the wrong number," Helma said, already pulling the phone away from her ear.

"Aren't you that librarian?" The young voice blared out of the earpiece. Helma paused, hearing something else behind the angry tones and pulled the phone back to her ear. "Yes, I *am* a librarian," she said. "How may I help you?"

"Where's my dad?" The voice was still demanding, angry, but Helma detected a touch of panic. "Is this Syndi?" she asked.

"Is my dad there?"

"Of course he isn't here; it's the middle of the night." Helma sat up and switched on the bedside lamp, which threw a pool of light around her bed and left the rest of the room in shadow. "When did you see him last?"

"This afternoon, at the police station."

"This *afternoon*?" Helma repeated, trying to cover her shock. "And you haven't heard from him since? He hasn't come home? He didn't call you?"

"No."

"How did you get home? Where's Joseph?"

"He's here. A policeman brought us back to Dad's house. Dad said he had to do something important and then he'd come right home and we were supposed to wait here. But he hasn't even called. Mom said she didn't trust him."

"Your father is completely trustworthy," Helma told her. "Completely. He always does what he says he will. And if he doesn't, it's because . . ." She stopped.

"Because something happened to him?" Syndi's voice sounded even younger. "Is he dead?"

"Of course he's not dead. There's a very simple explanation for this, some kind of a misunderstanding, I'm sure. I'll find out what it is. You go back to bed."

"It's only midnight. I haven't been to bed yet."

"All right. Either your father or I will be there in an hour, all right?"

"Do you mean it?"

"I always mean exactly what I say," Helma assured her. "What's Joseph doing?"

"Watching TV. Dad has expanded cable so he's been sitting in front of it all night."

"I'll see you in an hour," Helma told her.

"I'd rather it was Dad."

"It probably will be. Don't worry."

"I didn't say I was worried."

"I'm glad to hear that. Good night, Syndi."

"Yeah," and the phone went dead.

Helma hung up, missing the cradle once. Her hands were cold, and she was surprised to see they were shaking.

❧ chapter seven ❧

BITTER TIDINGS

In one graceful swoop, Helma swept back her covers and swung her legs over the side of her bed; her feet automatically sought the slippers she left strategically placed at her bedside. Wayne Gallant wouldn't have left his children alone unless he was *unable* to reach them. She felt the pounding of her heart as she reached for the phone again. Her hand to her breast, she gulped a deep fortifying breath and, as she released it, dialed the Bellehaven Police Department.

"Police," the voice answered. "Lehman here."

For once, Helma was grateful that a few of the policemen had overestimated her relationship with Wayne Gallant. Sidney Lehman was one of them.

"Officer Lehman, this is Helma Zukas. Is Chief Gallant in?"

There was silence, and Helma pictured the consternation on Sidney Lehman's young face. He would sit upright, perhaps even smooth the front of his shirt, and, even though she couldn't see him, compose his face into careful lines that betrayed nothing.

Helma took a chance. "I know there's been a problem. I need to speak to him."

"Well, Miss Zukas. Right now he's not able to come to . . . oh damn, sorry, ma'am. Carter Houston is on his way to talk to you."

"Where is Wayne?" she demanded, her voice echoing Syndi's "Where is my dad?"

"He's at the hospital. Carter can tell you—"

Helma cut him off, already kicking off her slippers, not noticing where they landed. "I'm on my way to the hospital."

"But Carter—"

"Sidney, call Carter back to the station. Carter Houston is not someone you should ever send to deliver bad news. Good-bye."

The hospital. The news coursed through Helma, freezing her. Then a shiver racked her body and she drew her nightgown over her head, tossing it behind her to the floor as she reached toward her bureau for underwear and slacks.

In five minutes she was descending the outside staircase of the Bayside Arms, passing dark windows of the other apartments, her feet rat-a-tat-tatting on the wooden steps, her hair only finger-combed, her jacket unbuttoned. TV laughter came from Mrs. Johnson's apartment and pulsing TV light shone on her curtains. The parking lot was silent, the street deserted. Every move Helma made—pulling out her keys, opening her car door—was magnified in the night.

She was about to turn on her engine when she spotted a car turning into the parking lot. Black or navy, no bar of lights on its top, but without a doubt from the smooth and steady, no, the *deliberate* way it was being driven, she recognized it as a police car.

Helma Zukas was not a sneaky person; she never *snuck*, but she *did* notice that the carpet on the passenger side was out of alignment, so she bent low to straighten it. When she rose again after the edge of the carpet was finally tucked straight and true beneath the passenger seat, it was to see Detective Carter Houston's unmistakable figure climbing the staircase of her apartment building. She was surprised he hadn't taken the elevator.

Ruth had once described Carter as a Fernando Botero painting, and when Helma looked up the artist, she saw that the resemblance was marked. His punching-toy body and tiny feet, his pursed-lip tidiness, slickly combed hair, and dark-rimmed glasses. Carter Houston had no visible sense of humor, especially regarding himself, and this made him an irresistible target for Ruth's teasing.

Whatever Carter had come to tell Helma, she'd rather find out for herself. She turned on her engine, put her car in gear and pulled out of her space, never looking back toward Carter, although as she pulled onto the street she *might* have heard a voice calling, she just couldn't be sure. And she had no time to find out, either. After all, she'd promised Syndi she'd have an answer for her in fifty-four minutes.

The hospital. Wayne Gallant in the hospital. Her breath caught each time she thought of the possibilities: An accident? A shooting? Or even a heart attack; he *was* in his forties.

Helma drove two miles over the speed limit all the way into downtown Bellehaven, once zipping through a yellow light and once making a left turn on a red light. The hospital occupied one side of a rough square, comprised of the library, the police station, and city hall. As Helma rounded the corner, not even glancing toward the library as she normally did to affirm that all was in order, she saw four police cars parked near the emergency room entrance. An ambulance was backed up to the door. Its rear doors were open but its lights were off.

Helma parked her Buick in an Emergency Room Only space and hurried toward the wide automatic doors. It was then that she realized she'd left her purse in her apartment. All she'd brought were her keys. She glanced without pausing into the open ambulance. No blood.

The receptionist at the desk was laughing with a green uniformed EMT. An elderly man sat in the waiting room, his hand to his forehead. The light was muted, the odor antiseptic, the colors unnoticeable.

"Excuse me," Helma told the woman, who wore a blue smock with a miniature teddy bear pinned above a name tag that read *Jane*. "I'm here to see Wayne Gallant."

The woman's eyes narrowed slightly as she considered Helma, then she smiled. "Are you family?"

"Excuse me," Helma repeated, "but the children are home alone." She pointed to the double doors leading into a hallway. "Is this the way?"

"He's out of surgery. Second floor, Room 224. Intensive care." She half stood, one hand grabbing Helma's arm. "Are you okay, honey?"

"Intensive care?" Helma whispered.

The woman nodded and pointed to the EMT. "Bill here can go with you."

Helma straightened. "No thank you. I'm fine, really. Two twenty-four?"

"That's right. The elevator's right around the corner."

"I prefer stairs," Helma told her.

The woman smiled. "Probably faster than the elevator anyway. The door's across the hall from the elevator."

No one was in the stairwell, and Helma took the steps two at a time, climbing until she came to the white steel door bearing a number 2 five feet tall.

The strong medicinal smells hit her as she opened the door, bringing quick flashes of her brothers smashing their bicycles into each other, her grandfather's heart attack, the birth of her first nephew.

But now, policemen filled the peach-colored hallway, talking together, one speaking on a cellular phone, another talking animatedly to a nurse. Helma spotted only one officer she recognized—Officer 087—and only because he'd once issued her an unfair traffic ticket.

She walked briskly to two policemen in conversation a distance from the others and said in a weak imitation of her silver-dime voice, "The children are at home. How is he?" They turned to her, their usually cool eyes filled with concern.

"Children?" the larger of the two policemen said, then his eyes widened. "Damn. I forgot his kids were here. Are they all right?"

"I'll take care of them, but how is *he*?"

"So-so. His leg's been set, and his left arm. Bruises and contusions. It's the head injury they're most worried about."

"What happened?" she demanded, but neither answered. "Is he conscious?"

The two policemen exchanged glances and the smaller one shook his head. "Not yet."

"When was he brought in?"

"About seven. Somebody spotted the empty cruiser an hour earlier."

"Thank you," Helma said, trying to comprehend the words he was saying, wondering why she had such difficulty making sense out of them. They were simple words, monosyllabic mostly, but she had to pick them apart one by one. Broken arm, unconscious, empty cruiser. She stepped away from the policemen and stood by the wall facing the closed door of Room 224, listening for sounds from inside, waiting. After five minutes the door opened and a tiny, short-haired nurse stepped out. Helma was beside her, her hand catching the door before the nurse was all the way through.

"I came as quickly as I could," she told the nurse as she stepped past her through the door into Wayne Gallant's room. "Thank you." And she pulled the door closed before the nurse could say a word.

If Helma had watched hospital dramas on television she'd have known the names of all the machines. But she'd research that later; at the moment they were all a blur of digital numbers, graphs, and electronic beeps. Her only clarity was the man lying on the bed.

She stood at the foot of the bed looking down at him.

She'd never seen Wayne Gallant completely "quiet" before. How could he take up so little space?

A monitor beeped rhythmically; that seemed like a good sign. His mouth was slightly open, his right leg and left arm bulky beneath the sheet. His dark hair was crusted with blood around a three-inch square that had been shaved above his left ear. Stitches closed a V-shaped cut. What had happened?

Hardly realizing she'd moved, Helma found herself beside him, her hand lightly touching his below the tubing taped to his wrist. His skin was cool and dry.

"Hello," she said.

He didn't move; his eyes didn't open. She spoke slowly, carefully separating each word from the next.

"Don't worry about your children. I'll see that they're taken care of. I'll be sure they're . . . fed and kept clean." The monitor beeped twice more and she glanced up at the wall clock. It had been twenty-five minutes since Syndi's phone call. "Get well," she whispered close to his ear, patting his hand. "Please."

When she left the room, only three policemen remained in the hallway, one of them Officer 087, who stood near the wall jotting in a notebook. They'd argued in front of a judge over her unfair traffic ticket and had avoided one another ever since. The policemen she'd spoken to when she arrived were gone, so she approached Officer 087, hoping he hadn't overheard her conversation with the first policemen. He warily watched her walk toward him, even leaning away from her and nervously touching his moustache as she stopped in front of him.

"Why did it take so long to find him?" she asked. Officer 087 frowned, and Helma continued, grasping at the one fact she knew. "An empty cruiser should have alerted more people."

"Danish Point is just enough out of the way, I guess."

Helma tucked that information away. Danish Point was a high, treed sandstone bluff that formed a small promontory into the bay, with gorgeous views of the islands and, on especially clear days, the Olympic Mountains. It was undeveloped, not yet city-owned because of its high price, but a piece of property that the public used anyway. "Why was the chief of police answering a call?" she asked. He didn't answer, and she continued, "*How* did you find him, then?"

"A high school kid and his girlfriend called it in on the girl's cell phone. Carter was closest and he took the call."

"Carter Houston?"

He nodded. "The chief was below, on the rocks. Carter—"

As if on cue, angry voices sounded down the quiet hospital hall and Helma turned to see Carter Houston round the corner, with Ruth beside him, six inches taller. She'd obviously been interrupted at work on one of her paintings: reds and purples, according to the splatters on the sleeves of her sweatshirt and leggings. Her hair was tied on top of her head, a smear of magenta paint above her ear. Carter wore, as usual, whether night or day, a black suit and striped tie. Both Carter and Ruth were red-faced. The three policemen drew back, watching the two approach.

"Would it kill you to give out just a teensy bit of information, like is the guy dead or alive?" She stopped when she saw Helma. "So how is he?"

"Resting comfortably."

Ruth raised her hands and let them drop. "Well, thank you for that enlightening bit of information. You're as bad as Detective Tight Lips here."

"What are you doing here, Ruth?" Helma asked. It was difficult to turn her mind to anything besides what was happening behind the door of Room 224.

Ruth jerked her head toward Carter Houston. "He brought me here and then refused to give me the details."

"I didn't bring you," Carter Houston contradicted.

"You—" He stopped and bit his lower lip, looking confused, almost bewildered.

"Same thing. You showed up at my house, woke me up looking for Helma and then expected me to just go back to sleep. Could *you* have? After *that*?"

"You weren't asleep."

"I might have been. It was that time of night."

Even in her distracted state, Helma sized up the situation. Carter Houston had tried to take command of the moment, and despite his exchange with Ruth, was holding onto his single remaining position of power, as keeper of the facts. "Is he still unconscious?" he asked Officer 087.

"Yes, he is," Helma answered for Officer 087. "So don't even consider bothering him. Let him rest."

"I wasn't about to 'bother' him," he told Helma stiffly.

"Good. I'd like to discuss how you found him," Helma said. "I understand you answered the call when his cruiser was discovered at Danish Point. Why was he driving a cruiser? And why did *he* answer a call in the first place?"

Carter gazed around at the other policemen in the hallway, his expression accusatory, his round face puffing red. The other three policemen avoided his gaze.

"Did he speak to you before the ambulance arrived?" Helma asked.

"I believe that's privileged information," Carter told her.

Ruth leaned down and, as if he couldn't help it, Carter Houston looked into her face. "Oh, come on, Carter," Ruth said in her huskiest voice. "What's it going to hurt? You know Wayne would tell Helma the whole story, A to Z."

"I'm not aware that he would," Carter said, pulling himself away from Ruth's dark eyes. He pursed his lips and stared straight ahead, going as inanimate as a royal guardsman at Buckingham Palace.

It was obvious that Carter Houston wouldn't be divulging any new information that night. Helma checked her watch. It was 12:46. "I promised the chief's children I'd contact them by one. I have to leave."

"There's a phone down the hall," Carter suggested, returning to life. "Then I'd like to speak with you for a few moments."

Ruth turned and snapped at Carter, " 'There's a phone down the hall?' You want her to tell a thirteen-year-old kid that his father's lying in the hospital on the very edge of death over the *telephone*?"

Helma stepped between Ruth and Carter. "I'll take care of it. Thank you, Carter." To Ruth, she said, "Wayne Gallant is *not* on the edge of death. And also, I believe the thirteen-year-old is Syndi and that Joseph is fourteen."

"I'm so grateful you clarified that," Ruth said. "And if you're leaving this place, I'm coming with you."

Carter's face softened in relief.

❧ chapter eight ❧

JAWS THAT BITE

"**H**ow bad is he hurt?" Ruth asked as soon as they were out of Carter Houston's hearing. She paused by the hospital elevator, one hand to the call button, then sighed and followed Helma to the stairs. "You've got to get over this thing about elevators. They're useful inventions designed by highly competent engineers . . . mostly, anyway. Remember that story about the . . . oh, never mind."

"Steps are beneficial for both of us," Helma told her.

"Yeah yeah. So you say. How bad is it?" she asked again.

"Broken bones and a head injury," Helma told her as she pushed open the steel door to the stairs. "He's still unconscious."

Ruth brushed her hands through her hair, bushing it out even wilder. "Geeze, a head injury. Do you know what happened? Carter wouldn't say a word. That man is without feelings."

"Carter *did* try to contact me," Helma reminded her. Their voices echoed in the concrete stairwell. "You have to allow him that."

Ruth grunted. "He was probably ordered to. So what *did* happen?"

Helma paused on the tiled stair. She absently removed a tissue from her pocket and rubbed away a fingerprint on

59

the wall. "It seems the chief left an interrogation to respond to a call, and a few hours later someone found his car up at Danish Point. He was on the rocks at the bottom of the cliff. It would have been nearly dark, so it was fortunate he was found."

"What kind of call was he answering?" Ruth asked.

"I haven't discovered that yet."

"You trying to take the paint off the wall?" Ruth asked, and took the tissue from Helma's hand. She patted Helma's shoulder. "Come on. Let's get out of here; it smells like sick people. He fell?" she asked, shaking her head in disbelief.

Helma swallowed. "He must have. What else?"

"Can you picture Wayne Gallant hopping out of a cruiser, strolling over to the edge of a cliff and *falling* over? Even with my vivid imagination, I don't see it happening."

They'd reached the ground floor and Helma stopped, one hand to the cool metal doorknob. "He did not *jump*."

"Definitely not. Not even those kids could make a man like him jump. A lesser man, maybe. No, my friend, I'm saying he might have been pushed. I mean, he's a cop. All kinds of funny things happen to cops. That's why they have unlisted phone numbers and don't hang out in public places."

Helma turned the doorknob and stepped into the shadowy lobby on the quiet main floor, saying over her shoulder, "I can't focus on conjecture right now. It's too soon. We have to reassure his children."

"I'll think about it for you," Ruth offered.

They reached Helma's car in silence. When Helma tried to unlock the door of her Buick, the key wouldn't fit in the lock. She fumbled with it for a few moments before Ruth took the key from her hand. "No way I'm riding with you when you're in this shape. I'll drive."

Helma hesitated, and Ruth cupped her hands around the keys and pulled them closer to her body. "Listen, I'll even wear my seatbelt and I promise not to drive over thirty-five."

Helma opened her mouth to argue but surrendered and walked wordlessly to the passenger side of the car. She closed her lips tightly to keep from reminding Ruth to re-lock her door, to pump the gas pedal twice before she turned on the engine, to realign the mirrors, and to refrain from shifting gears too fast. "He lives north of town," was all she allowed herself to say.

"Yeah yeah, I know. I'll get us there. You sit and think about how you're going to break this news to his kids."

But Helma's thoughts refused to settle. She noticed the trafficless streets, the empty sidewalks, wondering where everybody was, then reminded herself that it was nearly one in the morning. Briefly, she considered Ruth's assertion that Wayne Gallant might have been intentionally pushed off the cliff. But how? Was there a struggle? Unless he was surprised, it would take more than one assailant to force him off the rocks. And why had he answered a call to Danish Point in a police cruiser? He usually drove a plain car. But she couldn't settle her mind around those thoughts, either. She felt like Aunt Em, who sometimes referred to her own thoughts as "noodle soup."

Wayne Gallant's house sat along the bay on the north edge of town, bordering on expensive homes in Belle-haven, homes with a long view across Washington Bay to the opening that led through humpy islands and around the Olympic Peninsula into the open ocean and the wide world beyond.

"The next block," Helma reminded Ruth.

"I know."

"You might want to slow down."

"It's under control," Ruth said, and swung Helma's car into the chief's driveway without using her turn signals and barely touching the brakes. Helma gripped her armrest to keep from swaying into the door.

The house was lit from the second floor to the first. Every window glowed with light. The houses on either side were dark. A figure stood in a first floor window, facing the driveway. From the silhouette, Helma guessed it was Syndi. Her dashboard clock, which was as accurate as her watch, read exactly one o'clock. Fifty-nine minutes since she'd promised Syndi either she or the chief would call in one hour.

"Got your script ready?" Ruth asked as she stopped the car in the driveway beside the front door and turned off the car engine.

The figure disappeared from the window. "I can only tell them what I know," Helma said.

"Which is the very last thing they want to hear. Well, unless they're expecting even worse news. Soften it up for them, okay?"

Helma remembered Syndi's whispered question asking whether her father was dead. She clasped her hands into fists and walked the brick sidewalk to the wide porch and front door, expecting the door to be thrown open by Wayne Gallant's frightened children.

But the door remained closed when she reached it. Surprised, she rang the doorbell, hearing its distant Westminster chimes and also the sounds of music. Helma counted to twenty, ignoring Ruth's, "Yeah, you can just tell the little darlings are worried sick, can't you?" before she pushed the doorbell again, this time with two insistent rings.

Finally, Joseph opened the door. He might have been sleeping; his hair was such a tangle naturally it was hard to tell. "Where's Wayne?" he asked, holding the door partially closed and glancing behind Helma and Ruth.

"May we come in?" Helma asked. "I'd like to speak to you and your sister."

Joseph shrugged but opened the door all the way. His eyes were watchful even though he covered a yawn.

Inside, the television blared rock music, and on the screen, six women with bored faces were moving in unison behind a man who shouted a song about baby blue eyes.

Helma took in the living room in an instant. It was as if a camp had been set up among the chief's simple furnishings. A cordless phone sat on the coffee table in the midst of pop cans and chip bags and a box of sugar-coated cereal. Pillows from the couch were strewn on the floor. Syndi sprawled on the sofa, a blue blanket around her shoulders, staring at the television. If Helma had met this Syndi on the street, she wouldn't have recognized her. The heavy makeup had disappeared, and except for the carefully composed boredom on her face, she resembled what she actually was: thirteen years old.

The remote lay on Syndi's lap, but Ruth walked over to the television and with a jab of her index finger pushed the Off button beneath the screen. "So where is he?" Syndi asked when the screen went blank. The room was silent. In the corner nearest the kitchen, the pendulum of a grandfather clock swung back and forth, rhythmically ticking off the seconds.

"Yeah, where is he?" Joseph asked. He sat on the arm of the sofa, casually swinging one leg, his fingers creasing his pant legs.

"He's in the hospital," Helma said. "There's been an accident."

Both stared at her, neither moving an inch or a facial muscle.

"He has a few broken bones and a head injury. I'll take you to visit him tomorrow." The clock ticked, the refrigerator motor turned on.

Behind her, Ruth murmured, "Say a few positive words, like he's going to be just fine in a couple of days."

"We don't know that," Helma murmured back.

"So what?" she whispered, and in a louder voice she told Joseph and Syndi, "He's going to be fine in a couple of days." And when the two children continued staring at her, she added, "Probably."

"Did somebody shoot him?" Joseph asked.

"We don't know the details but it appears he fell," Helma told him.

"He *fell*?" Syndi asked. Her lip curled.

"If it makes you feel any better," Ruth snapped, "it was down a cliff, not out of his chair."

"Was he pushed?" Joseph, still seeking the drama in the situation, asked.

"We don't know yet," Helma told him. "We'll find out more tomorrow."

Joseph and Syndi exchanged glances, their faces expressionless, and suddenly Helma remembered seeing that same glance between her parents, between her father and his raucous brothers and sisters. Conversations without words.

Helma said it before she thought: "You can't stay here alone; you can spend the night with me."

"It looks like this vacation is over," Ruth said. "Where's your mother?"

"In Paris," Joseph told her, standing.

"France," Syndi added. "With her new boyfriend. He's rich."

"I'm okay here," Joseph told them, leaning too casually against the fireplace mantel, a pose. "Take Syndi."

"I'm not going," Syndi said from the sofa. "I'm staying here until Dad comes home."

"It may be a few days," Ruth said, more gently.

"I don't care."

"You can't stay here alone," Helma told them.

Ruth looked from Syndi to Joseph, frowning. "Yes, they can," she told Helma. "Just for the rest of the night. It's almost morning anyway. They're old enough."

"But they'll be alone."

"That's right, they will. What if," Ruth said, turning to Syndi and Joseph, "you spend the rest of the night here.

Then tomorrow after you've seen your father, we'll decide what happens next."

"How soon can we see him?" Syndi asked.

"I'll visit the hospital first thing in the morning," Helma told her, "to be sure it's all right, and then I'll come get you."

"What time?" Syndi asked.

"About eight o'clock. Is that too early?"

"It's okay," Joseph said. "You won't forget?"

"She won't," Ruth said. "That I can promise you."

On a pad in the kitchen, in large print, Helma wrote down her phone number, Ruth's number, the police, and the Bellehaven Public Library's, and then attached it to the chief's refrigerator with a *Bellehaven City Police* magnet. She checked the refrigerator and cupboards for food and found them well-stocked. The chief had obviously shopped with teenage appetites in mind.

"Are you sure you want to stay here alone?" Helma asked one last time before she and Ruth left.

"Sure, why not?" Joseph asked.

"Is it okay to leave all the lights on?" Syndi asked, still on the sofa. "I mean, if I don't feel like turning them off?"

"Sure," Ruth told her. "You can leave the TV blaring, too, if you want to."

Outside, Ruth gave in and surrendered the car keys to Helma so she could drive home.

"I don't feel comfortable leaving them without adult supervision," Helma said as they pulled out of Wayne Gallant's driveway. She glanced back at the brightly lit house for a moment before accelerating down the street.

"It's only for a few hours. What can happen? Besides, they're scared to death about their dad."

"They are?"

"Of course they are, couldn't you tell? Kids just hide things. Didn't you when you were that age? Never mind; don't answer that."

Helma felt the night's confusion metamorphosing into a thick exhaustion. She longed for sleep, to feel her cheek against her pillow and to drift into the dark warmth of her bed. The thought of that pleasant unconsciousness was overpowering.

"Hey! Watch out!"

Helma jumped. Ruth had grabbed the steering wheel. "Are you okay? You were drifting across the center line."

Helma corrected the car's trajectory and sat upright, blinking several times. "I was just thinking."

"Bull. You fell asleep. Pull over and let me drive."

"I'm perfectly capable."

"Yeah, right, I can see that." Ruth leaned over and turned on the radio, switching from the easy listening station to a station that played the same kind of music Syndi and Joseph had been listening to. Then Ruth rolled down her window and sang off key to accompany the radio. Cool night air swept through the car, and by the time they reached Ruth's neighborhood Helma was not only wide awake, she had a headache, too.

As she turned into the alley that led to Ruth's converted carriage house, which was behind one of Bellehaven's Victorian homes on what was called "the slope," Ruth said, "He's going to be all right, Helma."

"I don't know that yet."

"He's tough, and as they say, he's got a lot to live for."

"But what happened? Who—"

Ruth plugged her ears with her fingers. "Tomorrow. Figure it out tomorrow in the light of day. Get some sleep for what's left of the night; that's what I'm going to do."

As soon as Helma entered her apartment she began removing her clothing, meanwhile heading toward her bedroom. As she pulled her sweater over her head, a thought occurred to her and she phoned the police station. Sidney Lehman again answered the phone. "How's he doing?" he asked, when she gave him her name.

"Resting comfortably. I told his children, but they're spending the remainder of the night alone at his house. Could you arrange for a car to patrol, discreetly, around the house?"

"You bet. They okay?"

"I think so. I'll spend the day with them tomorrow."

"Oh?" He hesitated. "You sure?"

"Of course. I'm prepared."

Then, without even glancing into the night over Washington Bay, Helma crawled into bed in her underwear and at last fell into sleep so deep there was no room for dreams.

At six A.M., Helma's clock radio turned on and she awoke instantly, despite having had only four hours of sleep. She had a curious longing for black coffee, which she'd only tasted once in her life. Instead, she placed two tea bags in a cup and drank the strong brew while she plotted her day. The new pamphlet stand was the topic of discussion at the library's Monday morning staff meeting. It was vital that Helma be there since she was chairperson of the pamphlet stand committee and there was bound to be an argument over the size and number of slots, and exactly where it should be placed in the library.

But first she intended to do what she'd been waiting hours for: to visit Wayne Gallant in the hospital. It was 7:10 when she left her apartment, and a haze of fog hung in the air that would burn off by nine or ten. As she descended the steps to the parking lot, she heard the rhythmic pounding of feet.

TNT Stone jogged from behind a parked SUV. He didn't appear surprised to see her, and in fact she had the distinct impression he'd been watching for her.

" 'Morning, Helma," he called, and jogged to her side, stopping beside her to wipe his face on the towel around his neck. "About last night," he continued. "You can forget about it."

Helma frowned. The only event she could think of "last night" was Wayne Gallant's injury.

"I mean about clearing Mary Lynn," TNT went on. "I was out of line asking you to interfere; the police can take care of it. You just forget I ever mentioned it to you and enjoy your own life." He laughed and stretched out the words "Never mind" in parody of a well-known comedic routine.

His words were jovial but Helma felt his attentive gaze. "You're right," she said. "The police are experienced at solving crime."

TNT visibly relaxed. A sincere smile lit his face. "Great," he said. "That's great. Have a good day now."

Helma pondered TNT's change of heart as she drove to the hospital, curious that he seemed as determined that she *not* interfere as he'd been the day before that she *should* interfere.

But as soon as she turned into the hospital's parking lot, every thought of TNT, Mary Lynn, and her husband's murder slipped from her mind.

Helma did not ask if Wayne Gallant could have visitors; she did not pause at the main desk where a blue-jacketed woman sat with a foam coffee cup; she simply headed for the stairs and to Room 224 without meeting anyone's eyes. A woman of purpose.

His door was ajar. A sign hung on it but Helma avoided reading it in case it said, "No Visitors." She slipped inside the warm room.

He lay as he had seven hours ago, still connected to all the machinery. A pillow wedged against his right side had shifted his body weight. His cheeks were flushed and his breathing more rapid, as if his sleep were disturbed by unsettling dreams.

Helma sat in the chair near the head of the bed, cleared her throat and smoothed her skirt. "The children are fine," she told him. "I talked to them last night and told them you were here. I'll bring them in to visit soon. They're waiting for you to come home." She cleared her throat again. "I hope that will be soon."

A soft swish sounded behind Helma, and she turned to see a nurse enter the room, carrying a full plastic bag of clear fluid for the drip above his bed. She nodded to Helma and efficiently went about her business, explaining to Wayne Gallant what she was doing as if he were wide awake and attentive to her every word. When she was finished, she dropped her plastic gloves in the trash can and said to Helma, "I saw you last night. You haven't had much sleep."

"You were here last night?"

She nodded, and Helma remembered her: the small dark-haired nurse. Her name tag read, *Molly, R.N.* Her dark brown eyes were red-rimmed. "Twelve-hour shift. I'll be finished in a few minutes. Then it's home to snooze land."

Helma stood and followed the nurse out the door of Room 224 and out of Wayne Gallant's hearing range. "Excuse me," she said, catching up to the nurse. "Were you here last night when Chief Gallant was brought in?"

"I only work this floor so I didn't see him until they brought him out of recovery."

"Was he conscious?"

"Not really." She jotted numbers on a chart with a click pencil.

"Not really? Did he speak at all?"

"Just one word."

"Do you remember what that was?"

"Are you family?"

Helma looked up at the clock in the hallway. "I have to pick up the children in a few minutes. May I bring them in to see him?"

"Of course."

"What was it he said?"

The nurse set aside her pen and smiled at Helma. "Only 'tonights.' "

"That's all? 'Tonight's'? As in 'tonight's dinner'?"

"That's right."

"Could it have been singular?" Helma asked. "Just 'tonight'?"

"Possibly, but I'm pretty sure it was plural. Maybe he meant 'two nights.' "

"Thank you, it might be significant." Helma left the nurse, wondering how the word 'tonights' or even 'two nights' could be construed to have *any* meaning. She didn't allow herself to confront the secret desire that the syllables he mumbled when he lay gravely injured might have borne more resemblance to the word "Helma."

❧ *chapter nine* ❧

CLAWS THAT CATCH

At the bank of pay phones in the hospital lobby, an elderly woman was speaking loudly into one of the phones: "It was his gall bladder. I told him that but he wouldn't listen. You know how Frank is."

The chief's phone number was unlisted but Helma had surprised herself by effortlessly committing it to memory the first time he'd given it to her. She'd bring Joseph and Syndi to the hospital and afterward invite them to read in the library until her meeting was finished. Then she'd find someone to stay in Wayne Gallant's house with the two young people until either their mother returned from Paris or their father had recovered.

"Yeah?" It was unmistakably Ruth's voice, above the sound of a TV talk show in the background.

"I'm sorry," Helma told her. "I must have automatically dialed your number. I meant to call the chief's house."

"Well, you got that right. That's where I am."

"At Wayne Gallant's house?"

"The very place. I got to thinking about these kids. That's what they still are, despite their big people size and bad behavior. Kids. So back I came. I put them to bed properly and cleaned up their mess in the living room. You'd be surprised how well they take orders when you threaten them with bodily harm."

71

"Ruth," Helma said, surprised. "You . . . I wish I'd thought of that."

"Yeah, well, next time. Now I'm waiting for the sun to rise."

"The sun rose hours ago. Are Syndi and Joseph awake?"

"Nope. Sound asleep. How's the man? And no more of that 'resting comfortably,' please."

"He's still unconscious. The nurse said he mumbled the word 'tonight' or 'tonights' when he was brought in last night."

Ruth whistled. "Tonight's what? That's not exactly enlightening. Tonight's the night? And if he said 'tonight' last night, that means it's all moot anyway, because *that* 'tonight' has come and gone."

"If you struggle to speak when you're gravely injured, I believe those words have significance."

"Not always," Ruth contradicted. "You know how sometimes when you wake up and there's a song already playing in your head and you can't shake it all day? Maybe he had a *West Side Story* moment."

Helma ignored that bit of trivia. "Perhaps instead of the possessive 'tonight's,' " she suggested, "as in 'tonight's dinner,' he was speaking in the plural. Two separate words: 'two nights.' "

"As in two nights from now? Or then?"

"Correct. It may have been a warning or a partial message explaining how he ended up at the bottom of the cliff."

Ruth sighed. "I don't know, Helma, that's putting a lot of stock into an ambiguous statement. It's not even a statement; we're talking at the most, two words, maybe only one."

"English is an ambiguous language," Helma told her, "under the best of conditions. No, I know Wayne Gallant, and he doesn't speak without purpose. He might have said more to the police when he was found."

"That's why all the cops were at the hospital last night; it's a criminal investigation, not just their beloved leader taking a tumble."

"Carter Houston was the first to reach him," Helma told Ruth.

"Forget that, then. Even *I* couldn't wheedle any information from Carter. What's your plan?"

"Nothing at the moment. I'm sure the police have the investigation under control."

"Right," Ruth said. "I'd feel more confident of that if the chief were the investigator instead of the investigatee, but I'm willing to give them a day or two to wrap it up. In the meantime, what about the duo?"

"Who?"

"Syndi and Joseph. I can bring them to the hospital to see their dad. Then what? We can't just turn them loose on Bellehaven. Is there such a thing as a twenty-four-hour teenage baby-sitting service? Other than juvenile detention, I mean?"

"I'll find someone to stay at the chief's house with them."

"Well, good luck. Okay, so after the little darlin's wake up and eat their post toasties, we'll visit the hospital. After that, we'll come by the library to give you the latest, plus see what you've dreamed up."

"Thanks, Ruth."

"Betcha. Oh. You'd better tell TNT you can't get mixed up in his son-in-law's murder, not with this new development."

"I didn't plan to in the first place, but this morning he rescinded his request anyway."

"He did? He was sure eager last night."

"He changed his mind." A man stood behind Helma, impatiently jingling keys in his pocket.

"Now, *that's* curious, don't you think?"

"Maybe," Helma admitted. "I have to go now. Someone's waiting for the telephone."

"Mmm. Okay, but TNT . . . we can talk about it later."

The Bellehaven Public Library was situated only two blocks from the hospital, so Helma left her car in the hospital parking lot and, carrying the zippered bag that held her work pumps and the latest issue of *Library Journal*, walked to the library, entering through the door off the loading dock that led to the overcrowded staff room.

George Melville, the bearded cataloger, sat at his desk, where he commanded the indexing and classification of the library's materials. Cataloging, he frequently announced as if he'd just thought of it, had advanced from requiring active human thought to the ability to push the Enter key repeatedly in an electronic cataloging database.

He looked up from his newspaper as Helma entered, his usual bemused smile slipping into seriousness. He removed his feet from atop his open desk drawer and stood to meet her. "I heard about the chief. How is he?"

"He has several broken bones and a head injury," Helma told him, thinking as she spoke those simple words how inadequately they conveyed Wayne Gallant's condition. "The doctors will have a fuller prognosis when he's fully conscious."

George shook his head. "Rough. I know you don't listen to rumors but I heard he was chasing a convenience store robber who turned on him."

"If that's true, the police haven't released that information yet." One of the library technicians carried a new box of books past and gave Helma a small sympathetic smile.

"Why are you here, anyway?" George asked, frowning. "Nobody expected you to work today. Well, maybe the Moonbeam did, but she doesn't count."

The "Moonbeam" was the common sobriquet for Ms.

Moon, the director of the Bellehaven Public Library.
Helma had never called her that, although the name was
so common it no longer elicited comment. Helma sometimes wondered if even Ms. Moon was aware.

"What else could I do?" she asked, surprised by his
question. "I'm not useful at the hospital. I'll visit him
during my lunch hour and after work."

"Spoken like a library trouper, but don't be surprised if
you feel different in a couple of hours. Bad news takes a
while to soak in." He paused. "I know."

Helma looked at George curiously. Despite his cyni-
cism, he was a private man, and none of them had learned
much about his personal life, even after working with
him for several years.

George folded his newspaper into quarters and
dropped it in the trash can beside his desk. "Looks like he
won't be investigating this new murder, then. Did he tell
you about it?"

"Lewis Dixon?" Helma asked. "No. Did you know
him?"

"Only by sight," George told her. "Shame." He sighed
and shook his head. "The pamphlet holder meeting is still
on for nine o'clock sharp. The Moonbeam has declared
the whole staff should pass judgment on the design." He
rolled his eyes. "Nothing is so insignificant that we can't
form a committee to beat it down to its lowest common
denominator."

"It *is* an issue that effects everyone."

"Not me. Nobody reads pamphlets anyway. Look at
the reams we threw out last month. The only time patrons
take one is when they need scratch paper. And now we're
going to add a new piece of furniture to hold them?
Killing a tree to hold more dead trees."

"Maybe the pamphlets aren't used because they aren't
clearly accessible to the public."

"Then put it on video," George grumbled. "People
don't want to read; they want to *watch*." As Helma

walked away, George mimicked in falsetto, "Oh, Mister Librarian. I don't want to read all those big words in *Moby Dick*, don't you have it on video?"

Farther back in the workroom, Harley Woodworth, the social science librarian who George called Hardly Worth-it, sat in his cubicle next to Helma's, one elbow on his desk, shoulders back, in an executive pose. After Ms. Moon had taken Harley into her office a month ago to discuss his increasingly morose behavior, Harley had attended a three-day retreat on one of the more remote San Juan Islands, where he'd shouted himself hoarse, pounded drums, cried over his depressingly mundane childhood, and triumphantly stumbled across a bed of burning coals.

Not only had he returned with a slight limp from blistered soles, but with a whole new persona that still hadn't settled comfortably over his formerly health-obsessed, pessimistic self.

"Good morning, Helma," he said in his new lower-pitched, smoother-toned voice. No more announcements of his morning blood pressure, no more rows of vitamins and herbal concoctions lining his desk. His hair had grown around his ears. His pants, which he'd worn belted too high, had been replaced by pleated-front chinos, his striped shirts by collarless shirts and vests advertised in slick magazines.

"Good morning, Harley."

"I understand your police friend has been injured," Harley said. His eyes sparkled with keen interest but Helma noted his struggle to hold back the probing medical questions and conjectures he would have offered as the old Harley. He still retained his former habit of opening his jaws while holding his lips closed, which he did now. Twice.

"Yes, he has, but we're hoping he'll recover quickly," Helma told him as she placed her purse in her lower desk drawer and sat down to change from her casual shoes to her navy pumps.

When she heard furtive whispers coming from Harley's cubicle, Helma raised her head to see Deidre Templeton, the new Washington State history and geneal-ogy librarian, leaning across Harley's desk, her strident whispers buzzing, Harley nodding as he listened. Their position made Helma think of the figures in a painting she'd seen once, but at the moment she couldn't remem-ber where.

"Oh," Deidre said when she saw Helma, pulling back from Harley. "I didn't see you hiding down there."

"Good morning, Deidre," Helma said, ignoring the barb. When Deidre first arrived at the library, she'd announced, "I'd like to be called DiDi," and although everyone except Helma had tried it at least once, Deidre she'd remained. "It would be like calling my pit bull Fifi," George Melville had apologized to her. "If I had a pit bull."

Deidre was pale-skinned, with long pale hair she wore in two tight braids that began high on her scalp and joined into one thin braid that hung to her waist. She was thin and tense, and during moments of high anxiety grabbed the tail of her braid and brushed it back and forth across her cheek.

Deidre had joined the staff the Thursday before Harley had left for his life-changing retreat. Barely noticing Harley previously, Diedre had been dazzled by his trans-formation and had taken up the challenge of fostering the new Harley, adopting him with the same enthusiasm she greeted a tome of new genealogy lists.

"Then you're not staying at the hospital this morning?" Deidre asked Helma. "I thought you'd be needed there."

"I'll return later," Helma told her, watching Deidre pull her braid from behind her back.

"Then you're going to the meeting about the new pam-phlet holder?"

Helma was certain she saw Deidre nudge Harley. "Yes," Helma told her. "I'm the chairperson of the committee to select a design."

"Oh." Deidre stepped away from Harley's desk. "That's the way it'll be, then," she said mysteriously, and left his cubicle. Harley turned to his computer, his fingers racing across his keyboard.

The minutes until the meeting crawled past. Helma wasn't scheduled on the reference desk until that afternoon, and although library affairs were usually so engrossing they occupied all Helma's attention, today she couldn't keep her thoughts from traveling back to Wayne Gallant lying silently in his bed only two blocks away.

How had he ended up at the bottom of Danish Point? He wasn't a man who took foolish chances, and she couldn't imagine him in a physical confrontation with a criminal—not alone. But Officer 087 had said he'd answered a call, which was curious in itself. And to leave his two children? It didn't make sense.

"Tonights" he'd said. Or "tonight." She printed the two words in the margin of an ad for a new reference book titled, *Stephen King: A Concordance*. Beneath those two words, she added, "Two Nights," then other near-homonyms: doughnuts, too nice, do nice, dolmite, too tight.

Helma leaned back and studied the list, turning her pencil end over end. The words were meaningless. She needed clarification. Ruth was right: Wayne Gallant had probably spoken to the police when he was rescued. She tapped the eraser end of her mechanical pencil against the desktop, extruding an inch and a half of lead from the tip. If only he'd spoken to someone besides Carter Houston, she might learn what he'd said.

She picked up the telephone on her desk and had punched in the first four digits of the police department before she pulled away her hand and hung up the receiver. She needed more information, but from whom? It wasn't likely any policeman would be forthcoming over the phone. And so often the answers were in more than words. She needed to talk face-to-face so she could *see* the answers as well as hear them.

Finally, she retrieved a book on head injuries from the library's medical section and perused its index, reading portions on symptoms and prognoses. After finding articles that contradicted each other and offered no real insight, she closed the book, the unhelpful words "every case is unique" echoing in her mind.

At 9:05 all the librarians sat at the round table in the tiny staff lounge: George Melville to Helma's right; Eve, the curly-haired fiction librarian to Helma's left; and Roger Barnhard, the children's librarian, beside Eve. Harley and Deidre sat together separated from George Melville by an empty chair. Ms. May Apple Moon, the library director, entered the room, wearing a new smaller-sized dress. The former vegetarian had adopted a diet that she at first jokingly called "Meats and Grease" but which she now spoke of with the awe and fervency of a religious convert who's witnessed a miracle. Absolutely no fruit, vegetables, or grains. Her weight loss had been visibly instant but her giddiness over the dropping pounds was beginning to wear thin.

Ms. Moon stood, casting occasional glances at her reflection in the mirror on the wall opposite her and smoothing her palms over her hips as if she were checking to see if her bones had been uncovered yet.

"We have several pressing items on our agenda today," she began, "beginning with the fact that all of our public computer terminals are being monopolized by e-mail users rather than for research. We . . ."

Helma, whose habit was to record the salient points of each meeting she attended on a yellow pad for future reference, found her pencil poised over the yellow pad—

fifteen minutes had passed and she hadn't written a single word nor did she have the slightest idea what Ms. Moon was talking about. She caught the words "temporary access," and printed those in block letters on the second line of her sheet of paper. On the other side of her, Eve and Roger were exchanging notes. Helma glimpsed the drawing of a duck on the slip of paper Eve was passing Roger. George was writing the words "Beck's beer" on what appeared to be a grocery list.

If Wayne Gallant's fall wasn't an accident, was the person who pushed him still in the vicinity, waiting for an opportunity to finish the deed he'd begun? There hadn't been a guard outside his room that morning. She wrote "arrange police protection" beneath "temporary access," and saw George Melville's puzzled expression as he glanced at her pad. She casually laid her pencil across the words and again turned her attention to Ms. Moon, who was smiling at herself in the mirror and asking, "Are there any other issues we need to discuss?"

Beside Helma, George whispered, "Uh-oh," and nodded toward Harley and Deidre. "Something's on the wind."

Deidre swiped the end of her braid across her cheek like a paintbrush. Back and forth. Her spine was rigid and her pale eyes burned toward Ms. Moon. Harley sat beside her, opening and closing his jaws, his lips so tightly closed they'd nearly disappeared. He looked as if he had a stomachache.

"All right, then," Ms. Moon said, "it's time for a discussion of the new pamphlet holder. Helma, this is your committee, and also, I believe," she glanced down at her notes, which were written on paper edged with butterflies and mystic clouds, "Eve and George."

Deidre held the end of her braid clasped in both hands and stood. Her chair scraped against the floor. "Harley is on the committee," she announced at the same time that Harley said, in a weaker voice, "I'm on the committee."

Deidre remained standing while Harley slouched in his chair, his head sunk into his shoulders as he gazed defiantly into the middle distance.

"Harley has every right to be on the committee," Deidre continued, her voice rising to ringing fervency. "He distributes pamphlets as much as the rest of you and he has the same responsibility to the reading public as you all do. Our patrons look up to Harley; they trust his judgment."

"Wrap that woman's braid around her head and give her a sword and breastplate," George murmured, then began humming a tune that sounded Wagnerian.

"Everyone will have an opportunity to see the final design and comment on it before we request bids for its construction," Helma told Deidre.

"That's not the same thing," Deidre said, her voice ascending another notch. "Harley may have pamphlets in mind that are of an unusual size."

"And what size would that be?" George asked. Eve smothered a giggle, her curls undulating. "Now—" Ms. Moon began.

Deidre's face turned bright red. The tail of her braid twirled in her hands. She cut off Ms. Moon's words, nearly shouting, "Harley's voice must be heard."

Harley looked up at her, a confusion of admiration and consternation on his face. He reached forward as if he were about to touch Deidre's arm, then jerked away, clasping his hands tightly on the tabletop.

When Helma didn't respond, Deidre added, "Besides, your boyfriend is probably going to die and you won't have time anyway. Harley could be chairman."

Helma rose, ignoring Eve, who gasped and said, "What a rotten thing to say. That's mean; that's just *so* mean."

"Excuse me." It was Dutch, keeper of the circulation

counter. He stood at the door, his military bearing exaggerated. "There's a policeman here to see you, Helma."

"It's bad news," Deidre said with a trace of satisfaction.

George stood and pointed his finger at Deidre. "You. Shut. Up."

❧ chapter ten ❧

NEVER A WORD

Helma followed Dutch from the workroom into the library's public area. Dutch was an ex-Army sergeant who'd embraced both the mission of the library and Ms. Moon's leadership. Like the retired sergeant he was, taking position ahead of Helma turned his stride into a cadenced march, which suited her at the moment, relieving her of concentrating on the simple act of ambulation. She set one foot firmly in front of the other, only the clenching and unclenching of her hands betraying the turmoil in her heart.

Why were the police here to see her? The children. Had something happened to Syndi and Joseph? Perhaps her apartment had been burglarized or Boy Cat Zukas had mauled another cat. It could be her mother or Aunt Em. Aunt Em *was* eighty-four years old, after all, and her mother drove way too fast. She straightened a chair as she passed a library table, picked up a gum wrapper from the floor, cast a warning glance at a young boy pinching his little sister, all the time keeping a wall around the idea that something had happened to Wayne Gallant, that through the power of saying it aloud, Deidre had twisted fate and made it come true.

Dutch paused for Helma to draw abreast of him, then stepped behind the circulation desk and nodded his thumb-shaped head, first to Helma, then toward the foyer.

She turned to see detective Carter Houston sitting on one of the green and wood chairs, his back straight and feet tidily together, a book balanced across his knees. She glanced back at Dutch for verification and he solemnly nodded again.

Carter Houston stood when he saw Helma walking toward the foyer. Something in her expression must have alerted him because he held up a plump hand and quickly assured her, "I didn't bring bad news. The chief's coming to, I heard."

"The children?" Helma asked.

"Fine as far as I know. Your friend's with them, though," he added, sounding as if *that* were bad news.

"Yes, I know." She chose the chair opposite him and he sat down again, settling into the Naugahyde seat and picking a speck of lint from his sleeve. "I hear the weather's expected to change," he said. The expression in his eyes was hidden by the sun's reflection off his black-rimmed glasses.

"Carter," Helma said, catching him before he had time to prepare his defenses, "I was just about to phone you. What's your opinion of 'tonights,' the words the chief uttered at the hospital—and presumably when you found him as well?"

She watched Carter's face closely. He was a true professional, quick to conceal his emotions but not so fast that Helma didn't catch the slight narrowing of his eyes. She wasn't giving him new information, that was obvious.

"Can you at least tell me what type of call he was responding to, and why *him*? Why not one of the other officers? Was it a burglary? An accident? I'm guessing the original call wasn't to Danish Point or you would have found him sooner."

Carter merely gazed past her head, his lips pursed like

a fish's, one of the fish her father and uncles used to spear in Scoop River. Suckers, they called them.

"All right, Carter," Helma said. "Why did you ask to speak with me?"

Carter let out a breath like a sigh, pushed his glasses higher on his nose, and regarded her for a few moments before he held up the book that was sitting on his knee. That's when Helma noticed the book was sealed inside a clear resealable bag. She spotted the bar code on the upper left side of the front jacket, the blue ownership stamp of the Bellehaven Public Library on the end pages.

"This book," he said, and stopped, tapping the cover with his forefinger and holding it close enough for her to read the title but not to touch. It was an oversized book called, *Behind the Looking Glass*. Not a book from the children's collection but the annotated, analyzed version from the adult collection. It wasn't a new book; Helma had seen it several times in the past few years.

"Yes?" Helma asked, leaving it to Carter to dole out the information in his precise, some might say smug, manner. She'd seen bags like the plastic bag that enclosed *Behind the Looking Glass*: the sealable top and frosted area for writing date and details; it was an evidence bag.

"Is it familiar to you?" Carter asked, still holding up the book.

"Of course. It's shelved in the 820s, I believe. It was more popular a few years ago than now. It's an analysis of Carroll's *Through the Looking Glass*. Exhaustively so, I understand."

"The soup strained too thin?"

"Flannery O'Connor accused her critics of doing exactly that," Helma said, frankly surprised at Carter's allusion.

Carter nodded wisely. "Do you know who checked this book out?"

"Of course not. And even if I did, as a librarian I'd never divulge that information. We assure our patrons' complete privacy."

"But you could access the computer records and confirm who'd checked it out, correct?"

"It's technically possible, yes, but doing so is against the guidelines of the American Library Association Code of Ethics, the Revised Code of Washington, and the tenets of librarianship which are adhered to by every librarian of ethical persuasion."

Carter Houston pressed his lips together and a dimple formed in one cheek. He turned *Behind the Looking Glass* in his hands and gave Helma a meaningful look she chose to ignore.

Tami, one of the new pages, pushed a cartload of books through the foyer and looked curiously at Helma and Carter Houston from the sides of her eyes.

Carter waited until she was gone before he cleared his throat and held up the bagged book, turning its cover toward Helma as if it were sacred. "This book," he said, "was found at a crime scene."

"That makes no difference," Helma told him. "Our patrons put their trust in our policies. To betray their trust and expose their reading habits to police scrutiny would hinder their quest for knowledge. Haven't you ever wished to pursue certain sorts of information in complete privacy, even secrecy?"

Carter's eyes shifted to the left, then back again to Helma's face, but without meeting her eyes. "It's a vital link to this particular crime scene," he said, "the only clue we have. By knowing who checked this book out, we could solve this crime."

"Not necessarily," Helma disagreed. "I believe you're speaking of circumstantial evidence. Knowing the borrower's name wouldn't mean that person had committed the crime. Library books are frequently stolen or lost or even borrowed. Did you take fingerprints from the laminated book jacket?"

Carter nodded as if she'd asked a naive question. "There was a confusion of prints on this book, none of them usable to identify the criminal." Helma raised her eyebrows and he corrected, "The *alleged* criminal."

"Why ask me about the book's borrower?" she asked, preparing to rise. "Speaking to Ms. Moon would be more appropriate. Although any librarian here would refuse to divulge our borrowers' records." A fact of which Helma wasn't completely certain.

Carter folded the loose edge of plastic around the book and slipped it into the black briefcase beside his chair. "I thought you would be the most cooperative since you have an interest in this case."

Helma Zukas did not play guessing games or leap to take enticements that were suspiciously dangled in front of her. "Excuse me," she said, rising from her chair. "If there's nothing else, I have work to attend to."

"This book," Carter Houston said in the sonorous voice of one who relishes delivering a bombshell, "was found at Danish Point, where Wayne Gallant nearly lost his life. It's the only piece of evidence in our possession."

Helma dropped back into the Naugahyde chair. The air whooshed out of the seat cushion. "Evidence?" she repeated.

"The only piece," he confirmed, leaning down and patting his briefcase with a curious fondness.

Helma thought fiercely, recalling her Library Ethics class, the "Sanctity of Trust" workshop she'd attended, even the article she'd coauthored on "The Librarian-Patron Bond." Next, she thought of Wayne Gallant's still form beneath the white hospital sheets.

Carter leaned toward her. She smelled his shaving lotion, the same once-popular spicy brand her uncles and father had used. His voice dropped. "There may be a few facts about the case I could share with you."

"The police have a code of ethics as well," Helma reminded him, leaning away from him.

His face looked pained. "I'm not breaking any code, only sharing facts that will soon be made public."

"When you found him, did he say anything else besides 'tonights'?" she asked.

"I'm not saying I heard anything more," Carter told her coyly.

"Was the word 'tonight' in the possessive form?"

"I couldn't say," he told her.

"Why was he at Danish Point?" Helma tried.

Carter leaned back and placed his elbows on the chair arms. He might have been seated at a desk, speaking to a subordinate. "A complaint about a prowler was called in. Since it was Sunday and we were short staffed, he decided to take it."

"The *chief of police* decided to take it?" Helma repeated, confused. Carter watched her closely as she tried to puzzle it out. She recalled what TNT Stone had said, and asked, "Wasn't he questioning Mary Lynn Dixon; about her husband's death at the time?"

"I wasn't there," Carter said curtly.

"He left his two children at the police station to answer a call about a prowler while he was in the midst of a *murder* interrogation?"

"Whatever he did was his own decision," Carter said.

"But why? It doesn't make sense." She tapped her fingers on the wooden arm of her chair and looked at him expectantly. "Unless there was something unusual about the prowler."

"You'll have to ask him that when he regains consciousness," Carter said, and Helma couldn't tell from his face whether he knew the reason or not.

Dutch left the circulation desk and walked through the foyer, close to Helma's chair. He turned the jade plant near the window so the opposite side faced the light, then took several moments to realign the pot. Helma waited until he returned to the circulation desk before she continued. "The book was at Danish Point?" she tried. "How did you connect it to Wayne Gallant? People frequently watch the sunset or enjoy the view from that spot. Any of our patrons might have accidentally left it there."

Now Carter spoke with some reluctance. He rubbed his palms together. "The pages weren't warped, so the book hadn't been lying on the ground very long. It may have fallen from a car."

"In a scuffle?" Helma asked. There was more that Carter wasn't saying, more evidence; she could feel it.

Carter glanced toward his briefcase and said even more reluctantly, "Maybe."

"That doesn't mean that whoever checked out the book pushed Wayne Gallant over the cliff."

"We know that. But they could have been at Danish Point at approximately the same time. They may possess critical information." Carter watched Helma intently, and when she didn't say anything more, he asked, "Then you'll cooperate? You'll tell us who checked out this book?"

"I already explained that would be against the foundations of librarianship."

Carter Houston's cheeks puffed. He gripped his hands together until his soft knuckles turned white. "But I told you about—" he began.

"And I appreciate that," Helma assured him, "but I cannot betray my career."

Carter's mouth opened, then closed. He reached into his briefcase and removed *Behind the Looking Glass*, turning the front cover toward Helma as if it were a threat. "I'll talk to Ms. Moon, then."

"I'm sure she'll tell you the same thing."

"Are you? Really?" Carter rose from his chair. "We'll see."

"When I visited Wayne Gallant this morning I didn't see any policemen there."

He paused and frowned at her, his mouth pursed, his eyes rapidly blinking through eyeglass lenses. "And?"

"Shouldn't there be? If his fall was intentional—and you already referred to the site of his fall as a 'crime scene'—aren't the police concerned that whoever pushed him intended to kill him and might try to complete their intent?"

Such an open startled look crossed Carter's face before he could hide it that Helma knew the idea hadn't occurred to the police, or at least not to Carter. She pushed the moment, watching Carter closely. "Especially if this prowler had some other importance to the chief, as you suspect." But Carter was already smoothing his face into bland inscrutable lines.

"I'll talk to Ms. Moon now," he said, and headed for the circulation desk.

Helma watcher Carter Houston, the bagged book held close like a schoolchild's first text. She wasn't at all sure how Ms. Moon would respond to the police request. The circumstances were persuasive, and Ms. Moon had a weakness for civic responsibility, or at least the theory of it. There were dark and shameful stories of book-related employees who'd collaborated in famous cases: the New York "Mad Bomber," the Unabomber, Monica Lewinsky. And there were library heroines and heroes as well: the John Hinckley case, Sylvia Seegrist, the resistance to the FBI's "Library Awareness Program" in the 1980s. Ms. Moon and Carter Houston, despite their polar personalities, did have a certain sympathetic relationship.

The facts were indisputable to Helma: whatever material a library patron chose to read, whatever a librarian knew about a patron's interests, that information was as sacred as the bond between confessor and penitent.

There were occasions in life when decisions were made instantly, when there was no need for intense scrutiny or detailed lists of pros and cons. This was one of those moments. Without another instant of indecision, with no consideration of an alternative, Helma proceeded through the library without glancing left or right, no notice taken of misaligned chairs, giggling teenagers, or patrons arguing over whose turn it was to use a computer.

She pushed through the staff room door and marched to her cubicle, passing the now-empty staff lounge, only glancing once toward Ms. Moon's office, where through the open door she could see Carter Houston speaking to the director in hushed tones. Her computer still ran the screen saver of Melvil Dewey's famous quote of librarianship. She barely noticed Deidre leaving Harley's cubicle or Harley glancing soulfully in her own direction.

She sat down and rolled her chair close to her keyboard. Using her password, she logged into the library's circulation system. Without wavering, she pulled up the title *Behind the Looking Glass*. It was a simple procedure. Turning her head aside so she couldn't see the screen, or the borrower's name, Helma deleted the book's checkout history. Just that easily, it disappeared.

But there existed a second layer to the system where the record still resided. And also a third layer. To reach the third layer required a shutdown of the entire system and, in Carter's quest, a court ordered warrant, which would allow the undertaking to become a wider issue, with legal ramifications. The library world would rally, Helma was confident.

But the second layer could be accessed by using the director's password, which Helma happened to know after helping Ms. Moon untangle a computer knot she'd stumbled into the week before. Not that she'd *intended* to remember Ms. Moon's password, but it wasn't an easy one to forget.

"Hey, Helma, are you doing all right?" It was Eve, leaning into Helma's cubicle, her rosy face filled with concern. "Deidre is such a you-know-what. Don't listen to her, okay? The chief will recover even if it takes a while. Remember when I sprained my ankle that time? Skiing? I thought it would never heal, but now I can dance and everything."

"I'll be all right, thank you," Helma told her. Behind Eve, she still heard the quiet voices in Ms. Moon's office. She didn't have much time. "It's just that—"

Eve nodded. "I know." She touched her fist to her breast. "You really care about him a lot, don't you?"

Helma's hands fell away from her keyboard and she looked up into Eve's damp eyes. Eve's tears weren't unusual. She had once cried over a patron's convoluted tale of a lost book and a missing dog. Reading bad news in the *Bellehaven Daily News* sometimes left Eve sniffling into a tissue. "You're right," she told Eve, surprised how easily she could say the words. "I care about him very much."

"It'll be okay," Eve said, and left, holding her hand in a thumbs-up sign. Helma returned to her keyboard, feeling curiously comforted.

Moistening her lips, Helma delved into the second level, a murkier, more complex and fragile layer where a slight misstep could cripple the entire system. She entered Ms. Moon's password into the password box and clicked Enter, holding her breath, afraid that Ms. Moon had changed her password after sharing it with her.

But no, the screen blinked and Helma found herself in Level 2 without a guide. There were few help screens here. Moving purposefully but with caution, she again brought up *Behind the Looking Glass* and performed the Delete maneuver, looking away as she did so she wouldn't see the borrower's name.

But after what she felt to be an adequate amount of

time, when she turned her eyes back to the screen, the deletion hadn't been completed. And for an instant, in full view of Helma's helpless gaze, the borrower's name hung on the screen, before it blinked away forever.

❦ chapter eleven ❦

NEITHER MORE
NOR LESS

It was impossible for Helma to erase from her memory the name of the person who'd borrowed *Behind the Looking Glass*. She sat gazing at the Level 2 screen as if the name were still there among the pixels, glowing and pulsing and burning itself onto the screen. She didn't want to know; she wished with all her heart that she hadn't seen it. She removed a plain M&M from the ceramic box on her desk and sucked on it. A thought, like a blinking light, was asking, "Now what?" Then she sighed and bit the M&M in two between her front teeth, chewed and swallowed it. But she did know, so that was that.

Raised voices intruded into her thoughts and she leaned forward, swiftly pushing a few strategic keys on her keyboard, rising to safety from Level 2 until her screen showed only the library's desktop of icons.

"It was you, wasn't it?" Ms. Moon accused, standing at the entrance to Helma's cubicle, her hands on her hips, one foot tapping. Behind her stood Carter Houston, both their faces sternly set, eyes narrowed at Helma. The workroom was suddenly as silent as if it had been emptied of library staff. Even the air circulation system appeared to have shut down.

"I beg your pardon?" Helma asked. She took her hands from the warm keyboard and folded them together on her lap.

"Forty-five seconds ahead of me," Ms. Moon said, her wide mouth making exaggerated movements as she spoke. "*You* erased the name of the borrower of *Behind the Looking Glass*. And then . . ." She took a breath so deep it enhanced her height and girth by inches, shimmering the fabric of her dress. "And then," she repeated, "you used *my* password to sneak into Level 2 and erase the borrower's name there, didn't you? *My* password."

"Who was the borrower?" Carter Houston demanded. He still held the plastic-encased book in his hands.

"I turned my head when that information appeared on the screen," Helma told him, demonstrating exactly how she'd looked at the wall where her Great Libraries of the World calendar hung. She turned back to Ms. Moon. "I don't *sneak*. I simply did what any self-respecting librarian would be compelled to do, what I'd have expected you to do." She heard a gasp from Harley's cubicle.

"It's our responsibility to cooperate with the police," Ms. Moon said, "to support law and order. You of all people, considering your 'relationship' with the chief of police, should have been eager to do that." She shook her finger at Helma. "You weren't so clever. Not so clever at all. Maybe you erased the borrower's name from the circulation records and from Level 2, but it still exists in the computer's internal files. It can be pulled out by an expert."

"I'm aware of that," Helma told her, "but I believe that will take a court order, which necessitates arguing against a library patron's basic right to privacy. Many agencies will be interested in such an argument, including the

American Civil Liberties Union and the American Library Association."

"Curious but suitable bedfellows." It was George Melville, who now stood on the other side of Ms. Moon, his eyes sparkling. He stroked his beard and said to Ms. Moon, "But Helma's right. You'll need a warrant to search for that record."

As one, Harley and Deidre now rose from behind the shelves that separated Harley's cubicle from Helma's. Harley's jaws worked so hard he might have been chewing a wad of gum. Deidre held her braid end to her cheek. "But this is a criminal issue," Deidre said. "That's different, and there *are* precedents; other libraries have cooperated with the law in criminal cases."

"Much to our chagrin," George commented.

Ms. Moon flashed Deidre an appreciative look, and Deidre stepped closer to Harley and said, "Harley thought of that."

"And it's such an original thought, too," George commented. "Any other earth-shattering announcements? Thoughts on the right to bear arms? Freedom of the press? Separation of Church and State?"

"You always think you're so funny," Deidre spat out at George, who beamed that much more.

"What's going on?" Eve asked, entering the workroom through the door from the library's public area. "It's sure busy out there. Hi, Carter. I saw you at the pizzeria last night. Your Lhasa apso is such a little cutie."

"This is a serious library matter," Ms. Moon told Eve. "A sensitive and controversial policy issue has been circumvented by Helma Zukas."

"The rights of the individual are the library's highest priority," Helma said. "More so than institutional and societal rights."

"Who do you think pays our salaries?" Ms. Moon asked.

Helma opened her desk drawer and removed her purse. "I'm leaving," she said, standing and pushing in her chair.

Ms. Moon's mouth dropped open. "You're leaving the library?" she asked.

"You're walking out in the middle of this crisis?" Deidre asked Helma, her eyes on Ms. Moon.

"There is no crisis," Helma said, gazing first at Deidre, then Ms. Moon. "The matter is out of my hands. If you plan to carry it further, you'd be wise to contact the city attorney."

At that moment the staff door banged open and Ruth, with Joseph and Syndi behind her, entered the workroom. Ruth, who always liked to dress for her roles, wore a cotton shirtwaist dress that was almost subdued enough for the mother figure on a family TV series. Her lipstick matched Syndi's and her hair was in a modified page boy. She paused, taking in the group by Helma's cubicle before an eager smile lit her face. "Oh, this looks good," she said as she reached the little gathering. "What devilment have you stirred up now, Carter?"

Carter opened his mouth but Deidre beat him to it. "Helma's responsible," she told Ruth. "Helma's in trouble."

"Don't get your hopes up," George warned Deidre. "These things have a way of coming back and kicking you in the kazoo."

"This is a private work area," Ms. Moon informed Ruth. "It's no place for . . ." She waved her hand toward Syndi and Joseph. ". . . the public."

"Then we won't stay," Ruth replied amiably. "Think of us as having accidentally wandered through the wrong door at the wrong time, or the right time, depending on your perspective. It happens all the time in the movies. You know, when the innocent bystander walks into a room just in time to save the innocent victim from being shredded by the villains." She glanced from Ms. Moon to Carter, "Or whatever you're calling yourselves these days." She turned and made herding motions to Joseph and Syndi, back toward the door. Both young people remained where they were.

"Wait for me," Helma told her.

Ruth spun around, her eyebrows raised. "What is this, a rebellion?"

"You haven't requested personal leave," Ms. Moon told Helma.

"I'll take unpaid time, then," Helma told her, taking a step toward Ms. Moon. "Now if you'll excuse me."

"But you don't behave this way," Ms. Moon said, still blocking the entrance to Helma's cubicle, but on her face a look of uncertainty, even uneasiness.

"Don't or can't?" Ruth asked Ms. Moon, who spluttered.

"Don't. You're simply walking out of the library?"

Helma stepped closer to Ms. Moon. "I will if you'll get out of my way."

Deidre gasped and Harley grunted. George grinned so hard his beard rose upward like a smile. Eve made a sound like a squeak through her hands, and Ruth smiled indulgently at them all. Helma was aware of Joseph and Syndi watching the scene with avid interest while Carter and Ms. Moon stared at her with red and shocked faces.

Helma stood in front of Ms. Moon, inches from her, purse in hand, not saying another word, waiting. Ms. Moon's mouth opened and closed twice before she backed out of Helma's path into the narrow aisle. Carter Houston stepped back against a shelf of outdated cataloging manuals. Both were grim-faced.

Ms. Moon blocked the path to the back door, so Helma was forced to lead the way through the public area of the library to the front door. Ruth fell in behind her, humming the theme from *Bridge on the River Kwai*. Helma still heard Deidre's piping voice behind her. "See, this proves Harley should be chairman of the pamphlet holder committee."

As if voices had been raised, which Helma knew they hadn't, library patrons, with expressions of speculative curiosity, were attentive to their passing through the library: first Helma, then Ruth, Joseph, and Syndi. Activity at the circulation desk ceased; hands froze while stamping due dates in books. Dutch stood ramrod straight, watching them pass, and for a brief bizarre moment Helma was certain he was about to raise his hand to his forehead in a salute.

The moment the front doors closed behind them, Ruth stopped on the sidewalk and demanded, "What was that all about? What was Detecto-bot Carter Houston doing in the library?"

"He wanted me to divulge the name of a library patron."

"Oh." The interest in Ruth's face waned. "Is that all?" she asked, and started walking down the sidewalk ahead of Helma. "Did you do it?"

"It's against librarians' ethics."

Ruth picked an aster from the library's flower bed and waved it toward Helma. "So then I assume you *didn't* do it?"

"Of course not."

Ruth stopped again. "Wait a minute. I'm blinded by the high drama of you shucking off your chains and strolling unfettered out the library doors. Why did Carter want the name of a library patron?"

Helma glanced toward Joseph and Syndi, who'd slipped back into their sullen roles but stood only five feet away. Joseph turned parking meter handles and Syndi picked at the red polish on her fingernails.

"Oh. The kids are listening. You two, go wait by Helma's car in the parking lot."

"How are we supposed to know which one it is?" Joseph asked.

"I bet it's a Honda," Syndi said, her lip already rising in a sneer.

"Shows what you know," Ruth told them. "It's the oldest and cleanest car there. You'll know it when you see it, trust me."

"Did you take the children to the hospital?" Helma asked Ruth.

"If you ever hope to be on good terms with these two, don't call them children; just use their names, okay? Or say 'kids,' or even 'teenagers.' But yeah, we were there. They did their best to stay cool but it didn't work." Ruth shrugged and a sad expression crossed her face. "Poor kids. Tough to see your dad flat out like that. I mean, remember my dad? I *expected* to find him passed out in an alcoholic stupor in some dark corner or maybe even get a call to pick him up at the hospital emergency room, but these two think their father is some kind of a superhero."

"Carter said he was regaining consciousness."

Ruth nodded. "Compassionate of him to tell you that much. He wasn't talking yet but he smiled at Joseph and Syndi. You going over to visit him?"

"For a few minutes. Were there any police there?"

"One came as we left. Why?"

"I just wondered."

Ruth glanced sharply at Helma, then looked to be sure Syndi and Joseph were actually gone and said, "Okay, tell me what was going in the library."

Helma sighed. Ruth wouldn't let up until she'd heard all the facts. It was easier just to tell her and get it over with. "A library book was found at a crime scene and the police wanted to know who checked it out."

"And hotshot detective Carter asked *you*?"

Helma nodded.

"Why you, the paragon of librarianship? He should have known better. Why didn't he just go directly to his soulmate, Ms. Moonbeam?" Ruth snapped her fingers.

"Because he thought he could convince you to release the name. Because . . ." She placed her fingers on her temples like a psychic. "Wait, wait, don't tell me. Because it involved our beloved chief of police, so he believed that you—of all people—would cooperate. Am I right?"

"I can't speak for his motives." Two women carrying bags full of library books passed them, turning curiously to look at Ruth. One of them smiled widely at Helma and said, "Hello, Miss Zukas. I found that company's name after all and they're sending me my money back."

"That's good news," Helma said, uncertain what the woman was talking about.

"Loved by one and all," Ruth commented, watching the two women walk into the library. "Back to business. Did the cops try checking the book for fingerprints?"

"Carter said most of the fingerprints were too muddled."

"Most? But not all, am I right? Maybe a couple proved to be the chief's himself. I know, the book was overdue and Wayne Gallant, desperate to win your affections, tracked it down, and when he tried to wrest it from the delinquent's hands, he or she bumped him over the cliff and ran away in terror at what they'd done."

"The book wasn't overdue. Carter said they found it at Danish Point where the empty cruiser was discovered."

"Ouch. What else did he say?"

Helma pulled a leaf from an Oregon grape plant and tore it along its filaments. "That the chief had responded to a caller reporting a prowler."

"Do you believe that? It sounds fishy to me, like Carter didn't think that one through before he answered. Why did *he* respond to a prowler call?"

"That's exactly what I wondered," Helma said. "Carter claims that because it was Sunday the department was low on staff so the chief offered to take the call." She dropped the remains of the leaf on the ground. "But at the time he was in the midst of questioning Mary Lynn."

"And it would take more than a common prowler to lure the chief away from something as juicy as a murder."

"Exactly. TNT or Mary Lynn may have overheard vital information."

"Yeah, better ask them, 'cause Carter sure won't share."

"He did verify that the chief said the word 'tonights' when he found him."

Ruth shrugged. "For what that's worth; to me, it's too cryptic to be useful. And that's who they believed dropped the book? The person who pushed him over?"

Helma nodded.

Ruth leaned down until she could look squarely into Helma's face. Helma smelled her musky perfume. "It's beginning to come clear to me why the Moonbeam and Carter were preparing to flay you when I walked in. You deleted the borrower's name?"

"I did."

"Hmm, but I bet you saw the name, didn't you?"

"I turned my head away," Helma told her, just as she'd told Ms. Moon.

Ruth straightened. "I know you, Wilhelmina Zukas. You can't futz with me. I'm oh so very aware you never ever lie but you don't always complete your stories, either. Maybe you turned your head away from the screen, but either you turned back too soon or the computer did a funny, right?"

Helma didn't answer, and Ruth said, "Thought so."

Ruth and Helma turned into the library's small parking lot. Syndi was leaning against the front fender of Helma's Buick, her headset over her ears, eyes distant. But Joseph walked around the twenty-two-year-old Buick, gently putting a fingertip to its hood ornament, gazing at himself in the chrome, peering through its windows. When he looked up at Ruth and Helma, his face was almost animated. "This is a classic," he announced. "Where'd you get it?"

"It was a high school graduation present," Helma told him.

"Cool."

"Be nice and maybe she'll let you ride in it," Ruth told him. She turned back to Helma. "You go to the hospital and I'll take these guys home with me and bring them over to your apartment after lunch, okay? I've got things going on this afternoon."

"To stay with me?" Helma asked.

Even though she was wearing earphones, Syndi responded, "We can stay at Dad's house."

"Uh-uh," Ruth said, shaking her head. "Ground rules as of now: you two stay with big people until your dad's out of the hospital." Syndi opened her mouth but Ruth held up a warning hand. "No negotiations. Absolutely none."

Syndi slouched back against Helma's car, turning up the sound until Helma heard its rhythm. In a lower voice Ruth said to Helma, "Never voice doubt; they pick up on it, the same way wild animals smell fear. Don't even *think* doubtful thoughts."

"Even when I feel them?" Helma asked.

"Especially then."

❧ chapter twelve ❧

EAGER FOR
THE TRUTH

Helma recognized the policeman sitting outside Wayne Gallant's hospital room. It was Cliff Bikman, who she'd helped find the GNP of Tasmania when he was a high school junior. He rocked his chair against the wall, tall, brown-haired, still lanky, but with an edge of hardness around his eyes. An elderly couple glanced warily at the policeman and then gave him a wide berth as they passed Room 224.

When Cliff saw Helma, the front two legs of the chair thumped to the floor. "Hello, Miss Zukas."

"Cliff. How long have you been here?"

He glanced at his watch. "Maybe fifteen minutes. Carter Houston ordered it about twenty minutes ago. I'm here for four hours and then another officer will relieve me. We'll be on duty around the clock. I brought some books," he added, pointing to the two paperbacks on the floor.

"Good idea. Have you talked to him?"

"Carter?"

"The chief."

"Oh." He shook his head. "He was asleep when I came on. But you can go in. You're on the list."

"List?"

Cliff was still young enough to blush. "Family. I mean, kind of."

In Room 224, Chief of Police Wayne Gallant lay on his back, the head of his hospital bed slightly raised. Helma stood at the end of the bed gazing down at him. One of the machines he'd been connected to had disappeared. His hair had been cleaned of blood and there was more color to his face. His eyes were closed.

"Wayne," she whispered. The light above his head was set on low, aimed toward the ceiling. It hummed softly.

He didn't move, and she stepped to the head of the bed, glancing once to be sure the hallway was empty before she leaned down and quickly, briefly, pressed her lips against Wayne Gallant's forehead, then just as quickly straightened.

His blue, blue eyes opened. "Hi," he said in a husky whisper, his eyes meeting hers without surprise, as if he'd been aware of her presence all along. He ran his tongue over his lips, and she offered him the glass of water sitting on his bed tray. He took two swallows through the bendable straw.

"Are you feeling better?" Helma asked.

He nodded and smiled slightly before reclosing his eyes, reaching out his hand toward her. Helma took his hand and stood that way, half leaning over the bed, holding his big warm hand in hers, oblivious to the growing ache in her back, the weight of her purse on her shoulder, the impersonal sounds of the hospital. It was all very pleasant.

Finally, she stretched out her leg and with her foot she pulled the chair near the window closer to the bed and sat down. Her knees pressed against the cold metal of the bed frame. Wayne Gallant's breathing shifted from shallow to deep, uneven. Helma saw sparks behind her eyes and realized she was breathing to match his rough respiration. She counted, evening her own breaths, willing his to match hers instead. She sat that way for fifteen minutes, breathing evenly and consciously, holding his hand. Just as she was about to extricate her hand and leave, the chief opened his eyes again and whispered, "Helma." He swallowed, and she held the glass of water so he could take another drink through the bendable straw. "The kids?" he asked when he was finished.

"They're fine," Helma assured him. "Ruth took them to lunch and then they're coming to my house."

His eyebrows rose but he only whispered, "Thanks."

"Do you remember what happened?"

A bewildered look crossed his features. "I fell," he said, but it was more of a question than a statement.

"This is very common," Helma said, remembering a portion of the book she'd read at the library that morning. "You tend to forget a traumatic event, sometimes for a short while, sometimes forever, especially in a head injury. It may come back to you later."

He closed his eyes again and Helma watched him drift off into a quieter, deeper sleep. She sat with him another ten minutes. Then, after settling his hand on his chest, rearranging the chair, and checking the levels of his medications, she touched his shoulder and left the room, glancing back once more at the door.

Cliff Bikman closed his paperback book when he saw Helma, and she spotted a canoeist on the cover paddling beneath a sky of clouds shaped like a skull. "Are you monitoring who goes in and out of his room?" she asked.

He tapped a clipboard leaning against the chair. "Right." Helma saw her own name and her arrival time written in close and slashing characters on the first column. Hers was the only name listed so far.

Down the hall at the nurses' station, two nurses were

deep in conversation; the hall in the opposite direction was empty. No one could hear them. Helma cleared her throat. "The chief's fall was certainly a setback when you seemed so close to acquiring new information," she told Cliff.

Cliff blinked and frowned. "What do you mean?" Before Helma could think of a suitable answer, he said, "Oh, you mean the Dixon murder. Yeah. When the chief's well enough to remember, I bet we make an arrest pronto."

The Dixon murder. Lewis Dixon, Mary Lynn's dead husband. Hadn't she known there was a connection? Helma tried to take in this news without showing her surprise. "But so far the chief hasn't remembered?" she asked, already knowing the answer.

Cliff shook his head. "He isn't even talking in complete sentences yet."

Helma thanked Cliff and on her way out stopped at the nurses' station. "Is Wayne Gallant's doctor available?" she asked a tall, thin nurse who was filling out patients' charts. The nurse glanced up at a board that was just out of Helma's view and shook her head. "Dr. Gulf? He was here this morning and won't be back until after six tonight."

Helma was aware that often it was the people who *did* the work who understood the subtleties and complications of a situation on a more practical level than their supervisors. Nurses and doctors, paralegals and lawyers, book shelvers and librarians.

"In a case like Wayne Gallant's," Helma asked the nurse, "how soon might his memory return?"

"It varies," she said. "With swelling . . . it takes time. Frequently, the patient never does remember the accident itself. The whole day might be a blank. And I've seen cases where months later the patient suddenly, out of the blue, recalls every single detail. We just have to wait and see."

"Thank you," Helma told her.

"He's a sweetheart," the nurse said. "You can just tell."

As she left the hospital, Helma met Carter Houston entering through the automatic doors. He held up one hand as if to beckon to her and then let it drop before completing the motion. Helma Zukas had never been the type of person who taunted and she disliked people who made a practice of doing so. But as she and Carter passed one another, she said, "I noticed there's now a guard at the door of Wayne Gallant's room."

"Yes," he said, avoiding her eyes. "I thought it would be a good idea."

"Did you?"

"Yes, I did," he said, and neither broke their pace.

Instead of going home, Helma drove through the south side of Bellehaven and turned onto a residential street, stopping within the first block to allow a red dog and two small girls on bicycles to cross the street in front of her. There were no signs that marked the roads to Danish Point, no direct route, only circuitous streets that led through residential areas that were being added on as the city expanded.

And then, as if backed up to the forest primeval, the suburbs ended and the street turned into a cracked and broken paved road that meandered above the bay. Here and there, long private drives led off the road to exclusive or old homes. Danish Point wasn't far from downtown Bellehaven in straight miles but it was a fifteen-minute drive by car.

The road eventually turned to gravel and curved into a wide and rough parking area that held only a bright pink Jeep. This must have been where the cruiser was found, she thought. No wonder it was noticed. Helma parked her car on the opposite side of the lot and got out, carefully locking her door behind her. A well-trod trailhead led into a wooded and rocky area, passing beside a clump of madrona trees. The air here smelled of low tide; seagulls dipped overhead and disappeared. She'd heard people report bald eagles soaring along the shore.

The trail opened up at the cliff: massive rocks of golden sandstone worn smooth by time and wind. In fantastic shapes like mud that had been poured and hardened where it lay, the rocks tumbled down to a shelf of sandstone that was covered by water during high tide. She banished from her mind the consequences if Wayne had fallen a few hours earlier or later.

Helma stood back from the edge of the cliff, keeping one hand on the smooth bark of a madrona as she gazed out at the view of water and islands. The Olympic Mountains to the southwest were invisible, their presence marked by a thick bank of billowing clouds.

No, she couldn't imagine it happening accidentally. She let go of the tree and edged farther out onto the broad rocks, feeling the pounding of her heart but studying the ground as she went, looking for something out of the ordinary: a dropped clue, the sign of a scuffle, anything.

But the scene was peaceful, serene, deserving to be one of Bellehaven's favorite and secret retreats. As she returned to the safety of the madrona, releasing her held breath, a young woman stepped out of a fainter trail to the north and smiled at Helma. "This is so beautiful," she said. "It's a healing place, don't you think?"

On her drive home, Helma pondered over the person who had checked out *Behind the Looking Glass* and might have left it at Danish Point. She would never divulge the borrower's name; there was no question of that. But what was she going to do with that knowledge? She couldn't confront the borrower and demand a confession; that might prove deadly. And it certainly wasn't ethical to use the name in her own investigation. The name was purely circumstantial evidence, she reminded herself, just as she'd reminded Carter Houston and Ms. Moon. The borrower might have lost the book or had it stolen or even loaned it to a friend.

She slowed for oncoming traffic before she passed a bicyclist riding too far into the automobile lane. Gray clouds still edged the distant islands, hovering, waiting to spark the change from sunshine to rain.

As Helma pulled into the Bayside Arms parking lot she realized it was imperative that she conduct herself as if she were completely ignorant of the borrower's name. To be true to all she believed in, both personally and professionally, she'd have to proceed as if she hadn't viewed it, as if she were completely ignorant, without resorting to the most obvious fact: that she'd already seen the evidence.

Walter David, the apartment manager, was on his hands and knees, weeding around a row of flowering kale, a baseball cap protecting his balding head. Moggy, his white Persian cat, lounged in a wicker basket eyeing Walter's every move as if it might pounce. Walter straightened his back, hands to his knees. "How's the chief?" he asked. Walter was one of a minority: a Bellehaven native, and an attentive native who knew the town's secrets. More than once he'd possessed local information that Helma couldn't have learned from any other source.

"Resting comfortably," Helma told him.

Walter nodded, satisfied. Moggy's round blue eyes blinked. Helma was not a lover of cats but it seemed to her that unlike Boy Cat Zukas, Moggy's eyes were especially devoid of personality.

"TNT said his son-in-law was actually murdered," Walter said.

"That's what I understand. Did you know Lewis Dixon?" Walter shrugged and tugged on the brim of his cap.

"I'd seen him here visiting TNT. Seemed like a nice-enough guy. Who'd want to kill an English teacher? Just retired, young wife." Walter's face wrinkled as if he'd just remembered something.

"But?" Helma prompted.

"Nothing, really. I knew TNT before he moved in here, because of the boxing. For a while a few years ago he sparred with a club of amateurs at the Y. Once, after I'd been swimming, I heard TNT tell some guy he'd better be good to his daughter, or else."

"Was the other man Lewis?" Helma asked.

"Couldn't say for sure, but it was an older guy, so probably."

"Did they quarrel?"

"No. It wasn't a threat; more like a joke, but you knew from TNT's voice that he meant it." Walter shrugged and rubbed his nose, leaving a smidgen of dirt. "But who'd pick a fight with a guy like TNT, anyway?"

"Not many men. Thanks, Walter."

"Sure. Oh. Ruth drove through a while ago, checking to see if you were home. At least I think that's what she said she was doing. Couldn't hardly hear over the rock music."

"She had two children—I mean, young people—with her?" Helma asked.

Walter nodded. "A girl, and one with . . ." he made swirling motions around his head.

"The chief's children," Helma told him.

"No kidding?"

As Helma paused in front of TNT Stone's open door, she heard the rhythmic creaking of machinery. She raised her hand to knock on the jamb and the creaking abruptly stopped. "Helma," TNT called.

He stepped onto the landing, a white towel around his

neck and perspiration dripping from his forehead. He wore sweats as usual, darkened by perspiration into Rorschach blots on his chest and back.

"How's Mary Lynn?" Helma asked, wondering how she could arrange to talk to the young woman again.

"She's here, out on my balcony. Maybe you could have a few words with her. You know, woman things." His voice dropped to a pleading timbre. "It really helped when you talked to her before. I'd be grateful. I just can't seem to say the right thing. Every time I open my mouth . . ." He made a fist and shoved it toward his wide open mouth.

"I'd be happy to," Helma told him. "Have you heard any more from the police about Lewis's death?"

TNT shook his head and looked away. "Waiting, waiting, that's what we do. But don't trouble yourself over it, not a bit. It'll be A-okay. You take care of your policeman."

"May I ask you a question about the chief?" Helma asked.

"Sure. Go for it." TNT grinned and sawed his towel back and forth across his neck.

"When Mary Lynn was being questioned, do you recall what was said when the chief left? Any words at all?"

He thought. Helma glanced over the railing and saw Walter carry a pail of weeds to the Dumpster in one hand, with Moggy cradled in his other arm.

"In my hearing?" TNT asked. "Not a word."

"You're sure?"

"Sorry." He stepped aside and waved Helma into his sparsely finished apartment. "Mary Lynn's on the balcony."

In his kitchen, a tower of red and white paper cups sat on the counter. Helma took one and filled it with water, then carried it to the balcony.

Mary Lynn sat on one of two white plastic chairs, her feet on a white plastic table. There was no other furniture or decorations, no plants. She gazed out at Washington Bay, not noticing Helma, her expression becalmed and numb. Her curly dark hair was now pulled back and bound, her clothing changed to a simple skirt and cotton blouse. She wore no makeup and looked even younger than she had the day before.

"Mary Lynn?" Helma said, barely louder than a whisper, not wanting to startle her.

Mary Lynn turned her head and looked up at Helma, without surprise or recognition.

"It's Helma Zukas from the next apartment," Helma reminded her.

Mary Lynn nodded. "I remember."

"I brought you a glass of water," Helma told her.

Mary Lynn dutifully took the glass and drank it all as if she were parched. Helma sat in the other chair.

"He was *murdered*," Mary Lynn said, still gazing out over the blue water. "Who would want to kill Lewis?"

"Did he have any enemies?" Helma asked.

Mary Lynn absently watched a seagull fly across the view. "Obviously, but I don't know who. Maybe a student he'd given a bad grade." She almost smiled. "But probably not. He was an easy grader. That's why I took his class in the first place. That's how I met him, in case you didn't know. I didn't expect to get hooked on English literature but he was a great teacher."

"Was he dating anyone else?"

"No one seriously." Her face went thoughtful. "He did date other women. Even my mother, if you can believe that. But *she* asked him out. It was after Lewis and I started seeing each other. She claimed she was concerned about the 'older man' aspect, trying to protect her little girl, but that was a lie."

"She lives with you and your husband?"

Mary Lynn squeezed the paper cup flat. "Over the garage. She's always running out of money. I didn't want her there—we've never been close—but she asked Lewis first, not me. And there we were." She rubbed her arms. "We're polite."

"Then she and Lewis did get along?"

"Lewis is—was—more tolerant." She spread her right hand and touched the pad between her pinky and ring finger. "This was the injection site. How did they do it? He wasn't knocked unconscious, the police said. Why did he *die*?"

"A massive dose would have deprived his brain of glucose. The autonomic functions—" Helma stopped.

"But wouldn't he have had time to come inside or at least call for help? The garden is close to the house, I would have heard him."

"I don't know. Perhaps he wasn't able to."

"Oh."

"No one saw him in the garden? Not even your mother?"

Mary Lynn snorted. "She was still asleep when I found Lewis. No, we live in a fairly secluded neighborhood. There are a lot of trees on the property."

"But the garden's in the sun?"

"Sure. It's difficult to garden in the shade." Mary Lynn frowned at Helma. "You sound like a policewoman."

"I thought it might be helpful to talk about your husband's death."

"In a way, it is. It makes it more real, which is good, I guess."

"Do you remember seeing the chief of police when you were at the police station yesterday?" Helma asked, gently trying to shift the conversation.

Mary Lynn nodded. "He was there for a while, listening more than he asked questions."

"What did he say when he left?"

"I wasn't listening, I was upset." She hugged herself. "I think . . . No, I'm sure he said the word, 'coincidence' . . . that whatever had happened was a coincidence and he wanted to respond. He did mention he was leaving his own car and taking a . . ."

"Cruiser?" Helma asked.

"Where was TNT at the time?" Helma asked.

"Sitting beside me, holding my hand."

Even in her distraught state, Helma reflected, Mary Lynn remembered Wayne Gallant's conversation, while TNT claimed not to have heard a word.

"Have you read Lewis Carroll?" Helma asked.

"Of course, when I was a child."

"More recently?"

"Why would I want to?" Mary Lynn asked. "It's too precious for me. Besides, Lewis Carroll was a man of suspect tastes."

"Many people feel the art and its creator are separate entities."

Mary Lynn snorted. "Like presidential politics. Well, not me." She nodded toward Helma's balcony. "Is that your cat?"

Boy Cat Zukas sat on the railing of Helma's balcony, which was separated from TNT's by a three-story drop to the rocky ground. He stretched, gathered himself, and casually leaped the distance, landing with perfect aim on TNT's balcony. He stared at Helma, tail switching, his cool golden eyes appraising her presence on the wrong balcony.

"Yes," Helma finally replied. "Has he been bothering you?"

"No. I like his company."

"Do you have a cat?"

"Three outside cats. Lewis was allergic, but maybe TNT will let me bring one here."

"TNT?" Helma asked, slowly understanding. "You're staying here with TNT?"

Mary Lynn nodded. "Friends are bringing over a few things this afternoon." She crossed her arms, hugging herself. "I'm never going back there again. Ever."

🌿 chapter thirteen 🌿

VOICE OF DREAD

"**T**hey're all yours," Ruth said, entering Helma's apartment ahead of Joseph and Syndi, who each carried a green backpack, Joseph's slung over his shoulder, Syndi's bumping along the floor. "I've done my auntly duty, right guys?"

"It was okay," Syndi answered, and out of Syndi's sight Ruth grimaced and made shooting motions with her finger.

"You're leaving?" Helma asked Ruth. Her apartment felt overful of people, all wrong, as if she'd prepared for an adult women's get-together and had, instead, been surprised by a group of elementary school students without a chaperone. What would she do now?

"Yes, I'm leaving. What did you expect? Coparenting? I have to change these clothes." She lifted the hem of her June Cleaver dress. "Then I'm meeting a friend. Not to worry. I'll check in later to make sure you've all survived your first few hours." She laughed heartily—and by herself. "Ta ta," she said cheerily, and left.

Helma, Joseph, and Syndi stood in Helma's kitchen gazing at the door Ruth had slammed.

"Well," Helma said, and cleared her throat.

Together, Joseph and Syndi turned their heads attentively toward her. Helma's mind went blank. What came next? Food, her mother always offered food. "Would you like something to eat?" she asked.

"Do you have any chips?" Joseph asked. "The barbecue kind?"

"We just ate," Syndi said, both to her brother and Helma.

Joseph shoved his hands in his pockets. "So?"

"So we're not hungry."

Joseph's shoulders slumped and he bumped back and forth against the counter.

"I have some fresh vegetables," Helma said, "on a tray, plus corn chips and pretzels." When that brought no response, she added, "Crackers?"

"That's okay," Joseph said. Helma wasn't sure from the words but his tone of voice sounded negative. She pulled the box of cheese crackers out of the cupboard anyway and set it on the counter.

"Would you like to play a game of Scrabble? There's a Scrabble board in the hall closet."

"Ruth said we're going to sleep here," Syndi said, ignoring the invitation to Scrabble.

"She did?" Helma asked in dismay before she could stop herself, and then, at the sight of the two wary faces, she tried to recover the moment by saying, "I know it's not how you expected your vacation to turn out, but you can still have a good time. The only problem we have is that this apartment has only one guest bedroom."

"I'll take it," Syndi said. "Joseph can sleep in the living room."

"There's a sleeping bag at Dad's house. If we go get it, I can sleep on the balcony," Joseph offered.

"I have extra bedding. You can have the sofa," Helma told him.

Joseph dropped his backpack on the floor and flopped on the sofa, half lying on it and taking up three-quarters of the seat. "This is okay, I guess." He picked up the television remote and turned on the television, flipping through the channels too fast for Helma to make out the programs. "Is this all you get?" Flip, flip. "Just basic cable, not expanded?"

"That's right. There are books in that bookcase that might interest you."

"Do you have any comics?"

Syndi gave her brother a dark look. "Don't be dumb," and Joseph made a face at her, grotesquely stretching his lips.

It was going to be a long few days. That's how Helma was determined to view their visit: only a few days. Any longer was too overwhelming. Had Ruth told Syndi and Joseph they'd spend *every* night with her?

Voices and thumping sounded from the landing, and Helma opened her own door to look out, hoping it was an intrusion in which she could involve Syndi and Joseph. Skip and another young man were attempting to coordinate the lugging of a large cardboard box that had once held a television up the steps, one man on each side. Skip carried the greater weight, and with greater ease.

"Almost there," Skip said. "Just a few more steps." Now that it wasn't matted with perspiration, Helma could see his hair was fairer and thicker than she'd thought.

The other, shorter and more slender, man grumbled, "A lot of little boxes would have been smarter."

"We would have had to make more trips up these stairs."

"I could have handled it."

TNT stood in the doorway of his apartment watching the men, an amused look on his face. "You young guys need to pump a little iron. I can give you a few pointers. Just ask me." He stepped out of the doorway onto the landing. "Now set it down inside so you can meet Helma, the lady who carried Mary Lynn through the rough spots."

They grunted and pushed the box into the apartment, bumping against the door jambs, and stood, both flexing their hands.

"We met," Skip said. "Good to see you again. This is Dean."

"Dean who studied Wilkie Collins?" Helma asked.

The slight man with the receding hairline nodded and shook Helma's hand. His hand was soft, his clasp firm. "Now it's Dean who manages Hugie's produce department."

"Hey," Skip teased him. "There's honor in a perfectly ripe tomato."

"Not to mention a living," Dean replied. He would have fit well in a university setting, with his preoccupied eyes and donnish looks.

"Didn't you used to date Mary Lynn?" Helma asked Dean.

"Yeah, in another lifetime. She's a good kid." He sounded old, curiously paternal, as if he were talking about a child, not a former love interest.

"Keep it down," TNT told them. "Mary Lynn's asleep."

"No I'm not." Mary Lynn stepped around the huge box and stood beside TNT. Her eyes were dark, distracted. "Hello, Dean."

Dean touched her shoulder. It was the sure touch of a man who has once known a woman well. "I'm really sorry about Lewis, Mary Lynn. Do the police have any leads on who killed him?"

Mary Lynn teared up and without a word turned around and stepped back inside TNT's apartment.

Dean slapped himself in the forehead with the palm of his hand. "Oh God, I'm sorry. That was stupid."

"Sure was," Skip agreed. "He died less than thirty-six hours ago."

"Give her a few days before you start talking about murders and killers," TNT advised them. "The police grilled her yesterday. Left her flat out on the mat."

"I heard the chief of police fell off his horse," Dean said.

"Just keep jamming your foot up your . . . throat,"

TNT said, nodding toward Helma. "This little lady's a special friend of the man's. In fact, that's one of his kids right there."

Helma turned to see Joseph standing on the landing behind her, watching. He wore his headset and bobbed his head in three-quarter time.

"Deaf to the world," TNT said.

"Sorry," Dean told Helma, rubbing his hands across his head, front to back. "I didn't mean anything against the chief."

Helma nodded. "I understand you're a former student of Lewis's."

Dean nodded. "Yeah, he was a good instructor. I saw him last week."

"You met to discuss nineteenth-century literature?" Helma asked.

"No. We disagreed on which works constituted the canon. We met in my produce department at Hugie's; he was buying tomatoes." Dean made motions with his hands that were incomprehensible to Helma but which she guessed were associated with activities he performed in Hugie's produce department.

"I was under the impression he had an extensive vegetable garden."

"He said something about powdery mildew ruining his tomatoes this year."

The *Bellehaven Daily News* had recently published an article about the hopelessness of treating the mildew-ridden plants. It struck seemingly overnight, when the plants were poised to bear ripe fruit, destroying entire crops.

"The police should solve this pronto," Dean said. For an instant Helma thought he meant powdery mildew, but then Dean went on to say, "If it was insulin, all they have to do is check all the diabetics in town."

"Not to mention doctors, nurses, home health aides, vets—" Skip added.

"Okay, okay," Dean conceded. "So it's a big crowd."

"Have the police announced that Lewis's death was caused by insulin?" Helma asked, surprised.

Dean looked at Skip, who shrugged. "Mary Lynn told me."

"You don't need a prescription for insulin," Helma told Dean and Skip. She had already called Jim, her favorite pharmacist, to be certain.

"If you can kill people with the stuff, maybe you shouldn't be able to get ahold of it so easily," Dean said.

"What about butcher knives and ball-peen hammers?" Skip asked. "Clotheslines and rocks? Not to mention guns." He stretched his back, turned from side to side and pointed to the van parked on the sidewalk. "Come on, Dean-o. One more load should do it."

"*Another* load?" TNT asked. "Where's she going to put all this stuff?"

"That's what her mother wanted to know."

TNT looked startled, even a little panicked. "Beatrice didn't help you pack up these boxes, did she?"

"No," Skip told him, "but she wanted to. She told us to leave her the house key and she'd have the next load ready for us." Skip held up his hand. "But Mary Lynn has warned us enough about her snooping around. We didn't let her in; locked everything up tight before we left."

"Good."

Helma returned to her apartment, followed by Joseph, who was still nodding to the music in his headphones. When she closed her door, Joseph clicked off his tape player and asked, "Why'd he say that about Dad falling off a horse?"

"You heard that? It's a reference to your father being a heroic figure. Most people consider him to be honorable."

"I don't get it," Joseph said.

Syndi looked up from the couch, where she'd taken her brother's place in front of the television. "It's like the knight in shining armor falling off his horse, stupid." She glanced at Helma. "Isn't that right?"

"The analogy is but not the name-calling," Helma told her.

"See, I told you," Syndi said to Joseph, and went back to watching a television game show.

"It's a beautiful day," Helma told them. "Why don't we go for a walk?"

"Are you serious?" Syndi asked.

"Yes."

Joseph looked down at his feet.

Helma's doorbell rang and she opened her door expecting to see TNT or Mary Lynn, but Helma's mother, Lillian, and Aunt Em stood on her doormat. Helma had to compose herself for a moment at the sight of her eighty-four-year-old Lithuanian immigrant aunt, her father's oldest sister, the last of that generation of siblings, standing before her in a pair of denims and a pink sweater set with faux pearls sewn around the neck. Her mother wore jeans, too, a long blue vest and short-sleeved shirt, and she'd dyed her hair again.

They both lived in the same retirement complex on the other side of Bellehaven, but not as roommates; there were too many old grievances between them for that. But they were bound together by their past, and after years of a huffy standoff, had forged a truce as tight as any actual sisters'. Mrs. Whitney, Helma's old neighbor, had become Aunt Em's roommate, and Helma ran into the three of them in Bellehaven uncommonly often.

"Oh my dear," her mother said, stepping forward and briefly hugging Helma. "We're so sorry to hear about your dear Wayne Gallant's accident. How is he? Do you know what happened?"

"That poor man," Aunt Em agreed. She still retained a slight Lithuanian accent that turned her *th*'s into *t*'s and *ing*'s into *ink*. "You're probably just sick at heart. Have you been to visit him yet?"

"Yes, I have. He . . ." Neither woman was listening, both of them busily maneuvering to peer around her, trying to see into her apartment.

"Where are they? Are they here?" her mother asked. "Can we meet them?"

"Who?"

"The children," Aunt Em said eagerly. "We were on our way to that new place on Broadway for coffee and ran into Ruth. She said the chief's children are staying with you."

"They are, but—"

"Oh good." Helma's mother gently nudged Helma aside, and she and Aunt Em stepped past her into the apartment, where Syndi and Joseph both sat on the couch. The two older women approached them as if they were stalking elusive animals, their shoulders bumping together, their eyes bright.

"Oh my, aren't you the prettiest thing," Aunt Em told Syndi. "And those eyelashes. I bet the boys' knees go weak when you click those peepers at them, don't they?"

Syndi blushed and Helma's mother sat down beside Syndi, studying the girl. "You have your father's hair. You lucky girl. Women pay a fortune to have hair like that." Syndi touched her hair as if she couldn't help herself.

And to Joseph, Aunt Em said, after critically eyeing him up and down, "I do think that someday you'll be better looking than your father."

"And taller, too," Helma's mother said. "Look at those feet."

Both Joseph and Syndi squirmed in embarrassment, but Helma watched, amazed, at the first unguarded expressions she'd seen on their faces. They *liked* her mother's and Aunt Em's attention.

"What are you planning to do this afternoon?" Lillian asked.

"We were about to go for a walk," Helma told her.

"A walk? Why, that's ridiculous, don't you young people agree? Wouldn't you rather go out for an ice cream cone? We know the best place. Homemade."

"Oh yes," Aunt Em added. "Fudgie's. Their chocolate espresso crunch ripple will knock your socks off. And then why don't we go for a swim? We have a pool in our building."

"They shouldn't swim after eating," Helma said.

"Nonsense. That's an old wives' tale. Besides, we have a lifeguard." Aunt Em winked at Helma's mother, who smiled and said, "Oh yes. Juan."

"All right," Syndi said, shocking Helma by rising from the couch. "My swimsuit's in my backpack."

"Mine, too," Joseph said.

"You can come, too, dear," Aunt Em said to Helma, but with less excitement than she'd invited Syndi and Joseph.

Syndi picked up her backpack from the kitchen floor. "You could go visit Dad," she suggested.

Helma hesitated. "Maybe I will," she agreed, watching Syndi give a satisfied nod before she headed down the hall to the guest bedroom with her backpack.

"I'll put my pack in there for now, too," Joseph said, following Syndi.

"Such sweet children," Aunt Em said, gazing fondly after them.

"And so well-mannered, too. This will be fun."

"They can be . . ." Helma began.

Aunt Em and Lillian turned expectantly toward her. "Can be what?" Aunt Em asked.

"They're worried about their father," Helma tried. "They may not be as happy as you wish they could be."

"Well, you can't every second you're awake," Lillian said. "You need to have a little fun. That's the best medicine."

"I have an errand to run, then I'll be here all afternoon, if you need to call me," Helma told them.

"I don't know why on earth we would," Lillian said.

"Myliu tave," Aunt Em said over her shoulder in Lithuanian. I love you.

After her mother and Aunt Em left with the children, Helma looked up Lewis Dixon's name in her phone book. The address was listed, and she jotted it down on a piece of paper beside her phone: 2716 Rose Briar Lane.

It sounded vaguely familiar, but Helma couldn't place it. She flipped to the map in the front of the telephone book and looked it up. Rose Briar Lane was on the south end of Bellehaven. She used her fingers to trace the quadrants: L6.

And there it was, a short dead-end road branching off the road she'd traveled that very morning, the road that led to Danish Point.

Helma held her finger in the L6 quadrant of the map, thinking. On Sunday, while Wayne Gallant had been questioning Mary Lynn, there'd been a call from the vicinity of the murder. Wayne was a hands-on police chief, and it was very like him to have taken the call himself, especially if he believed it might be connected to Lewis Dixon's murder. *Had* he confronted Lewis's killer at Danish Point? She had to discover who had called in the prowler complaint.

Helma changed into slacks, a pullover sweater, and the comfortable shoes she wore for walking. Then she watched from her window until she saw Dean and Skip returning with a load of Mary Lynn's possessions before she left her apartment.

She met the two men, each carrying a cardboard box, on the stairs, Dean lagging behind. "You look tired," she said sympathetically. "Is this your last load?"

"Definitely," Skip told her.

"That's good."

Helma took the same route she had that morning, noting again the way the land was being sculpted and reshaped into new suburbs. Bellehaven was experiencing another growth spurt, this time being "discovered" by Seattleites a hundred miles to the south, who'd once considered the town hopelessly provincial and who were now fleeing their tangled and crowded city squeezed between mountains and water. Here they struggled like misguided pioneers to fashion Bellehaven into all they'd left behind.

She almost drove past Rose Briar Lane. The small sign that marked the narrow road was partially hidden by a huge rhododendron bush. The lane was paved, barely, and it angled down toward the water. Madronas grew here, and firs. Helma passed the driveways of 2600 and 2682, glimpsing expensive homes through the trees and gated driveways, and beyond them, the blue waters of the bay.

The number 2716 was carved into a pillar of granite, and Helma turned in, driving through shadowed trees until the land suddenly opened up into a clearing an acre or two in size.

The Dixons didn't live in one of the palatial homes but in a well-kept older two-story wooden house with Victorian touches. A small orchard grew on one side of the house, a few trees heavy with apples. On the south side, lattices of drying pea vines and rows of browning cornstalks marked a vegetable garden. On the opposite side of the driveway stood a newer two-car garage and above it, a deck jutted from the front, with a long staircase to the ground. This was obviously Beatrice's apartment. Blinds blocked off the windows; there was no sign of movement. Helma didn't see cars, so she slowly drove toward the house. Gravel crunched beneath the tires.

She stopped between the two buildings, waiting for a few moments after she turned off her engine for the appearance of a watchdog. Mary Lynn had mentioned cats, but not dogs. Still, her mother might own a dog. Dogs who barked were rarely a problem; it was the quiet ones who slunk up from behind.

When no dogs materialized, Helma climbed out of the car and walked to the side door, which appeared more heavily used than the front door. A harvest wreath hung beside the glass-paned door, a wind chime from the eave of the narrow porch. *Welcome* was painted on an oval river rock beside the front mat.

Helma knocked. And as she hoped, there was no answer. Without glancing around again, moving briskly, she walked around the house to the south side, to the vegetable garden that stretched the length of the house. It was well-tended, weedless, the rows straight and true, with marigolds planted at both ends of green rows. To one side, her eye was caught by signs of disturbance in the earth. Here, stakes remained but the plants were gone, and Helma recognized a sickly gray tomato leaf lying in the dirt. Powdery mildew. The only way to protect the rest of the garden was to remove the affected plants.

A concrete bench sat in the center of the garden, and next to it, according to a plaque at its base, a bust of Walt Whitman.

Helma sat on the bench and gazed toward the house. One window was clearly visible: a second-floor double-hung window with white curtains. Her view of the lower windows was blocked by a stand of red and green Japanese maples.

She could clearly see the garage and the apartment above it, but there were no windows facing the garden. So whoever had killed Lewis could have done the deed unobserved. All they would have needed was the required amount of time. The murderer couldn't have absolutely counted on the insulin causing a heart attack, and if it hadn't, Lewis's death would not have been instantaneous—or pleasant. Whoever had killed him had been audaciously confident he or she wouldn't be observed. They were either incredibly lucky or intimately aware of the Dixon household's habits.

Helma gazed around at the gracefully designed garden,

the surrounding greenery. The bay wasn't visible from here, but she could smell the saltwater, and the air was so still she nearly convinced herself she heard the gentle lapping of waves. Even knowing this had been the scene of a murder, it was a peaceful place, serene.

"What in hell are you doing here?" a voice demanded from behind her.

❦ chapter fourteen ❦

THE KITTEN'S FAULT

Helma jumped up from the bench in Lewis Dixon's garden and spun around, nearly tripping over a cucumber vine creeping into the pathway. A woman stood at the edge of the brown cornstalks, one arm held across her waist cupping the elbow of her other arm, the hand of which held a cigarette. It was easy to see who she was. Like viewing a caricature of Mary Lynn: hair the same color, only less natural; the same style clothing; the same weight, although distributed differently. But where Mary Lynn's gaze was direct and youthful, the older woman's gaze was narrowed and suspicious.

"You must be Beatrice, Mary Lynn's mother," Helma said. "She said you lived in the apartment above the garage."

"She said that, did she?" Her voice was smoky, rough-edged. "She told you they made me sleep over the garage?"

"You must appreciate the independence," Helma tried. She noticed now that the cigarette wasn't lit, nor were Beatrice's fingers tobacco-stained, and Helma guessed it was the remnants of an old and powerful habit.

Beatrice snorted. "Independence all right." She waved her cigarette toward her daughter's two-story house. "Dean and Skip wouldn't let me inside my own daughter's house."

"There may be evidence inside that could be used to identify Lewis's assailant," Helma suggested.

"Is that why you're poking around out here? Looking for evidence? What, empty bottles of insulin? Yeah, I know the details."

It was growing apparent why Mary Lynn and her mother didn't get along. There was no sense of "mother-liness" about Beatrice, little warmth that Helma could discern. Mainly, the emotion that Helma felt from Beatrice was anger.

"It is a baffling case. How could anyone give your son-in-law—"

"Call him Lewis, not my son-in-law," Beatrice told her curtly. "He was almost older than me, for God's sake."

"Lewis," Helma amended. "How could anyone have given Lewis an insulin injection without him calling for help? He should have had time."

"I don't know anything about how humans react to insulin," Beatrice said. Too adamantly, Helma thought. "Maybe we just didn't hear him. Maybe he was bonked over the head." Helma took two steps closer to Beatrice, and now the resemblance to Mary Lynn was less striking. Her face was tracked by lines that from up close resembled scars. Her eyes lacked Mary Lynn's softness.

"The coroner's report didn't describe any other signs of trauma."

"Well, I wouldn't know anything about that, either, would I? But I sure heard Mary Lynn when she found him lying out here in the dirt." Beatrice glanced toward the area where Helma guessed the diseased tomato plants had been pulled from the ground.

"So when you heard your daughter scream, you came down to the garden?"

"Or course I did. I'm not that callous of a mother, despite what certain people believe." She gazed down at the plot of garden again. "It was awful," she said in a quieter voice. "The ants . . ." She jerked her head, put her cold cigarette to her mouth and took an imaginary puff before pulling it away. "So what do you want to hear from me that I haven't already said?"

That's when Helma realized that Beatrice had mistaken her for a member of the police department, someone with the right to question her. It must be the aura of authority that clung to all city employees, she thought.

"Did you see a car or hear any visitors Sunday morning?" Helma asked, wishing she'd thought to carry a notepad with her.

"No. Nothing and no one. But Lewis was one of those early bird types. It improves your sanity to get a good night's sleep, I believe. A freight train could have driven through and I wouldn't have heard it."

"Did Lewis ever speak of enemies?" A pitchfork leaned precariously against the Whitman bust, and Helma straightened it, pushing the tines more securely into the dirt.

"Not to me, but everybody has a couple, right? Lewis definitely had one. Old lover or something like that."

"Do you know of any old lovers?" Helma asked.

She shrugged and patted her hair. "Who knows. They could be everywhere. He never introduced me to any. And you can bet he didn't introduce them to Mary Lynn, either."

"You knew Lewis before Mary Lynn did, I understand." A late summer butterfly, rosy white, fluttered across the drying pea vines.

This time Beatrice jabbed the cigarette in Helma's direction. "If you're trying to imply something, spit it out."

"Were you and Lewis close?"

Beatrice's face reddened. "That's ancient history, and it never amounted to much anyway. When it's over, it's over. I don't hold any grudges." She straightened her shoulders. "False hopes, either."

"Are you employed?" Helma asked.

"I don't need to be."

"I see." Helma gazed around her, mentally cataloging the land surrounding the garden where Lewis Dixon died: the firs at the back of the property, twisted from the winds that blew in off the water, the view of the Victorian house and garage and driveway, the nearly invisible road. This was a very private place, easy to commit a murder here without being seen, but more difficult, it seemed, to come and go without being noticed.

"What else do you want to know?" Beatrice asked. "I've got things to do."

"You were the person who called the police yesterday, isn't that correct?" Helma asked, feeling her way. "Regarding a prowler?"

"Nope, wasn't me."

"Did you see anything unusual?"

"Not a thing. That was Brenda, the Hayden's caretaker."

Beatrice waved her hand toward the north. "Like I said before, Brenda phoned me first, but she's the jumpy type. She said she's not staying in the house overnight anymore. The Haydens won't like *that*, I tell you. That's what they're paying her for, and they won't be back from Turkey for another two weeks. But all that must be in the police records."

"I'm sure it is." Helma made note of the name, Hayden, then nodded toward the house. "This is an old house for this area."

"It belonged to one of the oyster farmers. That's what this used to be sixty, seventy years ago." A spark of interest crossed Beatrice's face. Helma wouldn't have expected her to be interested in local history. "An old Japanese lady came here last year, just flat out of the blue. Her son brought her to see where she'd lived before the war."

"In this house?" Helma asked.

Beatrice shook her head. "She knew the people who lived in this house but her own house was gone. It was closer to the water. The road's still just to the north of us but the family never came back after the internment. Sad, isn't it?"

Helma nodded. She'd read once that none of the local Japanese had returned to Bellehaven after they'd been interned in camps in eastern Washington during World War II. They'd left behind businesses, homes, gardens, oyster farms, and in some cases, generations of history.

"Did Mary Lynn and Lewis have a good marriage?" Helma asked.

Beatrice gave Helma a disgruntled look. "How many ways can you people ask the same question? Yes, they did. They were, as the song says, 'crazy in love.'" Helma noticed that the fact didn't seem to enchant Beatrice.

A soft breeze blew up from the water, flattening the grass and rustling the trees. Beatrice accompanied Helma to her Buick, and suddenly three cats high-stepped through the grass toward them. Two black and white and a smaller calico. "Are these your cats?" Helma asked.

"Mary Lynn's," Beatrice told her. Then, just as the cats broke from the grass onto the drive, Beatrice waved her arms and said, "Shoo, shoo."

The cats turned back toward the grassy field, but the littlest one, the calico, stumbled and staggered, comical if it hadn't been so oddly clumsy. Helma only tolerated one cat in her life but she'd never known any cat to be so clumsy.

"Are you like that detective on TV reruns, that Columbo?" Beatrice asked.

"What do you mean?"

"Your car. You don't often see cars that old driven by policemen—or women."

"Oh. I'm not a policewoman, I'm a librarian."

"You're what? A librarian?" Beatrice dropped her cigarette and ground it into the dirt with the heel of her sandal. "Why would a *librarian* be nosing around here?"

Helma unlocked her car door and climbed inside. "Just curious. Thank you for your time." And she closed her door and relocked it before she turned on her engine and slowly drove away so her tires wouldn't throw up any dust toward Beatrice, who was following the car and shouting, "You liar. I'm calling the police about this and don't think I won't."

A hundred yards from the Dixon's home, Helma spotted a navy-blue car pulled off the road, partially hidden behind salmonberry bushes. She was already past it before she realized what she'd seen. Then she hit her brakes and, with her arm on the back of her seat and looking through her rear window, backed up until she blocked the blue car's exit. No one sat behind the wheel but she spotted the antenna, the bag of cheesy chips, and the spiral notebook on the dashboard. She was looking at an unmarked police car. Where was the driver?

Helma turned off her ignition and got out, holding her keys in her fist the way she'd learned in self-defense class. The car was parked in the depression of an old road that led off toward the water. Helma wondered briefly if this was the driveway to the old Japanese woman's lost home. Moss grew on the edges of the shaded pavement.

As she stood beside the unmarked car's front bumper, considering its presence in such an out-of-the-way place, she spotted an unmistakable figure walking toward her along the old road. Carter Houston was less than fifty feet away when he spotted her. He stopped mid-stride, and even though he quickly hid the black binoculars behind his back, it was too late. She'd already seen them. Carter wore his black suit and tie, but on his feet were a pair of expensive new hiking boots. She waited until he drew even with the rear bumper of his unmarked car before she spoke. "You were spying on me."

"What are you doing out here?" he countered, but without his usual certainty.

"Looking."

"You're interfering with police business."

"I don't believe I am."

Carter sighed and set the binoculars on the hood of the car. "Is Beatrice the person who checked out *Behind the Looking Glass*?"

Helma didn't answer, and Carter continued, "I'd bet my career that you saw the borrower's name before you erased it. That was tampering with evidence."

"It would never hold up in court."

"The charge would be enough to damage your career."

"On the contrary. I believe it would elevate me to a heroine in the library field." She paused. "You're not threatening me, are you, Carter?"

The use of his name seemed to briefly embarrass him. "No. I am not. I'm only sharing general observations with you. What did Beatrice tell you?"

"The same as she told you. She didn't hear or see anything unusual until Mary Lynn screamed. She also didn't see a prowler yesterday. Why did the chief come out here alone?"

Carter absently tapped his plump manicured fingers on the hood of his car. "Wayne might have been trying to send you a message," he said without looking at her.

"What do you mean?"

Carter gazed above Helma's head as if he were seeing his words played out among the treetops. "Let's say he saw the library book in his attacker's car and managed to pull it out, knowing you'd be able to discover who checked it out and identify his attacker, and also the—" He stopped.

"And also the what?" Helma asked. "I thought you

only wanted to question the book borrower as a possible witness."

"Those are two possibilities," Carter said stiffly.

Helma thought about Carter's first proposal. "If Wayne did want me to know about the book," she said slowly, still working out the possibility, "he'd know I'd never divulge privileged information."

"But he'd expect you to do *something* with that information," Carter persisted.

"Hypothetically, yes, he might," Helma acknowledged. She waited until Carter brought his eyes down from the trees and met hers. "If you believed that, you'd be interested in every move I made."

"Hypothetically," Carter said, the old smug smile returning to his face.

As a matter of principle, Helma did not shop at Hugie's grocery store. To take advantage of Hugie's sale prices meant a shopper had to sign up for a Hugie's card, allowing the store to track his or her shopping habits. In light of her beliefs in privacy, Helma felt it would have been hypocritical, even though Ruth had signed up for several dead and distant relatives and proudly presented Helma with her "very own genuine bogus card."

But today she drove out of her way to Hugie's and entered the softly lit store. Classical music issued gently from hidden speakers; green-clad "associates" scurried the aisles, fixed smiles on their faces. In the produce department, artful arrays of fruits and vegetables were arranged by complementary colors: the leafy green made more vibrant by nudging deep red; the browns softened by beds of parsley; the oranges and yellows heightened in shadowy corners. Cool sprays periodically misted the bins, and the air was as damp and fragrant as a tropical isle.

She found Dean, dressed in his Hugie greens, critically

eyeing a display of shiitake mushrooms. "The portobello delivery truck is late," he said, nodding to her in distracted acknowledgment. "I hope the shiitakes and oysters can fill in the gap until they arrive."

"Perhaps if you fluffed the frilly paper background a little more," Helma suggested.

"Good idea," Dean said, using his fingertips to spread the paper tendrils, then stepping back and nodding at the results.

"Did you finish moving Mary Lynn's belongings?" Helma asked.

"We did. But TNT is feeling—"

"Oh no. You're out of portobellos," a woman gasped behind them.

"The truck's late," Dean soothed, "but I can have them delivered to you in time for dinner."

"Oh, please. I need eight ounces for my penne recipe."

'No problem. Come over to my stand."

Helma watched Dean usher the woman to a desk beside an exquisite pyramid of sweet corn. While she waited she couldn't help but choose two deep red apples and one perfect pear, the display was so enticing. Around her swirled well-dressed, fast-moving people, the majority slender and athletic, gray-haired, each one beginning to resemble the next, like fading brothers and sisters of an overlarge family.

When Dean was finished with the portobello woman, he returned to her side, his eyes sweeping vigilantly across the produce aisles.

"You've worked hard in this department," Helma told him. "It's very attractive." She held up her apples and pear. "I couldn't resist these."

He nodded. "Produce wasn't my original career plan but you get used to it. It grows on you, so to speak." He laughed shortly.

"It's difficult for anyone to make a living with literature," Helma said, "creating it or teaching it. I enjoyed early twentieth-century literature myself, although I did spend part of a semester studying Lewis Carroll."

"*Alice in Wonderland*?" he asked.

"And *Through the Looking Glass*," Helma said, watching Dean's face closely.

"Whoops, excuse me," he said, stepping away to chase a Portuguese tomato that had escaped from its display. "Ah yes," he called back to her. " 'Twas brillig and the slithy toves . . . ' "

"You know it?" Helma asked when he'd retrieved the tomato and tossed it in the trash basket beside his desk.

"Doesn't everyone?"

"I found it incomprehensible," she told him.

"That's its charm."

Helma wasn't so sure about *that*. "Did Lewis Dixon teach a course on Lewis Carroll?"

"If he did, I didn't take it. Ask Skip; he worked in the English Department office for a while. He'd probably remember."

"Thanks. Maybe I will."

Dean considered Helma, picking up a gleaming eggplant and polishing it on his green apron. "You're curious about Lewis," he said. "Dixon, not Carroll."

"Aren't we always curious when someone dies?" Helma asked. "I didn't know him, but now that I've become acquainted with Mary Lynn I'm naturally curious."

"I see," Dean said, still looking puzzled.

"You said that you and Lewis disagreed," Helma said. "Did you and Mary Lynn end your relationship when she met Lewis?"

Dean replaced the eggplant on its aubergine stack with enough force that he had to catch two others from rolling. "What I said was that Lewis and I disagreed over what constituted the canonical works of nineteenth-century literature, that's all."

"And then Mary Lynn married Lewis."

"Don't make more out of it than existed," he said tersely. "All that ended years ago. Now if you'll excuse me." He pointed to a woman breaking apart a bunch of bananas.

"It was nice to chat with you," Helma told him. "Maybe I'll see you again at TNT's."

"Okay," Dean said, already turning away to rearrange the pyramid of golden bananas.

As Helma stood at the register, a woman in the next line over nodded to her and asked, "Helma, how's Boy Cat?" It was Barbara Susebenn, her veterinarian. She carried a green plastic basket on her arm filled with fresh vegetables and a container of butter pecan ice cream.

Helma moved from her own line and fell in behind the other woman. "He's fine. Thank you."

"He's due for shots next month." The vet had a phenomenal memory for the animals under her care. When Boy Cat Zukas's first vet had retired, Helma had researched Bellehaven's veterinarians carefully, and Barbara was considered the best cat vet in town. She guessed that Mary Lynn would be equally careful choosing a vet.

"Mary Lynn Dixon is a new neighbor of mine," Helma said.

Barbara's face saddened. "What a shame about her husband."

"It is," Helma agreed. "Do you know Mary Lynn through your veterinary practice?"

Barbara shook her head. "We're in the same volunteer group."

"Oh," Helma said, disappointed that Barbara wouldn't know more about Mary Lynn's cats. "I saw her little calico cat when I was visiting their place in the country," she said anyway. "Poor thing."

"She told me about it," Barbara Susebenn said as she emptied her basket onto the checkout counter. "It's not as unusual as you'd expect. A lot of cats develop it. Dogs, too."

"Do they?" Helma asked, placing her apples and pear behind Barbara's purchases, wondering what *it* was. "What's the best form of treatment?"

"The old standard: injections. Don't look so surprised. Insulin works as well on cats as it does on people."

"I *am* surprised," Helma admitted as she absorbed this information. "I hadn't considered cats or dogs contracting diabetes."

"Most people don't." She handed the cashier a ten dollar bill.

"Do the owners give their cats insulin injections with the same types of needles that people use?" she asked.

"That's right." Barbara took her change from the cashier and waved to Helma. "I'll be looking for you and Boy Cat next month."

Helma went through the mechanics of paying for her apples and pear, her mind racing over the possibilities. It was curious and, she admitted, suspicious, that the subject of Mary Lynn's insulin-dependent cat hadn't been brought up by Beatrice. It was such a coincidence that surely someone had mentioned the diabetic cat to the police. It seemed completely obvious to Helma. Unless, of course, the police didn't know.

Outside Hugie's, she stood for a moment, shading her eyes and studying the cars in the parking lot. There it was, dwarfed beside a green SUV. She strode across the lot toward the plain blue car. Carter Houston saw her coming and slouched in his seat, opening a newspaper in front of his face.

But Helma tapped on the driver's window and he rolled it down, his lips pursed like a child who's been caught red-handed.

"I brought you a healthier snack than those," she said, nodding toward the crumpled bag of cheesy chips on the dashboard and handing him the apples and pear. "I'm planning to stop by the hospital now, in case you lose me in traffic."

He mumbled something at her, but instead of waiting for clarification or thanks, Helma turned and walked back across the lot to her Buick.

❧ chapter fifteen ❧

OUT OF BREATH

There was no change in Wayne Gallant's condition. He smiled, mumbled a few words Helma didn't understand but which sounded like "Olympic skating," and slept. Officer Cliff Bikman had been replaced by a solemn young officer who asked Helma for picture ID and took his job so seriously she was unable to get a peek at his clipboard listing names of the chief's visitors. The tiny black-haired nurse named Molly told her that several people had telephoned the nurses' station asking about the chief's condition, and that no, of course they didn't keep a log of who called, nor did they ask the callers' names.

There was nothing Helma could do but sit beside Wayne Gallant's bed and hold his hand, her mind a curious blank, as if the world, including that of the person who'd killed Lewis Dixon and possibly pushed Wayne Gallant over the cliff, stopped outside the door of Room 224. Even when she tried to imagine Mary Lynn's face, only a few wispy features presented themselves. "It's odd," she whispered aloud while Wayne slept on.

Helma checked her watch as she reached the hospital lobby. Her mother and Aunt Em weren't planning to return Syndi and Joseph for another hour and a half. She stopped at the bank of four public telephones. Every one was in use, and a pregnant woman waited, her foot tapping. Only one of the telephones had a phone book, and when Helma stepped forward to remove it discreetly from the shelf where a man in jeans and a ponytail was speaking on the phone, he slapped his hand on the book and frowned at her.

Helma did not relinquish her hold. "I'll bring it back before your conversation is finished," she told him in a low voice.

They stared at each other, and finally he lifted his hand as if the phone book were hot, and Helma removed it.

Standing in the foyer, she balanced the phone book and flipped through the pages. Beatrice had implied that Brenda, a caretaker at the home of the Haydens, had phoned in the prowler call.

There were five Haydens, three with addresses that were in town and two without addresses. Juggling phone book, pencil, and paper, she jotted down the two phone numbers without addresses.

"Can I have that when you're finished?" the pregnant woman asked. "I can never remember my mother-in-law's number."

"Of course, but please return it to the man at the second telephone." Helma closed the book and gave it to the woman, then hurried to her car, which she'd parked, as usual, in a space at the edge of the lot, where it was safer from door dings and scratches. In the twenty-two years she'd owned her Buick, it had only received a single scratch and still had the original floor carpets and plastic seatcovers she'd had installed after high school graduation. A man had once followed her home just to ask if she was interested in selling her car. But since it ran so well, she hadn't seen any reason to give it up.

But before she reached her car, she realized that something was wrong. Her car listed to the driver's side. Ten feet away, keys in hand, she saw why: both tires on that side were flat. "Oh, Faulkner," she said, stopping and staring at the cartoonlike image. There was nothing on the pavement behind her car that she might have run over. No nails or broken glass. On closer inspection she discovered that both tires had inch-long slits just above the whitewalls. "Double Faulkner," she said aloud.

Then she walked twice around her car, examining the body for scratches or dents. She'd parked at the far end of the lot; no other cars were parked beyond her Buick. Someone could have parked beside her car and, using their own vehicle as a shield, slashed her tires without being seen.

She glanced around the parking lot; there was no sign of Carter or his unmarked police car. She wished she hadn't told him where she was going, or he might have followed her and caught the vandal in the act.

"Oh, dear. That's a shame," a woman in a blue cotton jacket told Helma, studying the car and shaking her head. Helma recognized her as one of the women who worked the front desk at the hospital. "Would you like a ride?"

"Thank you but I'll call Triple A."

"It certainly is curious that *both* tires went flat at the same time, isn't it?"

Helma agreed and decided she'd think about that later. Right now she needed to phone AAA and Ruth. The library was only two blocks away but she wasn't prepared to face Ms. Moon. She felt the briefest longing for a cell phone. As she turned to backtrack to the hospital, a tiny flutter of white on her windshield caught her attention. A slip of paper was pinned beneath her wiper blade, hardly more than a scrap. Carefully, she bent back the blade and removed the paper. It was the insert from an allergy relief box listing ingredients and instructions. She smoothed the thin paper on the hood of her car and, seeing nothing but tiny print, turned it over. Again only small print, but there, halfway down in blacker, bolder type, was the word "Warning," followed by a list of the medicine's possible side effects. Someone had used a felt-tip pen to draw a double circle around the word "Warning."

Ruth beat the AAA wrecker to the hospital parking lot. "They'll figure it out," Helma said, waving a hand toward her listing Buick as she climbed into Ruth's car. "That's why I pay extra premiums."

"Is this Helma Zukas speaking?" Ruth asked.

"What do you mean?"

"Nothing," Ruth said, putting her Saab into reverse. "Ever wonder where the word 'wrecker' came from? Funny thing to call a tow truck. 'Fixer' is more appropriate. Or maybe something like Mobile Repair Unit: the MRU."

"In the early days of automobiles," Helma explained, "there were businesses that towed away cars to be broken apart, or 'wrecked' for salvage. They were 'wreckers,' and the word evolved to mean towing a vehicle for repairs, too."

"Oh, the fascination of our living language," Ruth said as she waited for the light near the hospital to turn green.

"Why would anyone slash my tires and leave me a 'warning' message?" Helma asked.

Ruth briefly turned to look at her. "Figure it out, Sherlock. Some guilty person is panicked because you're snooping around and asking questions. They stopped by the hospital to finish off Wayne Gallant and were thwarted by you or security so they took out their frustrations on you. They'll probably try something more extreme next time."

"That's frightening," Helma told her.

"It's meant to be. Let's stop by the police station."

"Not now."

"Then call them when you get home."

"I'll think about it," Helma said, to which Ruth made a rude sound.

As they passed the library, Helma spotted Harley and

Deidre sitting close together on a bench by the rose garden. Deidre was leaning forward, talking earnestly, and Harley was looking down at the ground, occasionally nodding.

"That means whoever it is knows who I am and what kind of car I drive."

"And probably where you live," Ruth added. "It wasn't a random act, *that* I'd lay odds on. Don't take that warning note lightly."

"But why *warn* me?" Helma asked. Out her window she idly watched a woman pushing a baby stroller and walking a dog at the same time. "Warning me only piques my curiosity and makes the situation more obvious."

"Two possibilities," Ruth said. "This person doesn't know you that well and thinks you're some mousy librarian who will naturally be scared off by a flat tire or two. Or, this person is aware the crime is going to come to light and is desperately trying to throw up roadblocks."

"Stalling for time," Helma continued, "until . . ." She looked at Ruth, who nodded gravely. Helma swallowed and finished, "They're waiting to see if Wayne Gallant survives." When Ruth didn't answer, she said, "They are, aren't they?" Not really a question.

"He has police protection," Ruth reminded Helma. "No one's getting in there to hurt him."

"I'd like to speak to Mary Lynn, but first can you drive me to Matt's Used Books on Third Street?"

"Now?" Ruth asked. "You want to buy a book right now? Why not wait and borrow it from your local library? It's free."

"This particular library book is in police custody."

"Oh. Looking for a clue, right? Sure, I'll stop."

Matt's Used Books was on a side street in the older part of Bellehaven, between an antique store and a restaurant that had gone out of business years ago. It was a warren of tiny rooms which Helma didn't intend to venture into. Books were piled everywhere, even in aisles and blocking windows. Normally, she would have avoided its haphazard stabs at order.

"*Behind the Looking Glass*," Matt himself repeated when Helma made her request. He had a silvery beard and wore his hair in a long ponytail that was still brown at the tips. "Sure, we've got a copy of that. It was popular a few years ago, remember? Back when people were looking for the meaning of life in Mother Goose and obscure kids' books."

"Lewis Carroll isn't obscure," Helma said.

"Maybe not to anyone over thirty. Kids don't read that hard anymore; the words are too big," he said, sounding like George Melville. "They want it nice. And easy." Then for no reason at all he broke into a song about leaving a good job in the city.

"If you have more than one copy," Helma told him, interrupting his song, "I'd like the cleanest one."

"Got it," he said. "I'll be right back."

He returned four minutes later, after Ruth had tapped her car horn twice. "I found two copies. This one even had a jacket."

"Thank you." The book was identical to the copy Carter Houston had shown her. Helma again pretended she hadn't seen the borrower's name and tried to analyze the transaction without bias. The person hadn't been intrigued enough by Lewis Carrol's work to *purchase* a personal copy. The book was inexpensive, so the person who borrowed it hadn't needed it for a school text they could make notations in; they'd just had a personal interest in the subject.

"So that's it?" Ruth said when she saw *Behind the Looking Glass*. "The book that turned you into a subversive?" She fanned the heavily annotated pages. "Why do some people like to strip our pleasures down to the nuts and bolts? Where's the fun of the mystery? Why do we have to *know*? Tell me that, would you?"

"It's our nature to attempt to understand all we see and hear," Helma explained.

"Well, thank you, Professor Zukas. Should we rescue your mother and Aunt Em from Syndi and Joseph before we go back to your apartment?"

"Or the other way around," Helma suggested, recalling Lillian and Aunt Em's enthusiasm.

"Tsk-tsk. Bad-mouthing old ladies doesn't become you."

"Let's wait," Helma told her. "They said they'd bring Joseph and Syndi back. I'd like to talk to Mary Lynn first."

"Why? What would she know?"

"She could explain why she didn't tell the police her cat was diabetic," Helma told her. "It's alive because it receives insulin injections every day. That car in front of you is making a left turn."

"I see it. But no kidding? Mary Lynn gives her cat shots of insulin? Isn't that just a teensy too coincidental? A woman's husband dies because of an unnecessary insulin shot and that same woman just happens to be giving her cat insulin shots? Do the police know?"

"Maybe not," Helma told her. "It's curious that neither Mary Lynn nor Beatrice mentioned it."

"I bet that would endear you to your cat—trying to coax him into your lap every day with a syringe in your hand."

Helma agreed. Boy Cat Zukas dodged out of her way if he saw a newspaper in her hand, a response left from his life before Helma.

Ruth shook her head as she turned into the Bayside Arms. "Nope, if I had a diabetic cat, I'd have it put down."

Helma didn't respond, remembering how in seventh grade, Ruth had kept her family's ancient beagle in diapers for a full year after her father had threatened to have it put down. It had tottered around Ruth's room and finally died in Ruth's bed.

"Oh look, the gods are on your side. Isn't that TNT himself getting into his Jeep, conveniently removing himself from the picture so you can talk to Mary Lynn without an eavesdropper?"

It was. And he *was* by himself. "If she doesn't have any other company," Helma said.

Ruth honked and waved as they passed TNT. He raised his hand in half a wave, looking distracted.

"I bet your kids drive you crazy whether they're young or old," Ruth commented as they climbed the steps to the third floor.

"It's a generational phenomenon," Helma said. "Until one or the other leaves home or dies."

"Gloomy observation," Ruth commented, looking at Helma curiously, "but probably true."

Mary Lynn answered TNT's door. Behind her tumbled an array of empty boxes waiting to be broken flat like the stack of flattened boxes that stood to the left of the door. TNT's exercise equipment was surrounded by piles of belongings. Two coats were draped over its silvery bars.

"May I speak with you for a few minutes?" Helma asked.

Mary Lynn nodded. "Come in, but everything's a mess. TNT couldn't stand it and deserted me for the YMCA." She looked away from Ruth and Helma, gazing at nothing. "We've decided to hold the funeral on Thursday. Lewis's sister's coming tomorrow, but she plans to stay in a motel anyway. I hope I'll be moved in by then." She spoke in short sentences without much emphasis. "Maybe she could stay out at the house. . . . This is such a mess." Then she went silent, her shoulders slumping. Even in her weariness and distraction, Mary Lynn was delicately beautiful.

"It'll all fall together, don't worry," Ruth said. "These things take on a life of their own." When Mary Lynn looked confused, Ruth clarified. "That's what happens with weddings, anyway; funerals are probably the same."

They stood beside the kitchen counter, their way to any other part of the apartment, including the balcony, blocked by boxes.

"I stopped at Hugie's this afternoon," Helma told her.

"You saw Dean," Mary Lynn guessed, evincing no surprise. "He's never forgiven—" She stopped.

"Never forgiven what?" Ruth asked eagerly. "That you dumped him for the teacher?"

"It wasn't like that," Mary Lynn said. Tears filled her eyes.

"You and Dean are friends now?" Helma asked, more gently.

Mary Lynn nodded. "Cautious friends. Skip smoothed it over between us." She smiled slightly. "Skip and I both do volunteer tutoring at the Y, so we see each other several times a month. Skip tries to talk Dean into tutoring, too. He's nostalgic for the good old student days, I think."

"I saw my veterinarian at Hugie's today, too" Helma told her.

"Is your cat sick?" Mary Lynn asked politely but without any interest.

"No, but we spoke of your cat."

Mary Lynn blinked. "Dickens?" she asked. She pulled a sweater from a box at her feet and pulled it over her shoulders.

"The little calico cat?"

"Dickens Dixon?" Ruth asked. "Diabetic Dickens Dixon?"

"That's exactly what Lewis called him," Mary Lynn told them. "He had a weakness for alliteration."

"Why didn't you mention to the police that you gave your cat insulin shots?" Helma asked, guessing she hadn't.

"I knew it couldn't possibly be a factor in Lewis's . . . death, and I didn't want to complicate the issue. Besides,

I didn't give Dickens his shots; I could never do that."
She shuddered. "Not a needle."

"Your mother did," Helma guessed.

Mary Lynn nodded. "She worked in a nursing home
once, a long long time ago, and she wasn't afraid of needles. It's not a secret my mother and I don't get along,"
She looked from Helma to Ruth, her eyes damp, "But I
swear my mother had nothing to do with Lewis's death.
So I didn't see any reason to bring it up."

"Are you trying to keep it from them?" Helma asked.

"If I tell them *now*, it looks suspicious," she said in a
small voice. "Doesn't it?"

"If you do inform them," Helma suggested, "the police
can investigate and relieve your mind of keeping secrets."

"Secrets can kill you," Ruth said. She'd picked up a
framed watercolor of tulip fields from the floor and was
tipping it from side to side, critically eyeing it. "You forget which is a secret and which is public knowledge and
you confuse it all and get yourself and everybody else in
hot water. Trust me."

"Do believe her," Helma added. "She's had experi-
ence."

"Thanks, friend," Ruth said, returning the painting to
the floor.

"You're welcome."

"Are you going to tell the police?" Mary Lynn asked.

"They'll discover it on their own during the investigation," Helma told her, "but they'd be much more understanding if you told them yourself."

"The longer you wait, the worse it looks," Ruth added.

Mary Lynn bit her thumbnail and rocked back and
forth. "I wish Lewis could tell me what to do." Neither
Helma nor Ruth responded but Mary Lynn said, "Maybe
that nice policeman would be easier to tell."

"And which nice policeman is that?" Ruth asked.

"The detective. He's a little plump and always wears a
suit."

"You don't mean Carter Houston?" Helma asked.

"Carter?" Ruth asked, her voice rising to a squeak.

"Yes. Him. He seems very compassionate."

Ruth opened her mouth and Helma shot her a warning glance. "Okay, okay," Ruth muttered.

"If Carter's the person you feel more comfortable telling, then he's the man you should talk to," Helma told her.

"Will I be put in jail for withholding evidence?" Two tears slipped down Mary Lynn's cheeks.

"Nah," Ruth told her. "They don't do that around here."

"What kind of insulin was injected into Dickens?" Helma asked.

"Is there more than one kind?" Mary Lynn wiped away her tears with the back of her hand. "I remember it had an N on the bottle. Does that mean anything? The vet gave it to us. One bottle lasted a long time, a few months, I think. My mother kept it in her refrigerator."

"How many shots a day?"

Mary Lynn shrugged. "I don't know. Two?"

"Have you talked to your mother since Lewis's death?" Helma asked.

"Only when I found him. She heard me screaming so she came outside. We called the ambulance."

"Then what?" Ruth asked.

"She went back to her apartment."

"After the ambulance left?" Helma prompted.

Mary Lynn shook her head. "Before they came. When I asked her to phone TNT, she refused to call him and went inside."

"She left you alone with the . . . Lewis *before* the ambulance arrived?" And when Mary Lynn nodded, Helma asked, "So *you* phoned TNT?"

Mary Lynn nodded again. "He arrived right after the ambulance. My mother didn't come outside again and I haven't talked to her since."

"Whew," Ruth said. "That's brutal."

Helma agreed that it was. She recalled Beatrice's unlit cigarette, her contrived resemblance to her daughter.

The telephone rang and Mary Lynn reached across a stack of cloth napkins to answer it. "Hi, Skip," she said. "No, he left. My moving in is a little confusing to him, I think, but he'll come around." She listened for a few moments, then said, "Sure. Canadian bacon but no olives. Extra cheese. See you then."

After she hung up, Mary Lynn said, "Skip's dropping off a pizza for TNT and me. Would you like to join us?"

"No thank you," Helma told her. "I'm having company. I hope you'll consider calling the police or Carter Houston. I wouldn't be surprised if Carter was near enough to be here in seconds."

As they walked back to Helma's apartment, Ruth said, "Speaking of Mary Lynn being open and honest with our local law enforcement, when are you going to tell them about the warning note on your car?"

"It's manageable right now," Helma said as she unlocked her door. "I don't want the police to muddy up what might be unfolding. In a different situation, I'd tell Wayne, but I'm not telling Carter."

"Helma Zukas, I'm shocked."

"Well, would *you* confide in Carter Houston?"

"Hell no, but that's not what shocks me. You called our chief of police 'Wayne.' After how many years, is this some kind of a breakthrough?"

"Well, that *is* his name."

🌿 *chapter sixteen* 🌿

IN THE SILENT NIGHT

"**W**ho are you calling?" Ruth asked.

"Hopefully, the woman who phoned in the prowler call to the police," Helma told her as she dialed one of the two Hayden phone numbers she'd copied from the hospital phone book.

The first phone number was answered by an answering machine. "This is the Haydens. Leave a message," a man's businesslike voice advised. Helma noted that on her slip of paper.

The second phone number was answered by a child.

"Are your mother and father in Turkey?" Helma asked.

"Mom says Dad's a turkey," the child told her, giggling. "Do you want to talk to her?"

"Not today, but thank you for answering the telephone," Helma said, and hung up, already crossing out the second telephone number.

"Find out what you wanted?" Ruth asked as she peered in Helma's refrigerator.

Helma tucked the slip of paper into her purse. "Partly. I'll try again later."

It was almost dark when Aunt Em and Helma's mother returned with Joseph and Syndi. Helma heard them climbing the stairs, not their footsteps but their voices—singing. It was a slightly bawdy song about an old gray mare, complete with sound effects. Aunt Em's raspy voice was the loudest, and Helma had a sudden childhood memory of Aunt Em and her father and their four brothers and sisters bellowing the song during an evening of overeating and too much drinking. Had she joined in? She couldn't remember, and sadly, she considered that she most likely hadn't.

"Now there's a song they don't teach in grade school," Ruth said, tipping her head and listening, "at least not in the classroom."

Helma rose and opened the door before they could ring the doorbell. She surprised all four of them as they were drawing out the last notes of the song. Joseph and Syndi snapped their mouths closed while Aunt Em and Helma's mother carried on until they ran out of breath, tipping their heads close together. ". . . no mo-o-o-o-re."

Joseph and Syndi slipped past Helma into the apartment, heading for the sofa Helma had just vacated. Joseph carried an open can of pop, Syndi a brown paper bag.

When Lillian caught her breath, she said, "You should have come with us, dear. We had such a good time."

"Oh yes," Aunt Em agreed. "I haven't laughed so hard in months." She shook her finger at Joseph. "You are so funny."

Helma and Ruth exchanged quick glances. Joseph sat curling and uncurling Helma's new *Time* magazine, his eyes downcast. Funny?

"Now, Helma dear," Lillian said, "I'm sure you went to visit him again so tell these two how their father's doing."

"He's slowly regaining consciousness," Helma told them. Syndi and Joseph intently watched her face, reminding her of the way she herself listened to people giving important information: watching for more than just the words, alert to the true message. "He's only spoken a few words but he asked about you and I assured you were fine," she told them, realizing they expected only the complete truth from her, not any platitudes, and if she didn't give them the truth, she would hurt what little chance they all had of getting along. "He's on less medication than this morning."

Aunt Em tsk-tsked. "He's so fortunate you're here, the people he loves most in the world." Syndi looked away from Helma's face and nodded.

"We have a swimming date tomorrow," Lillian said. "Two o'clock sharp, don't forget."

"We'll wait out front for you," Syndi told her, "so you don't have to come up here."

"Isn't that thoughtful. We're meeting Ethel for a doll collectors' meeting in half an hour. But you call us if you get bored or lonely here."

"I'll go with you," Ruth told the two older women.

"To the doll meeting?" Lillian asked.

"No, just out the door," Ruth told her and Helma's mother said, "Oh," looking relieved.

"Did you enjoy your afternoon?" Helma asked Syndi and Joseph after her mother, Aunt Em, and Ruth left.

"Yeah," Joseph said.

"It was okay," Syndi agreed.

"Are you hungry?" Helma asked.

Both Syndi and Joseph shook their heads. "We got some stuff," Syndi said, pointing to the brown bag on the table.

They spoke unnaturally, with long pauses. Helma didn't know how to change the conversation to the effortless way it flowed when Ruth or Aunt Em and her mother were around. What did they do differently that made it work?

"Would you like to telephone your friends in Oregon?" she asked.

Syndi shook her head but said, "Mom's going to call us from France at Dad's house. If she doesn't get an answer she'll be worried."

"We'll check his answering machine every day," Helma

told her. Syndi watched her closely and Helma added, "Do you have a telephone number where you can reach your mother? You can call her from here."

When Syndi said, "Sure, I have her number," Helma saw the quick, surprised look Joseph gave his sister. "But I don't think I'll call her yet," Syndi finished, ignoring the smirk on Joseph's face.

"Even if you didn't have her number, the police could find her if you needed her," Helma assured her.

"I said I have her number," Syndi said. "Can I hold your cat?" Boy Cat Zukas was peering in from the balcony.

"Of course, but he can be independent sometimes," she warned Syndi, who was already opening the sliding glass doors and lifting Boy Cat Zukas by his front legs. Just as he behaved with Ruth, the cat went limp, allowing Syndi to handle him in any manner she wanted. Syndi dropped on the couch with Boy Cat Zukas in her arms and Helma could hear the black cat purring from across the room.

"Can I watch TV?" Joseph asked, and Helma readily agreed, despite the suspicion that Wayne would have suggested a different activity and that she herself didn't approve of television-watching just to fill time. She felt somewhat mollified when Joseph tuned in a show about volcanoes.

Her phone rang and it was the mechanic who normally worked on her car. "Triple A brought your car here," he told her. "I've replaced those tires but those were nasty gashes. Did you call the police?"

"Not yet."

"I'd do it if I were you," he told her. "At least make a report. James is here tonight so we'll drop your car off on the way home. It'll be there when you wake up in the morning, good as new."

"Thank you," she told him. "I appreciate it."

"No problem, but think about calling the police."

With the two young people settled, Helma took a glass of iced tea to her balcony and sat down. It was dark now and the black bay was surrounded by the lights of Belle-haven. The air smelled moist; she couldn't see the stars, and she surmised the clouds along the horizon she'd spotted earlier in the day had now spread across the sky. If they didn't bring rain, they'd bring cooler weather. A siren sounded in town, and she idly swept her eyes along the curve of the bay, looking vainly for the lights of an emergency vehicle.

There was movement on TNT's balcony and Helma gasped.

"Sorry." It was TNT, sitting on his deck, much like Helma. She caught the glint of light off a glass in his hand.

"Good evening," Helma told him. "I think the weather's changing."

"If it does I'll be stuck inside," he said as if it were an indescribable punishment. "Not that I mind being inside, but right now this house ain't my home. The way I eat isn't good enough for her; she had to cook me some god-awful mess that was supposed to be healthy but it gave me a bellyache."

"Mary Lynn?" Helma asked.

"Who else? I love that girl, but after a man's been alone awhile he makes his own way of life, you know?"

"Yes," Helma agreed, "I think I do." Here they both sat on their balconies, she thought, because inside another generation had disrupted their lives and taken over their routines. "Perhaps it only takes a period of adjustment," she offered hopefully.

"If it doesn't kill you first. How's the cop?"

"Getting better, I think."

In the light from his apartment, Helma saw TNT rise and face her balcony. "Tell me something," he said, keeping his voice low. "Did his accident have anything to do with Lewis's murder?"

"It may have," Helma told him. "We won't know for certain until he regains consciousness. Before the accident, Wayne mentioned that he knew Lewis slightly. Were you aware of that?"

"Sure, a good cop knows a lot of people, but they also knew each other from the Y. We've all worked out there together, threw a few punches at each other."

"Were they acquaintances on a social level, too?" she asked.

"I couldn't say."

"Maybe Mary Lynn would know."

TNT held up his hand. "Wait a few days, could you? Like after the funeral. She's doing more crying than talking right now."

Helma refrained from saying she'd already talked to Mary Lynn once that day and she seemed perfectly capable of speaking.

"Besides," TNT said. "I need a little break from murder and confusion right now."

Helma agreed and they told each other goodnight, even though they both remained on their balconies. Helma continued to puzzle over Wayne and Lewis. Was there another connection between the two besides just sharing workouts at the Y? The YMCA's gym was the largest and best equipped in Bellehaven and most people who exercised used the Y. That fact didn't have much significance.

Which brought her back to the prowler and the subject of coincidence. Wayne had chased a prowler to Danish Point and in a scuffle was thrown over the cliff. End of story, no connection to Lewis's murder, except they were both in the same vicinity. But the book. And TNT's reluctance to let Helma talk to Mary Lynn. And Carter had implied . . . he'd never finished his implication. Helma rubbed her temples, assuaging the hints of a headache. And her punctured tires. Certainly the events were all connected; how could she believe anything else?

She sat on her balcony awhile longer, and when her glass was empty, returned to her apartment. Syndi and

Joseph still sat on the couch. The television program had been changed to a comedy with a riotous laugh track but which they watched solemn-faced. Neither looked up as Helma carried her glass to the kitchen.

She used the phone in her bedroom to call the hospital one last time. "He's sleeping well," the nurse told her, "but he's still not talking. Try in the morning, Miss Zukas," she said, although Helma hadn't given her name.

Then she phoned the Haydens' house again, but either the caretaker was true to her word and not spending the night there or she wasn't answering the telephone.

The spare room was always ready for a guest but she needed to retrieve bedding from the closet for Joseph. In the bedroom, Syndi had dumped her backpack on the bed: a jumble of underwear and shorts and tops, a makeup bag decorated with pictures of a rock group Helma didn't recognize. The tape player was tangled with a pair of socks, and off to the side was a stuffed elephant with most of the plush worn off the fabric. One eye was missing and its trunk was frayed at the tip. Syndi had obviously owned the elephant most of her thirteen years. Helma took the bedding for the sofa from the closet and left the bedroom, wondering what Syndi had named the elephant and if it always traveled with her.

Helma had difficulty falling asleep, hearing Syndi and Joseph's voices, then unfamiliar coughs and sneezes, the sounds of the bathroom and creaking of furniture. She felt like she'd only just fallen asleep when she awakened with a jerk, her body rigid. It was 1:38 in the morning, and a few seconds later the sound that had startled her reverberated through her apartment again.

It was a snore, deafeningly loud. Helma listened to two more, then slipped into a robe and slippers and quietly headed for the living room to see for herself that the noise actually came from a boy as young as Joseph. She peeked

into the guestroom because the light was still on. Syndi
lay curled on her side, sound asleep, the stuffed elephant
in her arms and Boy Cat Zukas curled against her back.
The cat opened one eye and gazed at Helma, then looking
too satisfied, closed his eye.

Joseph had moved the sofa so it faced the sliding glass
doors. In the morning, when he opened his eyes, he'd be
greeted by the crowns of the humpy islands beyond the
bay. He lay on his back, the blankets tucked beneath his
chin, his mouth wide open. He'd left the counter light on
in the kitchen. Helma watched and listened to him for a
few moments, then knelt beside the couch. "Joseph," she
whispered, "roll over." The snoring guttered to a stop and
Joseph closed his mouth. "Roll over," Helma whispered
again, and surprisingly, he did exactly that, turning so he
faced the glass doors, tucking his hand beneath his cheek
and settling deeper into his blankets.

Helma pulled the blankets over his exposed shoulder
and rose, satisfied. She briefly considered turning off the
counter light, then realized that if Joseph were to wake up
in the night, he wouldn't be able to find his way to the
bathroom. By its light, she noticed Syndi's paper bag on
the table and wondered if any of the food was perishable.

So instead of turning off the light, she unpacked the
bag. There was a banana with a brown soft spot near the
stem, three cellophane packs of crackers Helma recognized as the kind her mother collected when she went out
to lunch, two candy bars, a bag of cashews, and a bottle
of raspberry soda. Helma left the dry foods on the table
and put the bottle in the refrigerator.

Since she changed all the paper trash bags in her apartment every week, she turned the paper bag upside down
in order to fold it and save it for Tuesday. As she did, a
slip of paper fell out. A sales receipt, she thought, but
when she picked it up to throw it away, she saw the handwriting. She held it to the light. "This is a surprise for
your father—his favorite flavor," was printed on the pa-

per. Helma read it twice more to be sure she was seeing it correctly.

"This is a surprise for your father—his favorite flavor." The handwriting wasn't her mother's or Aunt Em's. She was nearly certain it wasn't Mrs. Whitney's, either. Syndi had been carrying the bag. *What* was for her father? The candy bars? The pop? She found a plastic sandwich bag and slipped the note inside for safe keeping, then hurried back to Syndi's room to awaken the girl. On the threshold, she had second thoughts. Why frighten her in the middle of the night?

But what if Syndi had eaten something from the bag? It had been seven hours since they'd returned from their outing. Certainly, if she was going to be ill, she'd have felt effects by now.

Helma silently crept to the bed and leaned close to Syndi's face. Her breathing was normal. As lightly as possible, she placed the back of her hand against the girl's forehead. No fever. When she was satisfied that Syndi was fine, she returned to her bedroom and phoned the police department.

Luckily, Sidney Lehman answered the phone again. It was obviously his week for the night shift. "I'm looking for Carter Houston," she said. "Is he on duty tonight?"

"Not officially," Sidney told her.

"Do you know where he is?" she asked. Sidney was silent a moment too long, and Helma said, "If he's in the parking lot outside the Bayside Arms, please call him and ask him to come up to my apartment; I have a bag of suspicious items for him."

"I'll do that," Sidney told her.

"Thank you."

Helma counted: three minutes later, light tapping sounded on her door. When she opened it, Carter stood on her doorstep, slightly rumpled but still in suit and tie, even if his tie was askew. He blinked as if he'd just put on his glasses. "What suspicious items?" he asked. After his first glance at Helma in her nightclothes, he looked everywhere but at her, frowning once at Joseph sleeping on her sofa but not commenting.

"Wayne's daughter brought home a bag of snacks after an outing today and this note was inside the bag," she said in a low voice, but Joseph didn't show any sign of rousing. She handed Carter the plastic encased note. Even he must have been reminded of the plastic encased book he'd shown *her*.

Carter read the note, then turned it over and studied the blank back. "Was it in this plastic?" he asked.

"No. I did that."

He nodded in approval. "What was in the bag?"

"These items," she told him, pointing to the snacks on the table, "plus a bottle of pop that's in the refrigerator."

"That's all?"

"And the note, which makes it all very suspect. Do you feel it would be wise to have them analyzed?"

"Where'd his daughter get these?" Carter hadn't moved to touch the other items.

"I'll ask her in the morning. She's asleep, exhausted after such a traumatic day, and she's sleeping peacefully; I checked. It may be nothing—one of my mother's friends might have given them to her, but once you've had them analyzed, we can ask her which item the note is referring to."

Helma donned her dishwashing gloves and returned all the items to the bag. "My fingerprints are on file so if you dust these for prints, you can eliminate mine."

"I'd like to question the girl," Carter said.

"Definitely not," Helma told him as she folded the top of the brown paper bag. "It can wait until tomorrow."

"It would speed up the investigation," Carter persisted, his chin thrusting forward in determination.

"She's thirteen years old and she's finally fallen asleep after seeing her father lying injured in the hospital. If Wayne were here, he'd definitely refuse you, just as I am."

"You're interfering with police procedure again, Miss Zukas," Carter told her.

Helma gave him the bag. "Good night, Carter. I promise not to leave my apartment for the next six hours, so you may as well take a break from your surveillance duties. If there's evidence of tampering with these snacks, call me after seven in the morning." And she gently ushered him to her door, holding it open for him and saying, "Good night again," then closing and locking it before he could get in a word.

Joseph slept on, oblivious, but when Helma peeked in Syndi's room on the way to her own bedroom, the girl was facing the wall, the stuffed elephant not visible, Boy Cat Zukas at the end of her bed licking his paws. Helma had the distinct feeling that Syndi was wide awake. "Syndi?" she whispered. There was no response, and Helma left the room.

It would be a while before she could get back to sleep. There was probably a perfectly innocent explanation for the items in the paper bag but she wouldn't rest easy until she was certain.

Finally, she pulled *Behind the Looking Glass* from her bedside table and began to skim through it, reading pages at random, not knowing what she was looking for but convinced it had a place in the puzzle, and within that puzzle existed both Wayne's fall and Lewis's murder.

"Alice's looking-glass world serves as Carroll's polemic against the absurdity of the capitalistic theory," read one line, "especially in the United States."

Another read, "The image of the baby's transformation into a pig is analogous with perceived upper class superiority to the inferior races."

Definitely, the soup strained too thin, Helma thought. She read on, but quicker than she would have believed she was sound asleep, her bedside lamp still on, the book open on her blankets.

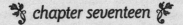

✤ chapter seventeen ✤

IF DANGER CAME

The morning sky was gray, featureless, which meant the drizzly weather would remain for the entire day, maybe longer. From Helma's bedroom window she could see the glistening leaves and the pavement shining with newly fallen rain. Sounds were muffled in the same way that Midwest snow softened them. Whatever she planned with Wayne Gallant's children would have to be inside, a development that felt daunting. She dressed in slacks and a sweater before leaving her bedroom. It was 6:45 A.M.

Syndi's bed was empty, but Helma heard the overexcited cadence of a television commercial and found them both in the living room watching early morning cartoons. The sofa had been pushed back into its usual place and the room resembled Wayne's living room the night she and Ruth had gone to his house. Joseph and Syndi sat on the sofa in the rumpled tangle of Joseph's bedding. A carton of milk stood on the coffee table, along with two used cereal bowls and spoons and an open box of raisin bran. Her grandmother's sugar bowl, its silver spoon lying in a glitter of sugar, balanced precariously on top of a *Time* magazine. Never had Helma seen such disarray in her apartment.

After she'd stood in the room a few moments taking in the scene, Joseph and Syndi became aware of her presence. "Hi," Joseph said.

"We already ate," Syndi added.

"I can see," Helma told her. "Clean up when you're finished, please."

"That bag I brought home is gone," Syndi told her, waving toward the kitchen table where she'd left it. "The one with the candy bars."

"Did you buy those snacks?" Helma asked her.

"Yeah. Dad gave us money," she said with a touch of defiance. "I didn't take money from any of those old ladies."

"They *wanted* to give it to us," Joseph said.

"Because they felt sorry about Dad, stupid," Syndi retorted. She jerked a pillow from behind Joseph and wrapped her arms around it.

"So?"

"So you shouldn't have taken it."

Before Helma could delve into *that* conversation, her phone rang. She turned her back to Syndi and Joseph, who continued to argue the moral implications of accepting money from old ladies.

"This is Carter Houston," he said briskly, all business. "The lab checked those items."

"Already?" Milk had been spilled across the counter, and Helma stretched the phone cord and wiped up the puddle with a piece of paper towel.

"We do operate twenty-four hours a day down here." He paused. "The raspberry soda was contaminated with arsenic."

Helma's vision suddenly narrowed to a tunnel; she felt behind her for a dining room chair and sat down, wrapping the phone cord around her hand. "Are you sure?"

"*I'm* not but the lab seems to be."

"I'm not questioning their expertise," Helma told him. "I'm not."

"Yeah, and you said the girl was carrying the soda in a bag?"

"Yes, what if she'd taken a . . ." She couldn't say it.

"Drink," Carter finished. She heard him inhale a deep breath. "I know. It would have made her damn sick, but for Wayne, in his condition, it might have been fatal." And more gently, Carter said, "We have to question her, to find out where she picked up the soda. Corky Danforth is on her way over. She's good with kids."

"I've met her," Helma said, grateful that Carter wasn't doing the questioning.

"In light of this," Carter said more briskly, more like the Carter Houston she'd come to know in the past three years, "reconsider your position on keeping the book borrower's name a secret. Passing on that information could save Wayne's life—or even the lives of his children."

"Don't use scare tactics with me, Carter," she warned. "I'm putting my trust in the Bellehaven police to solve this as quickly and efficiently as possible."

"Then cooperate."

"In every way I'm capable. Thank you for the information, Carter. Good-bye now." And she hung up, turning to see Syndi watching her, her eyes wide. "Don't be alarmed," she told them, "but someone from the police department will be here soon to ask you a few questions."

"Cool," Joseph said. He ate a handful of cereal directly from the box.

"It's about the bag I had, isn't it?" Syndi asked, folding the pillow on itself. "My candy bars and stuff? I was awake when that policeman came here last night."

"Yes, it is," Helma admitted. She briefly wondered how much to tell Syndi and Joseph, whether they'd be frightened, then decided a *little* fear was frequently beneficial. "There was a note in the bag saying the soda was for your father. A chemical had been added to it that would have made him ill. The police want to know how it ended up in your paper bag."

Syndi shrugged. "I don't know. I thought it was Joseph's."

"Raspberry, yuck," Joseph said around his mouthful of cereal.

"When did you buy the snacks?" Helma asked her.

"When we were with your mother and Aunt Em. Right at the beginning; they were worried we were hungry. But I didn't buy any pop."

"Did you leave the bag unattended anywhere?"

Syndi scrunched her mouth to one side while she thought. "Yeah, everywhere. I wasn't really hungry so mostly I left it in the car when we went swimming and for ice cream and when we stopped at the park."

Helma knew her mother never locked her car, not even on a shopping trip. "It's such a bother," she'd explained, "getting your keys out when you're carrying packages." And sometimes it seemed that *because* Lillian never expected to be robbed or vandalized, she wasn't. But it would have been so simple to open the car door and slip the bottle into the paper bag. Done in seconds.

Corky Danforth arrived while Syndi and Joseph were clearing away their breakfast detritus. Corky was a brilliant redhead with freckles that nearly matched her hair. Aside from her hair, she wasn't especially attractive, but she had an infectious laugh and an easy way about her that transformed her plainness into beauty the longer anyone remained in her presence.

"Hi, Joseph. Hi, Cindy," she said on entering Helma's apartment. She wore jeans and a sweatshirt instead of a uniform and was carrying a straw bag. Her red hair sparkled with drops of rain.

"It's spelled with an S," Helma told her. "S-Y-N-D-I," and was almost rewarded by a smile from Syndi.

"Got it," Corky said, grinning at Syndi. "I like it."

It quickly became apparent that Corky didn't intend to question Syndi and Joseph in Helma's apartment but planned to take them downtown to the police station. "There'll be someone there from CPS," Corky told her, "but you're welcome to come with and wait outside the office if you like."

When Helma declined, Corky told Syndi and Joseph, "I'll give you a tour."

"Dad's already done that," Joseph told her.

She winked at him. "I bet not the part *I'll* show you."

"Are we coming back here?" Syndi asked.

"You bet," Corky told her. She turned to Helma. "Unless there are other plans?"

"No, I'd like them to come back here," Helma said. "I'll stop by the library and the hospital this morning but I should be home by eleven-thirty."

"How about if I take these guys out for hamburgers after we chat? Bring them home around one?"

They agreed, and as soon as Joseph and Syndi left the room to change clothes, Corky's face turned solemn. "Have you left your apartment since Carter Houston was here?"

"No. Why?"

Gingerly, from her straw bag, Corky removed a plastic bag that held a wickedly jagged piece of glass about three inches long. "This was embedded in your welcome mat. It would have been tough to see as you walked out the door."

One end of the glass shard ended in a dagger-edged point. "How—" Helma began; the look on Corky's face stopped her question. "Did it appear to have been left purposely?"

"I'd say so." Corky returned the glass to her straw bag. "It wouldn't kill you, but chances are if you'd stepped outside barefoot or in slippers, you'd have received a nasty cut."

"Which would draw my attention from more deadly matters," Helma said, thinking of how she often stepped onto the landing in her slippers to retrieve the newspaper.

Corky looked at her curiously but only said, "That's right."

Helma was left in the sudden silence of her apartment. She turned on the radio to fill the space and then dressed for the library, thinking she should at least attempt to repair whatever damage she'd left behind at the library the day before. Pamphlet holders and circulation systems all seemed curiously remote.

But first she'd visit Wayne in the hospital. Her phone rang again as she was just about to leave her apartment. "This is Mary Lynn Dixon," the tentative voice said. "I told him and you're right, I feel better. It was the right thing to do."

"You told Carter Houston about your diabetic cat?" Helma asked.

"Yes, about Dickens and the insulin. I called him just a few minutes ago and he was very understanding, just like I thought he would be. He believed me."

Helma wondered if Carter ever believed anything until he was able to prove it. "That's good, Mary Lynn. I'm sure you'll rest easier now."

"We've had orders to be extremely cautious," Officer Cliff Bikman told Helma. "You're on the list and I know who you are but I've got to see picture ID and record your driver's license number." He ducked his head in embarrassment. "Sorry, but it's orders, like I said."

"I understand," Helma told him as she opened her wallet, "and I agree."

Wayne Gallant was running a fever. "It's not unusual," a new nurse named Gela told Helma. "We'll keep an eye on it."

"Have unauthorized visitors been in this room? Has he eaten anything that might have come from outside the hospital?"

"He hasn't eaten anything at all," the nurse told her, pointing to the drip that snaked into Wayne's arm from the plastic bag above his bed. "And the police guarding his door even checked *my* credentials before they'd let me inside his room." She patted Helma's arm as if Helma needed comforting. "Don't worry about him; he's snug as a bug here with us. A little fever is to be expected."

"Will this delay his recovery?" Helma asked. They stood in the doorway of Room 224 speaking in low voices. Even from there Helma could see the flush high on Wayne's cheeks: two unnatural red spots on his pale face.

"It depends."

"Everything 'depends,' doesn't it?" Helma said, her irritation with the uncertainty of it all chafing like raw flesh. "There aren't any clear answers. We can't plan or know; we're stranded, waiting for all the ducks to hit the ground."

"To line up, you mean. That's the way it is, all right," the nurse said, glancing up as a call button was pushed in another room. "I'll answer that and be back."

After the nurse left, Helma returned to Wayne's bedside. His skin was dry and overwarm, his breathing shallow. He didn't open his eyes despite her saying his name twice and holding his hand between hers. Helma sat watching his face, thinking of Carter Houston's request that she surrender the name of the book borrower. She couldn't; there was no question of betraying her code, but as she watched Wayne Gallant's chest rise and fall, her career-long convictions didn't seem as clear-cut as they once had.

Because of the drizzle, Helma drove to the library instead of walking and took the first shift on the reference desk dispensing information to the public. She was early and none of the other librarians had arrived. It was a quiet morning, one of those mornings when a loquacious elderly man, realizing she was not only paid to assist the public but was also a captive behind the reference desk, chose to explain in great detail why he needed to find the definition of the word "thrombosis" before his afternoon appointment with his doctor.

When the man was finally distracted by the most technical medical book she could find, Helma phoned the Hayden residence again, and after the fourth ring, the phone was answered. "Hayden residence."

"I have one more question about the prowler you reported on Sunday," Helma said briskly.

"Is this the police?" she asked.

"I'm sorry I didn't identify myself; my name's Wilhelmina Zukas. Have you recalled anything else that might make an identification easier?"

"No. Just that I saw somebody at the back of the property and I felt like they were watching me. People walk back there sometimes but they keep moving; they don't *sneak* around. The woman in the next house thinks I was imagining it, but I wasn't."

"I believe you. Could you identify the prowler as a man or woman?"

"I thought it was a man but I don't have a concrete reason, just a feeling. Maybe because he was wearing dark blue. That sounds retro, doesn't it? Blue for boys, pink for girls. Have you caught somebody?"

"No one yet, as far as I know. I understand you're not spending the nights at the residence?"

"I might. My boyfriend's going to lend me his dog; it's part rottweiler."

"Good idea. Thank you very much for your time."

Then Helma realigned the books behind the reference desk, sharpened all the pencils, and caught herself jotting down the number 224 again and again in various styles of handwriting on her yellow pad. She called the hospital and was patched through to the nurses' station on the second floor. Although she didn't give her name, she was told, "No change since you were here."

"Miss Zukas?" Helma glanced up into Dutch's face,

bracing herself for whatever complaint he surely had. In the three years Dutch had worked at the Bellehaven Public Library, he'd maintained a soldierly distance from every other staff member, and an unquestioning loyalty to Ms. Moon. He was in his fifties, steely-haired and gray-eyed, of impeccable bearing and no-nonsense humor. A tattooed dragon curled up his right arm and disappeared beneath his shirtsleeve.

"Yes?" Helma asked, politely, warily.

He stood at attention and nodded sharply. "The right to privacy is an American fundamental," he said, nodding sharply again. "I'm behind you all the way." Then he turned on one heel and proceeded back to the circulation desk before Helma could respond.

When her shift was finished, Helma returned to the workroom, and it was as if she'd stepped into a divided camp. Eve and George stood outside the staff lounge facing Harley and Deidre.

"You're serious, aren't you?" George was saying to Harley.

"Criminals relinquish their rights," Harley said in the voice of a man who's just spoken the opening line of a well-prepared speech. He shaped his right hand into a fist and pounded it once against his left palm. Deidre stood beside him, nodding her head, clutching the tail of her braid.

Harley opened his mouth to continue, and George Melville cut him off by saying, "Maybe after they've been tried by their peers and found guilty, but not before they've been legitimately identified as felons. Until then they're just like you and me, all of us equally protected by the law of the land."

"The right to privacy isn't guaranteed by the United States Constitution," Harley told him. "It's implied by the Fourth Amendment but it wasn't even a concept until Warren and Brandeis coined the phrase in an article in 1890."

"You've been doing your homework," George said, with just a touch of admiration impossible for a librarian to withhold in the face of well-executed research.

Harley shrugged modestly. "It was on the Internet."

"Besides," Deidre added, leaning closer and tapping her braid against Harley's arm, "the American Library Association says that compliance with the Code of Ethics is *voluntary*. There aren't sanctions or any fines if a librarian discloses a patron's record."

"It's the most sacred bond between librarian and patron," Helma interjected.

"But if you can save a life . . ." Harley said.

"Whose life?" Helma asked, but it was Deidre who snapped back the answer.

"Another victim's life, who else's? And you've already demonstrated that you believe lives are expendable by erasing the name the police wanted." She rubbed her braid against her cheek. "You'd rather follow some impossible ideal than save an innocent person."

"The library's obligation is to the individual," Helma told her.

"Oh yeah? And what if the next victim is a child?"

"It might have been," Helma said, and turned and walked away from them, feeling their eyes following after her.

She heard Eve ask Deidre, "What kind of librarian are you?"

"A reasonable one," Deidre answered.

Ms. Moon entered the workroom from the door that led to the parking lot. She carried a purple insulated lunch box that Helma already knew held a selection of high protein foods allowed on her new diet. She'd walked into Ms. Moon's office once at lunchtime and found the director seated at her desk with a substantial stack of naked roast beef slices, a container of cream, two boiled eggs, a square of cheddar cheese, and a leg of fried chicken spread out on the desk in front of her.

Now, Helma might have suddenly disappeared. Ms. Moon passed Helma on her way toward the little group of librarians and her office without acknowledging her, not a word, not even a grimace.

As if she'd heard every word of their conversation, Ms. Moon said to George, Harley, Eve, and Deidre loud enough for Helma to hear, "The process was begun this morning to obtain a search warrant for accessing the system's hard drive. It soon won't matter that an employee erased a borrower's name because the police will have access to every transaction."

Helma slipped into her cubicle and sat at her desk but leaned forward so she could hear George say, "When will it happen?"

"Maybe tomorrow," Ms. Moon replied. "Or the next day. The police are anxious to clear this up." There was a pause. "It would have been so much more reasonable to have cooperated in the first place."

" 'Cooperate' is a loaded word," George told her, "at least historically."

Ms. Moon's voice reached Helma loud and clear and frosty. "Are you implying that insurrection is of a higher moral value than cooperation?"

"I wasn't judging," George said, "only speaking pedantically."

Eve's voice cut across the workroom. "You mean like the American revolutionaries or the Nazis?"

"Try the allied powers of World War Two," Deidre told her.

There was silence for several seconds before Harley belatedly said, "Yeah," and the group broke apart.

Helma remained in her cubicle. If Ms. Moon were able to breach the computerized system as soon as tomorrow, the basic trust that library patrons felt toward their library—and librarians—would be destroyed. Her belief in her career would be a travesty. Tomorrow! Was there even time to make a difference? Helma pondered and contemplated, then looked down at her hands and realized she'd ripped a carefully researched, handwritten list of books on wild mushrooms into shreds. And she hadn't input it into her computer yet. She'd planned to place the list in the new pamphlet holder and give copies to the Merry Mushroomers. They didn't know she was compiling a list so they wouldn't miss it, but . . . Helma stopped. People couldn't care about situations they weren't aware of.

Reaching for her telephone, she dropped the mushroom list in her trash basket, ignoring the two scraps of paper that missed the basket and landed on the floor beneath her desk.

Ruth was still in bed but she mumbled something incomprehensible into the telephone. Helma bent her head over the receiver and spoke in a low voice—but only for the sake of privacy. "What's the name of your friend who writes for the *Bellehaven Daily News*?"

After two yawns and a groan, Ruth asked, "Man or woman?"

"Woman."

"Miki, why?"

"I'm curious how she decides which stories to write, whether they're assigned to her or she has her own ideas, or whether she hears leads from other people."

Ruth's voice came to life. "What have you got?"

"I haven't 'got' anything concrete but certain forces in the library may be cooperating with the police to tap into the library's circulation records."

"I thought you erased that."

"There's another layer that requires a subpoena to breach, at least in a situation like this."

"Oh-ho. And I bet it's being done quick and dirty before the public gets wind of it, am I correct?"

"You may be."

"Well, leave it to me. When you see the words 'anonymous source,' read 'Helma Zukas,' okay? Hey, what's that noise?"

Helma was already standing, the phone still to her ear, turning to see who was shouting near the door to the public area. Eve stood, too, her eyes wide. Deidre ducked down behind a cart of new videos and Harley was nowhere to be seen.

The door swung open and banged against the wall behind it. Through it charged Beatrice, Mary Lynn's mother. Her face was mottled red, her features twisted, and she was holding up her fists like a boxer. "Where's that Zukas bitch? I'm going to kill her."

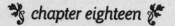

❧ chapter eighteen ❧

WITH SOBS
AND TEARS

As Helma stood in her cubicle watching the unfolding chaos in the workroom, still holding the telephone with Ruth's tiny voice shouting from the earpiece, she felt herself coolly withdraw into a pool of calm. The word "pandemonium" appeared in her mind and she idly considered its derivation, something to do with the poet Milton and the word "demon," she thought.

But only for a moment. Because Beatrice had spotted Helma and was heading toward her, hair tangled, eyes wild. She wore a pink sweatpants outfit with the neckline high, as if it were worn backwards.

"You went to the cops," Beatrice shouted as she approached Helma's cubicle. "You spied on me and then you told lies to the cops. I told you I'd do it and I will, by God. I'll have you arrested for trespassing and impersonating a police officer. You'll pay for this."

George Melville leapt up from his cataloging corner and advanced toward Beatrice, repeating, "Now now," in a soothing voice, one arm raised as if he held a large net. Ms. Moon stood in her office doorway, her mouth open.

The workroom door banged again and through it debouched TNT, Skip, and Dean, all three in spandex bicy-

179

cling clothes, like dancers bursting onto the stage. Immediately behind them marched Dutch, his face coolly passive. A group of patrons stood outside the door craning to
see in.

Helma didn't see a weapon on Beatrice, and since she
was being falsely accused, she held her ground, standing
at the entrance to her cubicle. Beatrice stopped inches
from her, one fist now turned into a pointing finger which
she jabbed in the air toward Helma. "You," she said, then
again, "You." She was smaller than Helma and had to
look up into Helma's face.

Helma had learned in workshops not to respond to the
accusations of irrational patrons, but this was different; it
wasn't simply a patron, irate over a library policy: *she*
was being personally accused. She kept her voice calm,
reasonable. "Mary Lynn, as the owner of the property,
could legally charge me with trespassing if she wished to,
but not you," she pointed out to Beatrice, "and I didn't
impersonate any other professional but a librarian—*you*
assumed I was a police official."

Before Beatrice could form an articulate response she
was surrounded by men. TNT reached out a hand to re-
strain her and she gave him such a withering look he
dropped his hand and stepped back, nodding to Skip and
Dean, who each grasped one of her arms, but neither with
much force.

"Let go of me, you idiots," Beatrice demanded, shrugging her arms until they did. "Do you know what she did
to me? She told the police I killed Lewis, that I used little
Dickens's insulin to give that great big man a heart attack. Hah! Little Dickens. Why, he must weigh four
pounds. I would have needed a barrel full of insulin for
Lewis to even notice."

Both Skip and Dean looked at Helma with raised eyebrows. "She'll just deny it," Beatrice said. Her voice rose
again, a decibel short of screeching. At that moment,
Dutch spoke up in military finality. "Lower your voice,

please, ma'am. This is a public building and there are children present." He stood ramrod straight, his face passive. Beatrice cast him the same withering look she'd given TNT but Dutch didn't even flinch.

"Dickens is a *cat*," Beatrice continued in a slightly lowered but unchastened voice. "Lewis was a man. There's no connection. Besides," she glanced at TNT, "if I had to kill somebody, it wouldn't have been *him*."

"Let's go outside to the parking lot to discuss this," Helma suggested. "We'll have more privacy."

"It's raining," someone, perhaps Eve, said. "Can't we stay in here?"

"Did you plant cops outside to arrest me?" Beatrice asked. It was a rhetorical question, spoken with a sneer.

Helma turned and walked toward the back door. As she passed Harley's cubicle she spotted him crouched down beside his desk, a heavy black book held in his hands.

"Is this safe?" George Melville asked from behind Helma. "Leaving the building?" Helma kept walking, hearing Beatrice's derisive laughter.

Helma didn't turn around until she stood in the center of the tiny staff parking lot next to the library, far enough away from her Buick that no one would lean against it. It still drizzled, a misty rain that Northwesterners barely noticed but which beaded like dew on hair and clothes, falling so lightly it could be shaken off without soaking through fabric or flattening curled hair.

The principles in the drama had all followed her: Beatrice, TNT, Skip, and Dean. Dutch stood five feet away like a sentinel, arms crossed over his chest, his eyes alert. George Melville and Eve stood on the loading dock, the others behind them.

Beatrice faced Helma. In her rage, her resemblance to Mary Lynn was less striking. More than just the fact that she was older, the aura of the unreasonable hovered about her. She wasn't trustworthy, and Helma sensed that she easily lied, without hesitation or perhaps even without awareness. "Why did you tell the police?" Beatrice demanded.

"I didn't," Helma told her. Around them, everyone was silent and attentive; no feet were shuffled, no throats were cleared.

Beatrice stood with her legs apart, leaning toward Helma. "Then who did?"

"What did the police tell you?" Helma asked.

"Tell me? It was in the middle of the night. Two policemen rapped on my door like the Gestapo, demanding I show them Dickens's insulin." She rubbed her arms at the memory. "They scared me so bad I nearly threw up. That bad."

"Did you show them the insulin?" Helma asked.

"Don't be stupid. Of course I did. It was the police. What an asinine question."

"Ma'am," Dutch warned quietly.

"Well," Beatrice said, brushing back a lock of hair and turning toward Dutch, "wouldn't *you* have waited until morning instead of scaring me out of my wits?"

Helma remembered what Mary Lynn had said about her mother sleeping in late every morning. Perhaps Beatrice spoke in relative terms. "What time did the police arrive?" she asked the woman.

"I looked at my clock so I can tell you exactly. It was 5:20, can you believe it? Nobody with an ounce of sanity is awake at that time of the night."

"Five-twenty?" Helma asked. "You're sure?" Mary Lynn had called her at 7:45 to report she'd just told Carter Houston about her diabetic cat. How could the police have talked to Beatrice at 5:20? "That's remarkably early for the police to be making house calls," Helma suggested.

"Don't you think I know that?" Beatrice squared her small shoulders and stood taller, the stance of defiance. "But that's what time it was. It wasn't even light out yet."

"I'm surprised."

"You can be if you want. But I didn't have one single thing to do with Lewis's death." She shook her finger again but her early rage was dissipating. She was winding down, unable to sustain her former fever pitch. "If you didn't sic the cops on me, I've got a bone to pick with the person who did, for certain." She turned to TNT. "Was it you? You've hated me since the day I bet against you in the Jenkins fight, haven't you? And now you're jealous because I live at Mary Lynn's house. Your beloved daughter, hah, and she isn't even related to you."

"Not by blood," TNT calmly answered. "The police were bound to find out about the cat sooner or later. It makes you look bad that you didn't tell them. Suspicious."

"Mary Lynn should have told them," Beatrice countered. "Dickens is her cat."

"So you both made a mistake." TNT began to bounce lightly from foot to foot as if he were warming up for the ring. "It still looks bad, like a punch after the bell."

"Well, I don't care how it looks." She turned in a circle, waving her arms to include everyone watching. "I'm warning you all. I'll go home now, but I'll be waiting for one of you to trip up, and then . . ." She slapped her hands together with a sharp crack, then turned and left the parking lot, walking in tight steps, shoulders back, toward the front entrance of the library. In silence, they all watched her leave, taking the drama with her.

"You knew she was on her way here to confront me?" Helma asked TNT and the two young men.

TNT gazed after Beatrice, who was just turning the corner of the building, on his face relief, amusement, and a shadow of sadness. "She showed up at your apartment first, making a hell of a ruckus before we went outside to see what had landed." He almost smiled. "She's a tough kid and she'd already been stewing a few hours so she was ready to blow."

Skip nodded. "She's calmed down considerably."

"And you were at TNT's apartment?" Helma asked Skip.

"I was, and Dean had just showed up."

Dean nodded. "Yeah, I was still in the parking lot—I could hear her from there, shouting for you to open your door and show yourself. We were meeting at TNT's for a bicycle trip to the Nitcum River." He glanced at his watch. "We might still have time if we get moving."

"And Mary Lynn?" Helma asked.

"She's not going," Dean told her.

"Helma's not talking about the bike trip," TNT told Skip and Dean, shaking his head, and to Helma he explained, "Mary Lynn's at home, *my* home. She wouldn't even go outside once she realized her mother was on the landing."

"I understood she told the police about her diabetic cat this morning," Helma said, still trying to account for Beatrice's and Mary Lynn's differing stories.

"Sure did. She was as happy as a Catholic who's made a good confession."

"You're saying she unburdened herself?" Helma asked. "And that was this morning, you're sure? Not last night?"

"Positive. Around 7:30. I overheard part of the conversation, all about that sick cat of hers. I'm not having a cat that needs shots in my apartment. If it was mine, I'd have it put down." Helma didn't believe TNT any more than she had Ruth.

A blue car pulled partway into the library parking lot and stopped, blocking the entrance. The crowd paused to watch it. Why was it that policemen always gave themselves away, even in unmarked cars? They drove with too much certainty, at the top of the speed limit, with *intent*.

Carter Houston stepped out of the driver's side. He was as impeccably dressed as usual but his eyes were red and bagged, his shoulders slumped by fatigue. The knees of his black suit pants were creased. He paused, his eyes passing over every member of the crowd before he approached Helma. She could see him calculating everyone's position, searching for a threat. "We had a call regarding a disturbance in the library," he announced. He glanced down at the notebook he held in his hand. "Actually, several calls," he added as explanation, and Helma imagined all the patrons in the library with their nuisance cell phones, dialing the police as Beatrice stalked through the public area.

TNT heaved a sigh and stepped forward. "It was my ex-wife Beatrice. You riled her by showing up on her doorstep at five this morning. She was looking for somebody to blame."

"In the library?" Carter asked, his eyes boring into Helma.

Helma nodded. "She believes I told you she gave insulin injections to Mary Lynn's diabetic cat."

Carter didn't even blink. "Why would she think that? Does she suspect you have privileged information, maybe information the police don't have access to—yet?"

"*Someone* told the police about Dickens the cat between one-thirty, when you were at my apartment, and five A.M. this morning," Helma told him. She took a breath. "And that information has nothing to do with the library borrower's name you're trying to extricate from the library's files."

"Maybe not directly—"

Their conversation was interrupted by Ruth's Saab screeching to a halt on the street in front of the library, backfiring as Ruth turned off the engine. Carter flinched. Ruth jumped from her car and strode toward the crowd in the parking lot, dressed in paint-spattered jeans and a black turtleneck, her hair uncombed, yesterday's makeup streaking. She looked far more threatening than Beatrice had, and the men, except for Carter Houston, stepped back.

"You left me twisting in the wind," she accused Helma.

"You didn't hang up the phone and all I could hear was a bunch of shouting and then it all faded away and there I sat, glued to the receiver until the mechanical voice ordered me to hang up. You could have all been wiped out by a mad patron for all I knew. What's going on?" She looked Carter up and down. "Need a good night's sleep there, don't you, Carter?"

George Melville joined them, his grin back in place. "Come on, Ruth. I'll give you the lowdown while they're talking."

"I don't want to miss anything."

"There's nothing to miss," Helma told her. "We're finished, aren't we, gentlemen?"

"Unless you've realized the true gravity of this situation and are finally prepared to share a certain name with me?" Carter suggested.

TNT, Skip, and Dean all looked at Helma, curiosity plain on their faces.

Helma was about to remind Carter that she'd turned her head away from the computer screen when the name of the borrower of *Behind the Looking Glass* had flashed across it, but the subterfuge—and she had to admit that's what it was—seemed pointless. The sooner it was all in the open, the sooner Wayne and his children would be truly safe. "I will never betray a patron's trust," she said. "Every single library patron's reading habits are privileged information."

"This would be the moment to sing a stirring library anthem," Ruth suggested. "Do you know any?" She scanned the tiny crowd, and when no one volunteered, she pointed to Harley. "That's a good job for you. Write one." Harley's mouth opened and closed.

"Your Saab's double parked," Carter pointed out to Ruth.

Ruth glanced at her car, still in the street, looking surprised to see it there. "Nobody's trying to gct out. Look at your own car. It's blocking the only entrance to this parking lot."

Carter held up his hands. "Listen, people. Let's break this up. Everyone back to your own business." More curious people had joined the gathering, some holding books in their arms, protecting them from the rain.

The crowd didn't move, too interested in discussing what had just taken place. TNT stepped close to Helma and asked, "What's this about your not betraying a library patron?"

"The police are interested in the name of a borrower, a possible criminal, or so they contend."

"And you're the only one who knows the name?" he asked.

"That's what the police believe."

Ruth shook her head. "Go for broke, why don't you? Tell the world."

"But it's true," Helma said, her voice loud enough to reach Ms. Moon, who watched from the workroom doorway, out of the drizzle, "I am the only one with that knowledge, probably the only person besides one—the borrower."

Several people regarded her with interest, and Ruth murmured, "Pin a target to your back, why don't you? A big red bull's-eye."

"Please disperse," Carter told the crowd, speaking louder. "Now."

People finally began to drift away, back inside the library, in the street, and to their cars.

"That's it?" Ruth asked. "I drove down here for this?"

Helma reached out and touched TNT's shoulder. "It was you, wasn't it?" she asked in a low voice. "You told the police about Beatrice and the insulin."

TNT tugged at his ear. "Now now," he cautioned, sounding like George when he'd tried to calm Beatrice.

"That's why you didn't want me asking any questions

about Lewis's murder. You knew Mary Lynn hadn't told the police about Dickens and you were worried I'd stumble onto it. Are you afraid that Mary Lynn actually *did* kill Lewis?"

"She's fragile," TNT said. "Even the questioning's too much for her."

Helma crossed her arms. "So when you discovered Mary Lynn was about to tell Carter about her cat, you decided to be preemptive and send them to Beatrice."

"Beatrice makes a better suspect, doesn't she?" TNT asked. He closed his mouth and tightened his jaws, then stepped away from Helma with a curt nod.

Carter's cell phone rang. He stood ten feet from Helma, and when he turned his back to answer it, she moved closer, listening.

"How long ago?" Carter asked, raising his wrist to look at his watch. "And you just tumbled to it now? Don't you watch TV? This happens all the time on TV. I'm on my way over."

It sounded like regular police business, and Helma was about to rejoin Ruth who was telling Skip and Dean about a jazz band at the Breakwater when Carter said, "And the chief's okay?"

He snapped his phone closed and headed for his car without turning to notice Helma, who was already running back to Ruth. She grabbed Ruth's arm and pulled her away from the two men. "Quick," she said, pointing to Ruth's Saab, still parked in the street. "You drive, and," she turned to see Carter backing his car out of the lot, "follow that car."

❧ chapter nineteen ❧

SUCH A TRICK

"**F**ollow what car?" Ruth asked as she and Helma raced toward her illegally parked Saab, which had by that time collected a growing line of cars behind it maneuvering to pass.

"Carter Houston's. Something's happened at the hospital."

"If that's where he's going," Ruth asked as she opened her car door—it wasn't locked, even her car keys were still in the ignition—"why the melodramatics? We'll simply drive to the hospital. Or if you're in a *real* hurry, you can walk over." Ruth put her car in gear and pulled away with a jerk before Helma had fastened her seatbelt. The windshield was beaded with raindrops too fine to warrant wipers.

"I need to be positive that's where he's going. He was on his cell phone, talking to the policeman at the hospital guarding Wayne's room, I think. He mentioned that 'it' happened all the time on television, whatever 'it' means."

"Was he pissed?" Ruth asked, turning a corner without looking and ignoring the blast of car horns.

"If you're speaking of the American slang term for angry rather than the British slang term for inebriated, yes, I'd say he was pissed."

"Well-spoken," Ruth said, and added smugly, "It's obvious to *me* what he meant. On TV, when some poor schmuck is in the hospital under police protection, you can bet the would-be assassin tries to sneak into his room to finish the job and he always goes for the camouflage factor: dressing up like a doctor or an orderly or a nurse. It's a given."

"But he said Wayne was all right," Helma said in a small voice, remembering that Carter had *asked* if the chief was okay, not *said* he was.

"Lookee there," Ruth said as she pulled into the hospital parking lot. "We beat the man."

And indeed, Carter's plain dark car had just turned onto the street in front of the hospital. He'd obviously obeyed the traffic laws, a nicety that rarely concerned Ruth.

Carter had the advantage because he was able to park in the Police Only spaces next to the emergency room entrance, but Ruth pulled into the Physicians Only space and they all reached the hospital doors at the same time.

Carter didn't appear surprised to see them, only weary. "What are you doing here?" he asked. "Or do I even want to know?"

"We're on our way to visit the man. What did you think?" Ruth said.

But Helma's first priority was the truth. "I heard you on your cell phone a few minutes ago," she told him. "Is Wayne all right?"

"This is police business," Carter said as he walked toward the elevator, Helma beside him.

"I don't care," Helma said. "Tell me."

Ruth veered off toward the stairs, and when she realized Helma wasn't with her, returned to stand in front of the elevator with Carter and Helma. "Love conquers all phobias, eh?" she asked Helma.

The doors separated; a bell dinged twice and a nurse pushing an elderly man in a wheelchair, his lap laden with a cardboard box of flowers and cards, stepped out. Carter entered, then Ruth. They turned to face the door, looking at Helma, who remained on the other side of the doors, looking in. No one spoke. Finally, Helma took two deep breaths and stepped inside the tiny, enclosed, windowless, unstable compartment. She closed her eyes while the doors dinged and slid together, and an invisible cable began hauling the flimsy box she stood in up to the second floor.

When she opened her eyes again, Carter was watching her and finally answered her question. "He's fine," he said simply.

Helma let out a sigh of relief. "There was a breach in your security?" she asked.

Again he considered her before he answered, rapidly blinking his round eyes. "Not an actual breach, no, but possibly an unauthorized person on the floor."

"What time?"

Carter folded his hands together. "You have a code of library ethics, Miss Zukas, that you find compelling enough to withhold evidence from the police. I, in turn, subscribe to a code that compels me to maintain silence regarding police matters."

"I understand and respect that," Helma said, "but I was also here in the hospital this morning. I may have noticed someone or something that could assist in your investigation."

The elevator dinged and the doors opened. "Thank God," Ruth said, standing back so Helma could step out of the elevator first. "It's getting pretty thick in here."

The second floor was busy. A young orderly pushed a bed around the corner, a man in a bathrobe walked slowly along, pushing his IV bags on wheels in front of him. A group of teenagers, some of them holding balloons and stuffed animals, spilled from one of the rooms into the hallway. Normally, Helma would have only noticed how loud they were and moved elsewhere but today she studied them curiously. Their clothing was so similar to Syndi and Joseph's that it all qualified as variations of a theme.

One boy wore dreadlocks, another girl's eyes were more heavily made up than either Ruth's or Syndi's. The longer she watched them, the younger they seemed to grow, only recently removed from childhood, leaping into adulthood.

"Helm? You okay?"

"Helma," she corrected with a start, realizing she'd stopped outside the elevator and that Ruth and Carter were waiting for her. "I'm sorry. Carter, you were about to tell me what the unauthorized person looked like?"

"No, I wasn't." He pushed his glasses higher on his nose. "But since you *were* here this morning, you may have seen something unusual. We can discuss that."

"Yes, we can discuss that," Helma echoed absentmindedly, already heading for Room 224.

Wayne's fever had stabilized, and he opened his eyes and smiled at Helma. "Getting better," he said in a raspy voice as she leaned over him.

"You are," she agreed, holding a glass of water for him. He took two swallows and closed his eyes again. She smoothed the sheets at his shoulders and glanced around his room. An unauthorized person. She checked the window; the room was two stories up from the ground and the windows didn't open anyway. The only entrance was guarded by a policeman. What had this unauthorized person planned to do? And how did they expect to get away with it?

Helma gently squeezed Wayne's hand and left the room. Ten feet from the door Carter, a heavyset dark-haired nurse and the policeman stationed at Room 224 were talking in low tones. Ruth slouched in a chair on the opposite side of the hallway, her eyes closed, looking like she was asleep.

Carter beckoned for Helma to join them. "This is Tom, the officer on duty, and Catherine, the nurse who noticed the irregularity. This is Helma Zukas. Can you describe for her what you saw?"

Catherine was a fair match for Carter. She looked exhausted, red-eyed and drooping. She was obviously staying on beyond the end of her shift. Her name tag was pinned to her sweater but she wasn't wearing a uniform except for sensible white shoes.

"You were here," she told Helma, "in Room 224. I work on the other side of the floor so you probably didn't notice me. But I'd just returned to the nurses' station for a new box of gloves and I saw you leaving. You paused to say a few words to the guard and I started back to the other side of the floor." She closed her eyes, remembering. "I heard the door to the stairs open and I turned to look, not that it's odd for people to take the steps but it catches your attention, you know what I mean? Especially early in the morning. But I didn't see anybody. But then I heard a second door and a few seconds later you opened the stairwell door and left."

"I don't understand," Helma said. "What did you see?"

"I really didn't see anything. It's what I found," Catherine told her. "There were more doors opening and closing than there were people on the floor." She shrugged. "Some people say I'm overly suspicious but I decided to take a look in the rooms. One winter we found a homeless man sleeping in an empty room. Room 218 is empty and that's where I found the scrubs and mask on the floor. I walked over to pick them up and found—"

Carter Houston touched Catherine's arm. "That's all for now," he warned. "The rest is police information."

"That's not necessary, Carter," Helma told him in her best silver-dime voice. "What else did you find, Catherine?" she asked the weary woman.

Catherine looked from Helma to Carter to Tom, the policeman. For a moment she looked confused, uncertain. Then she shrugged and said, "I know how to keep information to myself. If you three want to share it, that's between you. I'm going home now before I fall asleep right here on my feet."

"Thank you, Catherine," Helma told her. "Maybe we'll meet again sometime when you're on duty."

Catherine left them, and when she was barely out of earshot, Carter warned Helma, "Don't even consider badgering her later for information."

"There's no reason you can't tell me what she found," Helma told him. "I may have played an important part in this incident."

Carter grinned indulgently. "How do you figure that?"

"You figure it out. Catherine heard doors opening and closing. Obviously one of them was the unauthorized person who was planning to steal into Wayne's room. I left Wayne's room and this suspicious person saw me and realized I could identify him or her and dodged into an empty hospital room and abandoned the evidence."

Carter's brow wrinkled as he considered her premise. He nodded as if it pained him. "That's a possibility. Did you see anyone else? Someone in green hospital scrubs?"

Helma shook her head. "I didn't. But you may as well tell me about the evidence the nurse found in Room 218."

"That's privileged information."

Helma felt herself growing unaccustomedly hot. A prickling sensation raced up her spine and down her arms. Her jaw clenched. "You're being unreasonable," she said, shocked at how high-pitched her voice had grown, how it suddenly reminded her of Beatrice's.

"Then let's get out of here," Ruth interrupted, rising from her chair and joining them. "It's obvious Carter here does not intend to be helpful, so there's no point in taking up any more of his time."

"I'm not finished," Helma told her. But Ruth stepped between Carter and Helma and, facing Helma, gave her a deliberate, slow wink. "Or maybe I am?" Helma asked, watching Ruth. And to Carter she said, "Yes, I *am* finished."

Carter looked suspiciously from Ruth to Helma. "What's—" he began.

"Carter, Carter," Ruth said. "After all this woman's done for you." She shook her head in exaggerated sadness. "You never learn, do you?"

Carter didn't answer and watched them leave, suspicion still wrinkling his face. They passed Room 218 on their way to the stairs, and as Helma paused beside the door, Carter meaningfully cleared his throat.

In the stairwell, Ruth stopped on the top step and said dramatically, pressing her hand over her heart, "I know what they found in Room 218."

"You do? What?"

Ruth shook her head and glanced up at a light fixture in the ceiling. 'Let's get out of here first. This place might be bugged." And as they continued down the steps, Ruth said, "You may find this hard to believe but I can make myself invisible. Blend right in with the furniture and people forget I even exist. It's miraculous, really; you wouldn't believe the things I hear."

"Ruth, I've never seen you be anything but highly visible."

"Well, I was highly *invisible* a few minutes ago. Carter forgot I was sitting right there and you know how my presence drives him mad with passion."

"Drives him mad, anyway," Helma said, and Ruth stopped with her hand on the first floor door.

She turned and regarded Helma. "This situation is getting to you, isn't it?"

"What do you mean?"

"I don't know. Never mind." Ruth opened the door partway and said, "I mean you're acting like normal people do when they're under stress. Don't frown like that. It's okay to be normal; just don't be boring."

"Ruth, what are you talking about?"

"The facts of life. Come on outside and I'll share Carter's little secret with you. I bet he was the little kid who'd never warn you when the teacher was coming."

At midday the hospital lobby was busy with people coming and going, some carrying flowers and others sheaves of forms. Voices chattered, but as usual, when Ruth walked through the room, people momentarily silenced, watching her pass. Ruth nodded to an elderly man and winked at a tall young man.

As they exited through the hospital doors, two police cars pulled into the Police Only spaces and four policemen stepped out and walked rapidly toward the doors. One of them was Sidney Lehman, with whom Ruth had once had what she called, "a brief but vital moment."

"Hey, Sidney," Ruth said when they had almost drawn even. "Carter's waiting for you outside the chief's room. He just questioned Helma about what she might have seen this morning when the assassin tried to finish the job on Wayne. Any other news?"

Sidney stopped and grinned at Ruth. "Don't try and worm any information out of me, Ruth. The last time you did this, I nearly lost my job."

"I'd never want that to happen." She blew him a kiss. "Call me later."

Sidney saluted her and continued toward the hospital, hurrying to catch up with his fellow officers.

"Damn," Ruth said softly. "I guess I've tried that one too often."

"Tell me what the nurse found in Room 218," Helma said.

"Guess," Ruth said. She stopped and sat on a concrete bench facing a bed of mums. Cigarette butts littered the ground nearby.

"Oh Ruth, you know I don't play guessing games," Helma told her. "What was it?"

"A syringe. A full syringe. Can you at least guess what it was filled with?"

"Insulin?" Helma asked, sitting down beside Ruth. "Was it insulin?"

Ruth nodded grimly. "That's what Carter told somebody on his cell phone. There was a vial of it. Carter said what kind it was." She frowned. "Oh damn. I tried to invent one of those mnemonic tricks of yours but I forgot."

"Did you imagine a picture of the word?" Helma prompted.

Ruth nodded. "Yeah, one so ridiculous I wouldn't forget it." She squeezed her eyes closed and rocked back and forth.

"Was it a person? An animal? Or maybe nature?"

"I don't know."

"Ruth," Helma said sternly, "you have to remember. You must. Now think."

"Give me a clue."

"I can't. I wasn't there."

"So how many kinds of insulin are there?"

Helma had barely researched the subject of insulin. She'd meant to, but with Wayne's children, her world had suddenly grown too full. "I know there's a type called Regular and one called Lente and I think one that's an abbreviation: NP something."

Ruth shook her head. "No, none of those." She opened her eyes, idly looking around the hospital grounds. A grizzled man was pruning photinia shrubbery along the sidewalk. "That's it," Ruth said straightening. "It was a tree, a human tree."

"Human tree?" Helma repeated, then saying, "humatree, manbush, shrubman?"

"Almost, almost. No, it was log. Humanlog. That's it. Humanlog. See, I pictured this naked man carved out of a log floating down the river. Pretty good, eh?"

"Very," Helma agreed. "I'm surprised you forgot it."

She jotted the word "humanlog" in her notebook. She'd look it up at the library. She started to rise and then dropped down again as if the muscles in her legs had collapsed.

"What's wrong?" Ruth asked.

"I realized what might have happened if the timing had been different. Wayne . . ." She couldn't say any more.

"Yeah, but it didn't. And you know Carter—he'll have bars around Wayne's room by this afternoon. I heard the nurse say they'd changed all his IV bags and they were monitoring him. He'll be fine."

"But the children."

"Oh yeah, where are they?" Ruth looked around as if Syndi and Joseph might be hiding on the hospital grounds.

"At the police station with Corky Danforth. She wanted to ask them about the contaminated soda."

Ruth yiped. "Contaminated soda? What soda? What's going on?"

Helma told her about the bottle of raspberry soda intended for delivery to Wayne by Syndi. "What if Syndi had drunk it?"

Ruth brushed her hands through her hair. "Okay. Okay, they're fine for right now. Corky's good. But this means the whole mess has to be wrapped up fast. What should we do?"

"First, let's go to the library."

Ruth rolled her eyes. "Of course. The library. Now why didn't I think of that?"

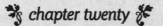

❧ chapter twenty ❧

TALK OF
MANY THINGS

Helma wanted to be at her apartment when Corky returned Joseph and Syndi. "We can't leave the children alone again," she told Ruth.

"Or worse yet," Ruth replied, "alone with your mother and Aunt Em. They couldn't protect those kids if somebody was determined to hurt them—not saying anybody is, of course," she amended. "Are you sure you want to go back to the library right now? The Moonbeam's probably not entertaining generous thoughts about you."

"Right now that doesn't make any difference, at least not to me."

"As long as you're home when the kids get back. Call me if you want me to meet them."

"Thanks, Ruth," Helma told her. "Did you tell Syndi and Joseph they'd be spending every night with me?"

Ruth frowned. "I didn't tell them where they'd be staying at all." She threw back her head and laughed. "Be flattered. Staying with you was *their* decision."

Ruth got back into her car. "Maybe Ms. Moon will have calmed herself with some relaxation mumbo jumbo and won't even notice you. I'll see you in a couple of hours."

It was a brief but troubled walk to the library. Helma

struggled to maintain her breathing, to keep the threats to Wayne Gallant and maybe even his children at bay, but her fears for them tumbled and buzzed inside her head. Finally, she tried to place the events of the last few days in order, imagining them as if they were listed in outline form, with Roman numerals and subheadings. At Roman numeral I, she mentally placed the arrival of Wayne Gallant's children at her apartment, but then replaced it with TNT's pounding on her door to request that she comfort the newly widowed Mary Lynn; then the children's arrival; followed by Wayne's fall, the contaminated raspberry soda, the slashed tires and broken glass, and the newly discovered insulin vial and scrubs in Room 218. Those were the major events. Beneath those she arranged the secondary events: diabetic Dickens Dixon, the prowler, Beatrice's injecting the cat, the word "tonights."

By the time she reached the door of the library's work room, the anatomy of the crime filled an imaginary sheet of paper. Her hair and clothes were damp but her thoughts were more settled. Order had been precariously restored and she had a plan of action. She went directly to her cubicle, nodding to George and Eve who were talking beside Eve's desk, ignoring the way Harley ducked his head when he saw her, not even glancing toward Ms. Moon's office.

Her computer was still humming, the Melvil Dewey screen saver streaming across the screen, and her telephone still off the hook. She returned the receiver to its cradle and immediately logged on to the Internet. The term "humanlog" brought up nothing except a suggestion that she rethink her search strategy. She reached for the telephone to call Ruth but instead heeded the computer's advice and did a search on insulin categories.

Helma was an efficient and experienced Internet searcher. Rarely did her final results end in extraneous hits, and this time was no exception. She clicked on a reputable website that described all the insulin types, and there it was: "Humalog," not humanlog, but close enough. It was a new insulin, the fastest acting available to diabetics, a type that began to lower glucose levels within five minutes. Five minutes! The next fastest insulin, Regular, didn't begin working for thirty to forty-five minutes. If a huge dose of Humalog were given to a nondiabetic, it would cause hypoglycemia that would be too severe for the body to absorb. Convulsions, coma, and possibly death if not immediately treated. And the effects on a man like Lewis, in good health but with heart arrhythmia, would assuredly be fatal.

But even Humalog took as long as five minutes to become effective. Five minutes should have given Lewis time to react: to struggle or at least call for help.

Helma clicked back and forth between the two most comprehensive websites, gathering more information on the several types of insulin and their effects. Then she sat in front of her computer, thinking about the cruelty of a person who could administer such a form of death, not just once but to attempt it again. Why? Because the chief knew who murdered Lewis Dixon. Self-preservation was probably a more compelling motive for murder than greed or revenge.

And if the murderer had been in the crowd during Beatrice's histrionics, Helma knew that he or she had heard her claim she knew who had borrowed *Behind the Looking Glass* from the library. That was the link: the book. She would never use the information she possessed, but she must find another connection, another proof. And she had to do it immediately, for Wayne and the children's sakes and for her own. Ruth was right: she'd painted a bull's-eye on her back.

Helma dialed the veterinarian's office, and not surprisingly, Barbara Susebenn herself answered. "Cat and Tonics."

"Hi, Barbara. This is Helma Zukas. I was wondering if you could give me information on cats and diabetes?"

"Symptoms, you mean? Is Boy Cat having a problem?"

"No," Helma quickly assured her, "at least not that kind."

"Ah," Barbara laughed. "Still beating up the neighborhood cats?"

"He can be contentious," Helma allowed, "but no, this is a reference question. What kind of insulin would you prescribe for a cat?"

"Depends. Usually Lente because the cat will only need injections twice a day. Sometimes NPH. Whichever the cat responds to best. A diabetic animal is a challenge; it can't tell you how it's feeling and it usually won't put up with its owner drawing blood to test its glucose level several times a day. The insulin injections are bad enough."

"Would you ever prescribe Humalog?" Helma asked. She looked up and saw Ms. Moon standing in her office doorway talking to Deidre. The look on the director's face was not pleasant.

"Humalog?" the vet repeated. "That's the new fast-acting insulin. No way. It's too hard to administer effectively. The poor cat would ride a roller coaster between hyper and hypoglycemia and that's too dangerous to the animal's life. Plus you'd have to give the cat injections several times a day. No, I've never heard of anyone using Humalog on a cat."

"Thank you very much." Helma hung up and glanced at Ms. Moon again. Ms. Moon was staring back. Glaring, actually. Helma looked away, grabbed her telephone book and looked up another number to dial.

It rang five times and then was answered by Beatrice, who sounded out of breath.

"This is Helma Zukas," she said. "Don't hang up."

"Why not?" Beatrice's voice challenged.

"Because we need to talk," Helma told her. "I'd like to come visit you. I could be there in ten minutes."

"You stay away from me," Beatrice shouted into the phone. "I don't want to talk to you."

Helma pulled the receiver away from her ear. "We have to talk. It's a matter of life and death."

"No," Beatrice said, and cut off the connection.

Helma replaced the receiver and stared at the telephone. She *had* to speak with Beatrice. If she showed up in Beatrice's driveway, could she convince the woman to talk to her?

"Helma?"

It was Deidre. The braid end was in her hand. She took a deep breath. "Ms. Moon said you were to remain the chairman of the pamphlet holder committee."

"It really doesn't matter to me," Helma said, surprised to realize that was actually true. "You or Harley or anyone else can be chairman. I'm far too busy at the moment."

Deidre nodded as if this were bittersweet news. "You have a life," she said.

"But, Deidre, so do you." Helma turned off her computer and reached for her purse.

"Harley's the first man I've—"

Helma closed her desk drawer with a clunk. "A man is not necessary to have a life," she told Deidre as she stood and placed her purse over her shoulder. "Don't believe that. Men come and go. So do children. *You* make your own life valuable, nobody else."

Helma's phone rang and she picked up the receiver. A few seconds later and she'd have been gone.

"All right. You can come tomorrow. Around eleven." It was Beatrice.

"Today would be better."

"No. Tomorrow or forget it. And I mean it."

"All right," Helma reluctantly agreed. "Tomorrow at eleven."

"And don't bring the police."

"I won't even inform them, I promise."

"Good."

Ms. Moon appeared at the entrance to Helma's cubicle. "Leaving us so soon, Helma?" she asked, nodding toward Helma's purse.

"I am," Helma told her, "and I'll be late tomorrow as well."

She stepped past Ms. Moon and headed toward the door to the staff parking lot. Behind her, Ms. Moon said, "Well." Then again, "Well."

George stood as she passed the cataloging corner and winked at her. "Look what happens to priorities when the person you love is in peril," he said.

"I beg your pardon?" Helma paused to ask.

He grinned and actually reached out and squeezed her arm. "Go for it, Helm."

"Helma," she corrected and left the building.

It was almost twelve-thirty when Helma returned to the Bayside Arms. She expected Corky to return Joseph and Syndi within the half hour. And then her mother and Aunt Em would pick them up for their swim date at two o'clock. Helma couldn't let them go alone, not this time. She wondered if her swimsuit was still in the bottom drawer of her bureau. It was a suit she'd bought in college, but she was still the same size so it should fit.

The misty rain had momentarily stopped but there was no sign of a break in the featureless silvery clouds. TNT's apartment door stood open, and Helma remembered, as she often did at the sight of an open door, how in Michigan during the warmer months, no door or window was left unscreened, how they'd closed the doors as quickly as they could behind them, how there'd been a progression of insects all spring and summer long: mosquitoes, gnats, deerflies, flies, bees. Fall and winter had been a relief because the insects were gone until the following spring. But in Bellehaven a mosquito was a rarity, biting insects and flies few. Only the wasps were a nuisance in late summer whenever the sun shone and food was eaten outside.

TNT stepped outside and launched into an apology before he even said hello. "I'm damn sorry I didn't have a chance to head off Beatrice before she got to the library, or even to call and warn you," he said. He used both hands to pull down his sweatshirt, which was riding up over his stomach. Helma could hear low voices from inside his apartment.

"I understand," Helma said. "but it turned out all right. We spoke on the telephone later."

TNT pulled back his head in surprise. "You did? She called you?"

"Actually, I phoned her.' "

He looked doubtful. "So everything's copacetic between you two?"

"I doubt we'll become close friends," Helma told him. Behind TNT, Helma saw Mary Lynn rise and approach the door.

"I never knew Beatrice to have a friend she could keep, anyway," TNT said. "She's been a fireball all her life, isn't that right, honey?" he asked Mary Lynn, who leaned against his shoulder, her dark hair falling forward.

"I try not to pay that much attention to her." Mary Lynn appeared more composed, even serene. "Would you like to come in for a glass of iced tea?" she asked Helma. "He has real glasses now."

TNT aimed a playful punch at Mary Lynn. "Don't be cruel," he told her.

Although she had little time, Helma accepted the invitation. Frankly, she was curious to see who else was in the apartment, who Mary Lynn had been speaking to. "You didn't go on your bicycle trip to the Nitcum?" she asked TNT as she entered his apartment. He no longer wore the tight bicycling clothes he'd worn to the library but was back in gray sweatpants. Helma imagined his bureau drawers filled with gray sweatpants and sweatshirts.

The flattened boxes were gone but other boxes were stacked against the living room wall. Two comfortable-looking chairs sat near the recliner, and the exercise equipment had been pushed farther back into the corner.

Skip sat on the stool at the counter, still dressed for bicycling, but Helma was beginning to suspect that like TNT's sweats, bicycling spandex was the major component of Skip's wardrobe. He smiled at Helma. "Hi again."

"Nah," TNT told Helma. "No bike trip today. We rescheduled it for Friday. Dean didn't think he'd get to work on time. No problem for us since we aren't working." He raised his hand to include Skip.

"Don't bad-mouth me, TNT," Skip told him. "I'm leaving in a few minutes to help Joe Miner scrape paint off the bottom of his boat. That's gainful employment."

"I stand corrected," TNT told him. Another playful punch, this one aimed at Skip's shoulder. "Have a seat," he told Helma, waving toward one of the new chairs.

Mary Lynn poured Helma a glass of iced tea and gave it to her and then sat in the other new chair. "The funeral's Thursday," she told Helma.

Helma nodded even though Mary Lynn had already told her. "It'll be a comfort to have friends and relatives with you," she said.

"Let's not get gloomy," TNT quickly said. "Tell Helma about that writer you and Skip were just talking about, the one who people thought was a man."

"George Eliot?" Mary Lynn asked. "I'm sure Helma is familiar with her."

"Is that right?" TNT sounded genuinely surprised.

"What drew you to Eliot?" Helma asked Mary Lynn.

"Her recognition of heroism in ordinary people," Mary Lynn answered without hesitation. "At least in her fiction."

"Not to mention the glories of redemption," Skip said, "even if it kills you."

"Especially if," Mary Lynn added.

"And Swinburne?" Helma asked Skip.

"His sea poems are what attracted me first," Skip told her. "I've always been drawn to the sea."

"Not his lifestyle?" Mary Lynn asked. A spark of mischief lit her eyes.

Skip blushed. "I don't even *like* monkeys," he told her.

TNT glanced between Mary Lynn and Skip, bewildered. "Keep it clean, kids. Seen any good movies lately?"

But Helma wasn't finished. "Lewis Carroll was a contemporary of theirs," she said.

"Different circles," Mary Lynn commented. She frowned. "He worked too hard at what he wrote."

" 'Mark this day with a white stone,' " Skip quoted. "That's what he wrote in his diary when he had a good day."

"Then you both studied Carroll?" she asked.

"A little," Skip said.

Mary Lynn nodded, twisting her wedding band. "All my days lately have been onyx," she said. "Black stones."

Skip left before Helma. "I'll bring that Housman poem over tomorrow," he told Mary Lynn as the door closed behind him.

"Thanks." Mary Lynn turned to Helma, her eyes suddenly dampening. "Skip thinks he has a poem that could be read at Lewis's service. But A. E. Housman? I don't know."

"Do you two discuss literature often?"

"We try to. We hoped the kids at the Y would be more enthusiastic, but . . ." She made sweeping motions with her hand above her head. ". . . flies right past."

"Skip told me about your other friends during your academic years," Helma said.

"Oh yes, we were going to burn up the world with our brilliant literary theories. Read and write and illuminate literature's deepest secrets. Can't you see it? And now look at us. Jan's in London, waiting tables, I hear. Dean's at least employed and paying his own way." She shook her head. "It isn't the way I thought it would be."

"It rarely is," Helma, who'd faced down that youthful idealism long ago, agreed.

"Sure it is," TNT interjected. "If you don't get what you want, you just change what you want."

"I believe there's a song that goes something like that," Helma said as she stood in the open doorway to leave. "Thanks for the iced tea. Oh," she said, turning to Mary Lynn. "Why didn't Dean and your husband get along?"

"I told you—literary differences. Lewis didn't consider Wilkie Collins's work an example of great literature." She looked down at the floor.

"And?" Helma prompted.

Mary Lynn sighed. "There were 102 applicants for twenty-three slots in grad school that year."

"And Lewis didn't recommend Dean," Helma guessed.

Mary Lynn nodded. "Is that your phone?" she asked, tipping her head at the faint sound of ringing.

It was. "Excuse me," Helma said, and hurried to her apartment door, her keys at the ready. The phone was on the fifth ring when she picked it up.

"Hi, Helma," the cheery voice said. "This is Corky. We have a plan and I wanted to run it past you. How about if I join Joseph and Syndi on their swimming outing with your mother and aunt?"

"For pleasure or protection?" Helma asked.

"A little of both. They're good kids and I haven't been swimming in ages. You'd think with all the water around here, we'd all be half amphibian."

"Perhaps we're wet enough without purposely having to dip into the water."

Corky laughed. "Then it's okay?"

"Of course." Helma thought a second. "But can you conceal a weapon in your swimsuit?"

"Don't worry. I'm never without protection."

Helma hung up, feeling guilty relief that she didn't have to participate in an outing with Joseph, Syndi, her mother, and Aunt Em. She and her mother alone could be an uncomfortable combination, and Aunt Em was always an unknown quanity. Add to that two children her mother wished were more closely related and who themselves seemed weary of Helma, and the results could be, as Ruth liked to say, "deadly."

Boy Cat Zukas sat on Helma's balcony, gazing into her apartment. His fur shone with a silvery mist of delicate raindrops. But when Helma opened the sliding glass doors, the cat refused to come inside and instead stood and paced her balcony, raising his feet as if the balcony floor were hot. Helma doubted the emotional acuity that many people attributed to their animals but Boy Cat Zukas certainly did seem agitated. She glanced to either side of her balcony and spotted nothing unusual, nothing out of place, no small dead animals. TNT's balcony was vacant. Boy Cat Zukas then leaped to the balcony railing and gazed down at the ground toward the corner of the apartment building. His throat rumbled the way it did sometimes when he spotted an out-of-reach bird. He hissed once, his eyes round and golden, and then abruptly returned to normal, balancing precariously on the railing and concentrating on licking his paws.

Helma peered down at the ground where a well-pruned photinia hedge grew close to the building. The leaves closest to the corner shivered as if the hedge had recently been disturbed. Helma left her balcony and raced through her apartment, throwing open the door onto the landing and gazing toward the corner, scanning the ground, the shrubbery. In the misty grass a path was visible where someone had recently walked from the corner of the building to the paved parking lot near the Dumpsters. And then the trail was lost. Nothing looked suspicious in the parking lot. Mrs. Webber was just getting out of her car, her silver hair protected by a clear plastic bonnet. A UPS truck was pulling into the Bayside Arms driveway. No other person or car moved. Helma stood on the landing for five minutes, watching, feeling the cool, moist air on her face and waiting. But there was nothing.

Helma phoned the hospital and made sure Wayne was still resting comfortably and that the police officer was at his station in front of Wayne's room. "Would you like to speak to him?" the nurse asked.

"Wayne?" Helma asked, surprised.

"No," the nurse said in a gentle voice. "I'm sorry. I meant the policeman."

Helma declined and had barely hung up the phone when Ruth called. "Are Joseph and Syndi back yet?" she asked.

"They're with Cocky," Helma told her. Boy Cat Zukas still sat on her balcony railing like an Egyptian figure, and while Helma knew it was foolish, seeing him there made her apartment feel more secure.

"I gotta tell you what happened." She paused.

"And?" Helma politely asked.

Ruth took a deep breath. "I know this is going to seem pretty trivial in light of teenagers and murder, but remember Paul?"

Paul from Minnesota had been a mismatched love of Ruth's. He was the only man Helma had ever seen Ruth cry over, a man completely unlike other men she was drawn to: Paul was quiet, soft-spoken, nonartistic. And a man Ruth hadn't spoken to in over a year. The mere mention of Paul's name sent Ruth into a melancholy fugue.

"Of course I do," Helma said. "What's happened?"

"Well . . ." Again the deep breath. "He's sending me a plane ticket to come to Minneapolis."

"Are you going?" Even as she asked, Helma knew it was a silly question. "You've missed him."

"Yeah. It was like my will had been taken over by aliens," Ruth said, a bewildered note in her voice. "Words like 'Yes,' and 'When's the flight?' just fell out of my mouth. I had no control, none."

"So when *is* the flight?" Helma asked.

"Friday morning. Early. I'll stay in Seattle Thursday night with Pika and Tom. I'm going out right now to buy new underwear; maybe a jacket. It might snow in Minneapolis this time of year, you just can't be sure. You know what else this means, don't you?" Ruth asked.

"New shoes?" Helma countered.

"Very funny. No. It means we have to wrap up this murder thing by Thursday morning, noon at the latest. When that plane leaves, I'm on it."

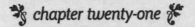

chapter twenty-one

A DISH AND
CARVING KNIFE

While she waited for Corky to return
with Joseph and Syndi, Helma pulled *Behind the Looking
Glass* from her blue bag and opened it at her dining room
table. Once more she attempted to find a connection between the text and Wayne Gallant. But instead she found
herself caught up in Alice's nonsensical world of
changelings, talking eggs and verbal conundrums, admir-
ing Alice's remarkable restraint. Lewis Carroll's mind
certainly was curious.

Corky didn't bring back Joseph and Syndi, it was
Helma's mother and Aunt Em. "That other woman
wanted to," Helma's mother said as Joseph and Syndi
headed for their spaces on the sofa with hardly more than
a nod to Helma. "but we told her it was our responsibility." The two older women were dressed more conserva-
tively, in elastic-waisted pants and pastel shirts. They
brought inside with them the slight chlorine odor of the
swimming pool. Aunt Em held a square covered dish.

"But, actually," Aunt Em said in a conspirator's voice,
"it was so we could warn you."

"Warn me?" Helma asked in dread. "About what? Did
anything happen while you were swimming?"

The television was turned on to an afternoon movie channel, and as soon as the sound of background music filled the apartment, Helma's mother moved closer to the refrigerator, beckoning Helma and Aunt Em to follow. Neither Joseph nor Syndi paid any attention.

"About *her*," Lillian whispered.

"Syndi?" Helma whispered back, glancing over at Syndi whose thumbnail was between her front teeth again, her eyes on the television.

"No," Lillian said. "The other woman, that Corky. Do you know she's a *policewoman*?"

"Yes, I do," Helma said.

"You do?" Aunt Em asked, disappointment sagging her face. She set the covered dish on the table. "And you let those children go out with her anyway?"

"Can you just please tell me what this is about?" Helma asked. "Why shouldn't they have been with her?"

"Because she works with the chief of police, silly," Aunt Em said. She fingered her amber necklace. "You don't want his children getting all cozy with another woman, especially one he can talk to about his career. She may not be as pretty as you are, dear, but she *is* younger. And that still counts in this world."

"That's right," Lillian said, nodding sagely, with Aunt Em joining her. "Men can be so blind. They're susceptible to firm flesh."

Helma sighed and looked up at the ceiling for a moment. "Did she tell you why she was with Joseph and Syndi?" she asked.

"Only that she was a friend of his and you were at work," Lillian told her. "You have to be more attentive. Your own career just isn't worth it if you lose him."

"My career is very satisfying," Helma reassured the two older women, "and I'm not concerned about losing Wayne Gallant to another woman."

Aunt Em leaned over and gripped Helma's wrist. "Never, ever let down your guard," she whispered. "It doesn't pay to be too sure of yourself; that's when people fall. You should do . . . you know . . ." She mimed opening her blouse, and then with her hands performed the function of a push-up bra. ". . . dress a little sexier. Make him *see* you."

"We need to go shopping," Lillian suggested. "Just the three of us."

"Good idea," Aunt Em agreed.

Helma gave up. "In a few weeks," she told them. "After Wayne recovers." She pointed to the covered dish Aunt Em had set on the dining room table. "What did you bring?"

"*Kugelis*. I baked it," she told Helma, not looking at Helma's mother.

There were countless variations of the salty Lithuanian potato dish that often fostered a blatant competition between cooks. Helma wouldn't dare say she preferred Aunt Em's *kugelis* to her mother's, but she did.

"Thank you," she told Aunt Em, imagining a slice fried and topped with bacon, onions, and sour cream.

"A snack for the children," Aunt Em told her. "They loved it."

Helma had already planned a dinner of broiled salmon and broccoli, so she fried the *kugelis* for Syndi, Joseph, and herself, and they ate it as an appetizer, the whole pan. "This is better than french fries," Joseph said, spreading the sour cream.

While she ate her dinner and Joseph gobbled and Syndi picked, Helma asked, "You didn't tell my mother or Aunt Em why you were with Corky?"

Syndi shook her head and tucked a piece of salmon beneath a stalk of broccoli. "It might have scared them."

"Yeah," Joseph added as he reached for a third roll. "They could have had heart attacks."

Helma considered them while she took a sip of iced

tea. "That was very thoughtful of you. Were you able to help Corky with the case?"

Joseph shrugged. "I don't know. She didn't tell us anything, just asked questions."

"Did you see Dad?" Syndi asked without looking at Helma.

"I did," Helma told her. "His fever's down and he seemed stronger. We'll visit him in the morning."

She nodded, still not looking Helma's way.

Both teenagers helped clean up after dinner but neither wanted to play Scrabble or any other game. Syndi curled up on the sofa with Boy Cat Zukas stretched across her lap, and Joseph sprawled beside her, every once in a while making fun of his sister or commenting to the television. Helma sat in her rocker and finished skimming *Behind the Looking Glass*.

The phone rang: the first of Ruth's calls that night. "Do you think I'm crazy?" she demanded without saying hello.

Helma twirled the cord around her index finger and sat down in the chair next to the telephone. "Not if it's what you want to do," she told Ruth.

"Yeah," Ruth said. "You're right," and hung up.

When Helma returned to her rocker, Joseph pointed to *Behind the Looking Glass* sitting on the seat and recited " 'Twas brillig, and the slithy toves . . .'"

" 'Did gyre and gimble in the wabe,' " Syndi continued without taking her eyes from the television screen. And they continued, alternating verses, without faltering, for all six stanzas, right down to, " 'And the mome raths outgrabe.' "

Helma couldn't help herself; she applauded, and in fact even spontaneously bowed first toward Joseph and then Syndi. "That was very impressive," she told them. "Very."

"Dad taught us," Joseph said. "He used to read *Through the Looking Glass* to us all the time. We know

"The Walrus and the Carpenter, too." He looked at Syndi and she shook her head but recited the last three lines. " 'But an answer came there none, And this was scarcely odd, because, They'd eaten every one.' "

"Dad can say nearly all the poems because his dad or somebody taught him," Syndi told her.

"I didn't know that," Helma said.

"I know him better than you do," Syndi said, raising her chin.

"Of course you do," Helma told her. "You've known him your whole life; I've only known him a couple of years."

Helma couldn't have said the three of them were actually *holding* a conversation. It was a different type of discourse than she had ever experienced; there was no plan or shape or topic, or even flow.

"That little white spot under Boy Cat Zukas's chin looks like a star," Syndi said once, and Joseph looked over and said, "Kinda."

"Do you have shoes like that?" Syndi asked Helma, pointing to a pair of high-heeled sling backs on a television starlet.

"No, I don't believe I do," Helma told her. "Do you like them?"

"Not really. Mom has some."

"More chips?" Helma asked during a commercial, and both children shook their heads.

"I want a car like that," Joseph said, holding up a magazine that he was reading the same time he watched television. "That is so cool." Helma knew that neither she nor Syndi were expected to respond.

Helma browsed her book when they weren't speaking, idly looking at Sir John Tenniel's illustrations. The White Knight bore a marked resemblance to Tenniel. Joseph looked over her shoulder on his way to the refrigerator for another bottle of root beer. "That's the White Knight," he said. "When I was *really* little, Dad used to scare me when he acted out the battle of the Two Knights."

"Someday you'll probably recite this to your own children," Helma said, and Joseph walked away, disinterested, the possibility too remote to comprehend.

Their conversation was relaxed and fragmented, the television playing in the background. Cool; was this what being "cool" was all about? Helma wondered.

Once, when Helma went to the kitchen to refill the nut bowl, she opened the curtain that overlooked the parking lot and after a few seconds saw the dome light go on in a plain dark car parked near the covered parking area. Carter Houston, she guessed, and wondered if he'd turned on his dome light to signal her that he was watching.

Syndi removed a slip of paper from her pocket and showed it to Helma. "Your aunt Em gave this to me. Do you think I could make it some time?"

Helma took the paper and gazed at it. At the top it read, "Lydia's Kugelis." Lydia was Aunt Em's mother, Helma's grandmother. Even Helma didn't have this recipe. She read it over, committing it to memory:

Lydia's Kugelis

5 lbs peeled white potatoes
1 large can condensed milk
*1 lb bacon chopped, with grease, fried with ½ large
    chopped onion*
1 Tablespoon salt
4 eggs

Grate potatoes, mix everything together. Bake in a greased pan for 10 minutes at 400° and 2 hours at 350° until golden brown.

"You can make it tomorrow, if you want," Helma told her. "This is a very old recipe, slightly modernized," she added, noting the condensed milk instead of cream.

"Cool," Syndi said.

Finally, after Ruth's third call—"Can I borrow your blue suitcase?" Helma yawned and stood, holding *Behind the Looking Glass* in her hands. "I'm going to bed," she told Syndi and Joseph. "Turn off the lights when you're ready and don't be alarmed if the phone rings in the night; it'll only be Ruth."

"What if it isn't?" Syndi challenged.

"If it involves you or anyone you love, I'll wake you up," Helma answered, and Syndi nodded.

Helma was brushing the left lower quadrant of her teeth, gazing at herself in the mirror and thinking of her meeting with Beatrice the next day when it hit her. She removed the toothbrush and wiped her mouth, then said aloud to her reflection, "The Two Knights."

Throwing on her bathrobe, she hurried back to the living room. "What did you say about your father acting out the scene of the knights?" she asked Joseph.

"Yeah, you know. The White Knight and the Red Knight. They have this stupid battle and keep falling off their horses over and over."

"The Red Knight is vanquished," Syndi said.

"Thank you. Good night," she told them, and left the room, thinking.

The Two Knights. Two nights. Tonights. That was what Wayne Gallant had said, not two nights, or tonights, but Two Knights. Helma had skimmed that part of Lewis Carroll's tale after reading in the annotations that it represented a foreshadowing of communism.

In her bedroom, Helma immediately sat on her bed and opened *Behind the Looking Glass*, flipping the pages until she found chapter eight, "It's My Own Invention." She couldn't be bothered with the annotations, only the original text. The Red Knight and the White Knight were on opposing sides yet they were evenly matched. Two foolish fantasy men enraptured by the Rules of Battle and yet unable to remain on their horses. They tumbled to the ground whether they were knocked off by one another or not. Significantly, the White Knight was triumphant.

The tale continued beyond the White Knight vanquishing the Red Knight, but Helma believed the importance of the story lay in the brief passages that contained both knights. She read them again and again. At first the Red Knight tries to take Alice prisoner, but the White Knight saves her. Was that important? Who was Alice? Mary Lynn? And what did the knights mean when they kept referring to the Rules of Battle? According to the annotations, it was an early reference, a prophecy perhaps of democracy vanquishing communism. In 1872?

After a while Helma began to feel she was extrapolating as much from the text as the author of *Behind the Looking Glass*. She turned off her lamp and pulled the blankets up to her neck, wondering if tomorrow Wayne might be well enough to tell her the significance of the Two Knights.

And as she dozed off, she realized that knights or no knights, she really only cared that Wayne recover.

At ten-thirty the phone rang again and Helma answered on the first ring.

"Do I look better in my blue dress or my yellow dress?" Ruth asked.

Helma imagined Ruth with dresses spread across her bed. She couldn't really recall what either dress looked like but she preferred blue herself so she said, "Blue, I think."

"Okay, I'll take the yellow one, then. Thanks," and she hung up.

But the peace lasted only a couple of minutes before the phone rang again. "What if he's been sleeping with somebody else?"

"That's a possibility," Helma agreed, smothering a yawn.

"Yeah, well it's my health we're talking about here."

Helma was too tired to suggest anything other than, "Why not just ask him?"

"Great idea," she said, and hung up again.

A movement at the bedroom door startled Helma as she returned the phone to the cradle. It was Syndi, and in the light from the hall, Helma could see she was wearing shortie pajamas. "Was that about my dad?" she asked, and put her thumbnail between her teeth.

Helma sat up. "No, it was Ruth. She's going to visit an old boyfriend and she's scared to death."

"Why?" Syndi asked.

"Because she really cares about him," Helma explained.

"Oh." Syndi nodded as if she understood completely. "Okay. Good night."

"Good night, sweetheart," Helma said, the word "sweetheart" curiously slipping out without a pause.

When Helma awoke for real, it was to singing, the high, pure voice of a choirboy. She sat up, listening. It was light in her room, and after a few moments she identified the voice as Syndi's, flying high over the sound of the shower. She sang a rock song that sounded familiar but her voice was lovely, un-self-conscious and lyrical. Helma lay back, smiling. As Ruth liked to say, "Who'da thunk it?"

The rain had stopped but the sky was overcast, and when Helma looked through her balcony doors at the bay, it was to view a silvery stillness. The bay lay as quiet as a lake, reflecting the silver sky. It might not rain this day but the sun probably wouldn't shine, either.

Joseph had tucked into a bowl of cereal and Helma was on her second cup of tea and still Syndi hadn't joined them. She'd been in the bedroom so long since Helma had heard her singing in the shower that Helma asked Joseph, "Do you think I should check on your sister?"

He shrugged. "Nah," he said between spoonfuls of cereal. "She takes forever sometimes."

Just at that moment Syndi emerged. "Good morning," Helma began. "Would you like a bowl of—" She stopped, staring at Syndi. "You're wearing—" she began again.

"These clothes were in the closet," Syndi said hurriedly, blushing. "Is it okay if I wear them?"

"Of course you can," Helma said, still staring at the blue A-line skirt and overlong fisherman's knit sweater, favorite remainders from her high school days twenty years ago. Had she really worn her skirts that short? The sweater, hand knit by Aunt Em, covered all but three or four inches of the skirt.

"Cool," Syndi said, dropping into a chair. "Who left them here?"

"Someone a long time ago," Helma told her. "I know she doesn't want them anymore so you can have them. Raisin Bran or Shredded Wheat?"

The *Bellehaven Daily News* thumped onto the landing outside Helma's door. She checked her doormat, then the parking lot when she stepped outside to retrieve the paper, but there was no police car. She unbanded and opened the paper distractedly, her mind on the day ahead. There, at the bottom of the front page, a heading caught her attention: *Librarian Refuses to Surrender Name,* and beneath that, *Police Preparing to Raid Files.* Helma quickly scanned the article, breathing easier as she discovered there was no mention of her by name, only "an unnamed librarian." Ms. Moon was quoted by name, however, defending her position, "We always try to cooperate with the authorities. The issue is under advisement." Ruth's friend at the newspaper had sensationalized the story, definitely, but if it drew attention to the problem long enough to stop the police from subpoenaing the library computer's hard drive, Helma was satisfied.

Lewis's murder was no longer on the first page but now on the third. *No New Leads in Prof's Death*, the headline read.

Wayne Gallant reached out his hands to his children and smiled. Tubing dangled from both arms and they touched him gingerly. Helma was sure another one of his machines had been disconnected but she couldn't say which one, only that now there was less beeping and fewer plastic bags of solution. His bed was raised so he sat almost upright.

"Are you okay now?" Syndi asked. Her voice held no moodiness, only hope.

"Better," he said in a dry voice. "Seeing you makes me better. You look nice, pumpkin."

"Thanks."

"You still need to borrow my comb?" Wayne teased Joseph, and Joseph shook his head shyly, then asked, "Do you think I ought to comb it out?"

"Not if you like it," he said. "Can you hand me that glass of water?"

Joseph did, and after a sip, Wayne asked, "What have you been doing?"

"Not much," Joseph said.

"We went swimming," Syndi told him. "With Helma's mother and aunt."

"Was it fun?" Wayne asked. He briefly closed his eyes.

"It was okay," Joseph said.

Out of the blue Syndi asked, "Do you remember what happened to you yet?"

Wayne frowned and shook his head. "I should, but I can't."

"It's all right," Helma assured him. "You will later."

He nodded and smiled, but the smile was tired, an effort.

"We'd better let you rest," Helma said. "We'll be back tonight."

He didn't argue. " 'Bye, buddy," he said, giving his son a slight nudge.

"Okay," Joseph said.

" 'Bye, Daddy," Syndi told him, and he reached out to hug her.

"Have fun today," Wayne told his children. "Can you two wait in the hall for a minute?" A flash of the hard look crossed Syndi's face but the two left without argument.

"Are they staying with you?" he asked Helma.

"They are," she told him. "Syndi's in the spare room and Joseph's on the sofa. They're doing fine. My mother and Aunt Em have taken them out a few times. We're going to the museum today."

He nodded but his thoughts were elsewhere. "How did I fall?" he asked.

"We don't know but the police are working on it, especially Carter."

"Good man under all that," Wayne said. He spoke slowly, with great concentration. "Trust him."

"Do you know what 'Two Knights' means?" Helma asked.

"Tonight?"

"Two Knights, the red and the white, from *Through the Looking Glass*. You mentioned them when you were brought into the hospital."

"Alice," he said, and Helma nodded. He could scarcely keep his eyes open. "I don't know why I said it."

"Later," Helma said. "You'll remember later. Rest now." But he was already asleep. She kissed his forehead and left his room to join Joseph and Syndi, who stood in the hallway arguing.

"They've had croquet for *years*," Syndi was telling Joseph.

"How do you know? Have you ever played it?" Joseph challenged.

"You don't have to play it to know it's been around forever," she said.

"I saw it on the Internet," Joseph said.

"So what? George Washington's on the Internet and *he's* old."

"Sorry," Ruth said, meeting them at her door, all in a flurry, a huge leather bag over her shoulder. "I really meant it when I said they could hang out here for a couple of hours this morning but this is absolutely the only time before Friday that I can get waxed—and don't look at me like that, kid; it's a girl thing."

"But I'm planning to meet Beatrice in twenty minutes," Helma told her.

"How about my friend, Jenna?" Ruth offered. "She's probably off work after lunch."

"I don't think so." Helma suddenly saw the looks on Joseph and Syndi's faces, the look of children who guessed they were in the way. "Would you two mind coming to the country with me?" she asked, hoping they wouldn't notice her change of tactics. "I thought it might be too boring for you, but maybe you'd like it after all."

"Will there be animals?" Syndi asked.

"I know there are cats," she said hopefully.

"Okay."

"Hey," Ruth said, pointing to Syndi. "Didn't that sweater used to—"

"You're right," Helma interrupted her. "It was left at my apartment. It's Syndi's now."

"Sure thing. And it looks great on you, Syndi, better than on the original owner."

Helma drove slowly on her trip to the Dixons' to visit Beatrice, glancing in her rearview mirror every little while and giving Carter Houston plenty of opportunity to keep her Buick in plain sight.

chapter twenty-two

THE DRUMS BEGAN

After seven minutes Joseph said, "This isn't the country, like farms and ranches." His headphones hung around his neck but he hadn't put them over his ears all morning. He was looking out the window at the suburbs and side streets. Syndi sat in the backseat reading a magazine she'd pulled from her backpack, and Joseph sat up front with Helma. The two young people had argued over which of them had front seat privileges, finally asking Helma to intervene. "No, thank you," she'd told them. "It's not a problem that's of interest to me; negotiate it between yourselves." Whatever method they'd used, at least it hadn't been loud.

"Not yet," Helma told him. "We should be there in about five minutes, but this is the only route. It won't be farm country with fields and cows, more like undeveloped land close to the water. Although they did farm oysters many years ago."

Which brought conjecture from the two about how to round up oysters and whether oyster farmers were called oysterboys.

"You don't drive very fast," Joseph commented.

"Is there a reason I should?" Helma asked.

Joseph shrugged. "I bet this car can go ninety, easy."

"Possibly," Helma agreed, "if there were a reason to." As they passed into an open and high area of grassy fields, Helma stopped herself from speaking the phrase most common to Northwesterners when they had visitors: "If it were a clear day, you could see Mount Baker from here."

This time Helma took note of the Haydens' driveway just before the Dixons'. A gate mounted on a steel post was swung closed across it. It appeared to be padlocked.

Although there was nothing definable, when Helma turned into the long driveway the Dixons' home looked deserted, the owners gone for an extended time. She parked close to the garage that Beatrice lived above. Behind the building, rather than inside the garage portion, sat one of the less expensive small cars, a yellow two-door. A bumper sticker read, *If you can read this you're too close.* Helma guessed it was Beatrice's.

"I don't see any animals," Syndi said from the backseat. "They don't even have a barn."

"I didn't promise you a farm," Helma reminded her as she opened her door, "only a home in the country."

"And cats," Joseph added.

"Yes, I saw three of them last time I was here." Joseph started to get out and Helma said, "Wait a minute, let's be sure she's home first." She couldn't presume that Carter had followed them, that he was standing by in his unmarked car prepared to leap to their defense. Here she was, in a remote area with the chief of police's two children. What if Beatrice wasn't home and she had driven blithely into an ambush?

Helma Zukas was an alert and observant woman. She often sensed danger or intruders or disorder. So now she stood beside her car and slowly turned in a circle, absorbing the Dixons' homestead, vigilant for danger. A slight breeze tinkled a hidden wind chime; the grass was still wet from yesterday's rain; in the distance came the sound of a straining engine. She took a step away from the car toward the garden and spotted Beatrice's overbright hair. She sat on the bench near Whitman's bust, holding a heavy mug and watching her. Helma felt a prickle of annoyance race up her arms. "Hello," she called to Beatrice.

"Who's with you?" Beatrice asked in her raspy voice.

Helma wasn't accustomed to shouting a conversation, even outdoors, so she took several steps closer to the garden. "The children of a friend. May they play with your cats while we talk?"

Beatrice shrugged. "There isn't much else for them to do around here. There weren't any children, you know. It's a good thing, now. It isn't easy to raise a child alone; just ask me." She sipped from her mug. "Last time I saw them, the cats were on Mary Lynn's front porch; they'll probably be in the wicker basket next to the swing."

"I'll be right back," Helma told her and returned to the car where she told Joseph and Syndi where to find the cats.

Syndi got out of the car and looked over at Beatrice. "Is that lady okay?" she whispered. "Should we stay nearby?"

"She's fine, just lonely, but thank you. The littlest cat's name is Dickens."

"Like in Charles?" Syndi asked.

"That's right," Helma said, surprised Syndi had made the association.

"Come on," Joseph said, "let's look around."

Helma returned to the garden and sat down beside Beatrice. She wasn't holding a cigarette between her fingers, but a dried flower stem. Her eyes were tired and without makeup. She appeared more haggard, yet curiously, more attractive. "What do you want?" she asked Helma.

"Just to talk," Helma said. "I believe you're the person who holds the key to Lewis's murder and the attack on the chief of police."

"The only thing I know is that I didn't do it." Beatrice's eyes were hard, unrelenting.

"Who knew about the cat's diabetes?" Helma asked.

Beatrice snorted. "About Dickens? Everybody who knew Mary Lynn. She liked to talk about that little cat as if she saved its life, when *I'm* the one who has to poke the poor thing every day." She shook her head and ground the flower stem against the seat of the bench. "How do you think that cat feels when it sees me coming?" she asked, echoing Ruth.

"Frightened," Helma acknowledged. "What do *you* think happened to Lewis?"

Beatrice looked up at the trees between the garden and the house. "Somebody wanted something he had. Or maybe they didn't want Lewis talking about some old secret. They were hoping it would be declared a heart attack, weren't they?"

"It appears that way."

"Then they weren't planning to leave town. They intended to be here after he died."

"That's a very good deduction, Beatrice," Helma said. "You've been thinking about this."

Beatrice sighed. "Every minute," she said, in a way that caused Helma to glance sharply at her.

"Wayne Gallant mentioned he knew Lewis," Helma said. "Do you know how?"

"Did he ever spar with TNT?" Beatrice asked.

Helma frowned, trying to remember. "He might have. In fact, I think I overheard them talking about it when TNT first moved in."

"A lot of men got together to box for a while. Like a club. I think they even had a name. The Kings or something. Like a gang of boys."

"The Knights?" Helma asked.

"Maybe. I don't remember. TNT and I split up a long time ago."

"Did Lewis spar with TNT?" Helma asked.

"Sure he did."

"Everyone tells me Lewis was in good shape," Helma

said, turning toward Beatrice. "Did he exercise? Perhaps jog?"

"He had bad knees," Beatrice told her. "He walked more than he ran."

"Around here?"

"I guess so. He exercised early in the morning, before I and half the world even opened our eyes."

Joseph and Syndi stepped around the corner of Mary Lynn's house. Syndi was carrying Dickens and the other two cats followed head to tail behind her. "What could Lewis have had that someone else wanted?" she asked Beatrice.

"Not much that I know of," Beatrice said. "He didn't collect valuable pieces of art or antiques. Mary Lynn talked him into buying the house. Books, he loved to garden. And of course he had Mary Lynn."

Helma rose from the bench. "Did Lewis know how you felt about him?"

Beatrice looked away, back toward the line of firs at the rear of the property. "He did. He was kind."

Carter Houston was parked in nearly the same spot as last time Helma had driven out to visit the Dixon home: at the end of the lane she now thought of as the oyster farm road. He sat in the driver's seat, his head leaning against the window, asleep.

Helma pulled her car in front of Carter's and stopped. "What are we doing?" Joseph asked.

"I'd like to talk to the policeman sitting in the car behind us."

"We met him yesterday with Corky," Syndi said, craning to look through the rear window. "He's kind of fussy."

"Good, then you know him," Helma said as she got out of the car.

"What did she mean by that?" she heard Joseph ask Syndi.

Carter was awake and rapidly smoothing his hands over his hair when Helma walked up to his window. "Hello, Carter. Wayne said I should trust you."

Carter squared his shoulders and straightened in his seat, as much as he could while sitting down. "That's right," he said stiffly, but a flash of pride crossed his face.

"Good. Then will you watch his children while I take a little walk?"

"What?" Carter sputtered indignantly. "Watch his children? What do you mean?"

Helma pointed to the oyster farm road behind his car. "I need to walk down that track a little way. Would you mind sitting in my car with Syndi and Joseph while I do it?" Carter opened and closed his mouth. "Or," Helma said, "they could sit in your car with you." She glanced at the bag on his passenger seat. "You have enough snacks to feed them and you both. You know how hungry teenagers get."

"Why are you taking a walk out here?" he asked.

"Carter," she admonished, and he blushed.

"All right, all right," he said, opening his door and heaving himself out.

Helma reached back into his car and pulled out a bag of pretzels. "Here, share these."

Helma hurried along the old track. Golden weeds brushed against her pants and even a rare grasshopper whirred out of her way. The track was partially over- grown, probably used now by partying teenagers. But there was a beaten path through the growth, wide enough and worn enough to indicate someone often walked here. She tried to imagine the scene when there'd been an oys- ter farm at the end of the road, reaching out into the wa- ter. She didn't look back until she reached the first clump of madronas. The land had dipped slightly and the track had curved; neither her car nor Carter's were visible any longer.

Helma slowed her pace, and in fact began moving

stealthily along the edge of the track, peering through the trees toward the Dixons' property. At first she saw nothing, only a rise of land and wild shrubbery. She scratched her arms on wild blackberry bushes when she stepped into the underbrush to get a better view. "Oh, Faulkner," she said as she pulled a thorn from her sweater and returned to the more navigable track.

Fifty feet farther up, saplings grew in the middle of the road, but both tire tracks were clear depressions in the ground, the track on the left more worn. Here, the view began to open up, and she found herself looking at the house that must be the Haydens'. The track had curved more than she realized. She could see the blue striped umbrella of a patio set on a deck and the cedar siding of a large multilevel house. So her position approximated the spot where the caretaker had reported seeing a prowler in a blue jacket. The prowler hadn't been studying the Haydens' house but was on his way to the Dixons'. Why? Lewis was already dead.

It wasn't long before Helma spotted the roof of the Dixons' house through the trees. A little farther and the track rose, giving her an excellent view of Lewis Dixon's garden. Beatrice still sat on the bench, her head bent. There was a dark shape on her lap that Helma guessed was Dickens the cat.

She surveyed the scene for several minutes, noting how easy it would be to slip through the bushes and into the garden and away again without being spotted. Then she began to search among the weeds and beneath the bushes, for what she wasn't sure. Maybe a twig twisted while the killer waited for his opportunity, or a dropped valuable. Had the prowler returned because he'd accidentally dropped something that would identify him?

Helma hunkered down, studying the forest floor, scanning for disturbance, pretending she was examining the haphazardness of Mother Nature as if it were her own apartment. Anything that didn't match the disorder of rotting vegetation and autumn colors. Rain had fallen since Lewis Dixon's death so she didn't expect to find tracks or crushed vegetation.

By her watch, she'd left Carter ten minutes ago. Still she kept on looking, slowly moving back and forth across the track, checking once in a while to be sure the garden was still visible, that she hadn't gone too far astray. A beer bottle caught her attention but it was too old, then a piece of metal, but it too had lain on the ground for a season or more. And once, she parted the matted grasses over a bulge and found a tumble of stones, some still cemented together, an old foundation.

Two knights. As she searched, she thought of boxing and sparring and what Wayne Gallant might have meant. Had there been *two* men involved in Lewis's murder and the attempt on Wayne's life? Two men from the Knights boxing club? The White Knight had vanquished the Red Knight, she remembered. But then, Beatrice hadn't been sure of the name of the group of men who sparred with TNT; the word "knights" might have nothing to do with boxing.

That's when she saw it. Caught on the broken branch of a low shrub when it had been dropped. A rag, the kind that might be used to check car oil. It was wet from the rain and dragged the branch downward. The rag was also black with smears of grease. Helma broke off a second branch and carefully used it to lift the rag from the shrub.

She stood upright with the rag successfully snagged on the branch, and less than ten feet away Skip Riems stepped calmly from behind a tree. She gasped but didn't move, didn't drop the rag. "That bicycle chain gave you a lot of trouble, didn't it?" she asked him.

"I don't know what you're talking about," he said. He wore biking clothes: dark brown that blended with the forest. If he were to run into the brush and trees, he'd be invisible in seconds. His hair was damp, as if he might have been wearing a helmet, but Helma didn't see any sign of his bicycle.

"I thought it was curious that you didn't have a cloth with you to wipe the grease off your hands when you came to the Bayside Arms looking for Mary Lynn. Even when I was a child, our chains were a problem. I carried a rag to clean up the grease when the chain came off. Otherwise, it made a mess."

"What did you ride," Skip asked with a taunt in his voice, "a single-speed?" He stood casually but as if he were prepared for movement, his arms at his sides, his stance light.

"Actually, I did. I inherited my older brother's bicycle."

Skip raised a hand toward the rag, and Helma pulled the stick out of his reach. "I don't think so," she said. "The police might consider it evidence."

"Of what? That I ride my bicycle on trails all over the county?"

"That you were here before, perhaps on Sunday morning when Lewis died, and again later in the day. Were you looking for this rag?"

"You can't prove that from a greasy rag." He was watchful but not overly concerned by Helma's accusations.

"Or a book? *Behind the Looking Glass?*"

"You already know I wasn't the person who checked out that book."

"But the person who *did* would connect it to you in a second. Do you still belong to the Knights?" she asked.

He laughed and swiped again at the rag, but Helma was too quick. "Don't try to trick me into answering any questions," he told her, dropping his hand. "I've heard about your fantasies, that you consider yourself a Miss Marble or somebody. You're a cop groupie, that's all."

"If you mean Miss Marple," Helma said, "she was a fictional creation of Agatha Christie's, a mistress of deductive reasoning; thank you, but I'm certainly not of her caliber. But if you're impervious to trickery, can you simply tell me what you're doing here?"

"Maybe the same thing you are," he said.

"Which is?" In the distance Helma heard a truck shifting gears. It was close, maybe on the same road where her car was parked in front of Carter's, but it felt miles away from where she now stood.

"Looking."

"That's not a very satisfactory answer." Helma watched as Skip casually rubbed his arm. He was too casual. To be that relaxed, he either didn't believe her to be a threat or he considered himself capable of negating any threat she posed. She didn't see a weapon, unless it was hidden behind his back, tucked into his cycling pants. A weapon might possibly be hidden nearby, with his helmet and bicycle. No, if he had a weapon it was closer, within easy reach.

"You sound like an elementary school teacher," he laughed shortly, "or a librarian."

"Either is a profession I'd be proud to belong to," Helma told him. "*You* sound like a disgruntled man who's wasted an education and never been able to hold gainful employment," she took a breath, "or hold onto a girlfriend." This was the kind of taunting that Syndi and Joseph engaged in, exactly the behavior she discouraged; there *was* a certain childish satisfaction to it.

His face reddened but then he relaxed and smiled at Helma. "Think you'll anger me into spilling the whole story to you?"

"Why should you? I already know it. You killed Lewis because you're in love with Mary Lynn. He wasn't attacked in his garden as everyone believes, but on this road, during his morning walk. He died in his garden, struggling to reach home before the insulin took effect."

"Do you know how crazy that is?" Skip asked, still casual.

"Do *you* know there's a policeman waiting at the end of this lane?"

She could tell from his face that he hadn't considered that possibility, that he couldn't see the road from this position and hadn't walked far enough up the lane to spot Carter. She swallowed, remembering that Syndi and Joseph were also waiting at the end of the lane.

"You've been watching me, trying to deter me with silly tricks," she said. "A shard of glass in my mat, slashed tires, afraid that I'd connect the pieces and inform the police. You followed me here."

"On a bicycle?" Skip laughed. "Get real."

Helma shook her head. "No, it makes sense. It takes fifteen minutes to drive here because the route is so circuitous. On a bicycle, by taking shortcuts and trails, you could probably be here in five minutes, ahead of me."

"But how did you know I'd walk down this lane?" She watched Skip's eyes and didn't see a flicker of acknowledgment. "You knew I was getting close to the answer and you managed to creep near enough to the garden to hear my conversation with Beatrice, didn't you? You heard me ask about Lewis's exercise habits. You were lucky."

"And you're not," was his cool comment.

"Wayne Gallant drove up here looking for a prowler and found you. He could have identified you as Lewis's killer so that's why you tried to kill him, too. Where did you get the idea to use insulin? From Mary Lynn's cat? Coroners look for signs of it during autopsies now, did you know that? Insulin as a murder weapon is passé, I'm told."

"Not if it works."

"It didn't. You loved Mary Lynn. And now you've lost her forever."

"I haven't lost anything." He moved a foot closer to Helma, and she retreated a step.

"You will when the police find out," she said.

"They won't. And there's no policeman at the end of the lane, either; why should there be? There are only two kids back there, Wayne Gallant's kids."

Cold raced through Helma's body. "You—" she began.

As if on cue, Helma heard her name called. "Helma? It's me. Those stupid guys sent me to look for you 'cause I'm a girl. Are you okay?"

Skip put his hand behind him and Helma screamed, "Run, Syndi! Get Carter! Run as fast as you can."

She didn't know if Syndi heard her, but Skip had pulled a small pistol from behind his back and was aiming it in the direction of Syndi's voice. He took a step forward, and with all her might Helma rammed against his side, flailing her arms at Skip and feeling his flesh beneath her fists, unable to recall a single thing she'd learned in self-defense class about remaining cool and calculating.

"Run," she called one more time before she saw, in slow motion, the butt of the pistol descending toward her face.

Helma stumbled; she put out her hands to stop herself but she crumpled to the ground as if she had no will. Curiously, she felt no pain, although she felt moist warmth on her face, trickling down her cheek. Skip paused and then stepped across her, his gun raised in the direction Syndi had taken.

"No," Helma cried, and with all her might she raised her arm; it felt without muscle, there was no strength to her hand, but she was able to reach high enough to bump Skip's leg, to trip him and send him sprawling to the ground.

But only an instant later he was on his feet again, the gun still in his hand. Helma watched as if the scene were playing out in a dream. Skip stopped, alert, surprise and rage on his face.

"Drop the gun," a voice shouted. The voice had menace and resolve; she couldn't believe it belonged to

Carter Houston, but that was who stepped into view, his gun held in front of him, his mild and fussy manner transformed into the cold demeanor of a lawman fully prepared to shoot if his orders weren't obeyed.

Skip fired his gun and almost simultaneously Carter fired his. The shots were deafening at such close range. Skip fell backward, the gun falling from his hand. The last thing Helma saw before she slipped into unconsciousness was Syndi and Joseph running toward her from behind Carter, disobeying his orders of "Get back."

Helma awoke with her head on Syndi's lap. She was still on the track, stretched out on the damp grass, a red handkerchief pressed to her face. Except the handkerchief wasn't actually of red cloth; it was covered with blood. Helma tried to raise her head and immediately gasped at the intense dizziness.

"You're not supposed to move," Syndi told her. "Carter said so. Not until the ambulance gets here."

"I don't need an ambulance."

"That other guy does. Carter shot him."

"What?" Helma did sit up then, despite seeing black and purple blotches in front of her eyes. "Where is he?"

Syndi pointed behind Helma. There was no terror in her voice, only interest and maybe—definitely—excitement. "Over there. More policemen are coming, too."

Skip sat leaning against a tree, his face pale and his eyes closed. Blood seeped from his thigh, spread across his cycling pants and stained the grass around him. Carter stood above him, holding his gun unwaveringly on him and talking on his cell phone. Joseph stood to the side, glancing from Skip to Carter, his eyes wide. "Wow," Helma heard him say.

"Are you all right?" Helma asked Syndi, and winced, feeling the pain in her right cheek. She gingerly touched her face and felt the lump over her cheekbone. Her right eye already wouldn't open all the way.

"Yeah." Syndi sat on the ground beside Helma, taking off her shoe. She pulled off her sock and handed it to Helma, taking away the bloody handkerchief. "Here, you're going to get blood all over yourself." When Helma had pressed the sock against the cut, Syndi told her, "I did just what you told me to. I ran back for Carter." She shrugged. "I might have been screaming my head off."

"Like a banshee," Joseph added.

"Carter heard you," Syndi said, "and he was already running down the track toward us. I ran right past him so I missed what happened next."

"I didn't," Joseph said, stepping away from Skip and Carter. "I was right behind Carter."

"He told you to stay in the car," Syndi said.

"I certainly did," Carter said fussily over his shoulder, not moving the gun from Skip. "Your father—"

"I'll tell him I disobeyed," Joseph offered. "He'll believe me." He turned back to Helma, his face turning bleak. "Skip whacked you really hard in the face with his gun and you went down. I thought he killed you. Then Skip shot at Carter and missed. Carter shot him . . ." Joseph held up his index finger. ". . . once. I took care of you until Syndi came back."

"Thank you, thanks to both of you," Helma told them.

"That's Carter's handkerchief," Syndi whispered. "It's ruined now, isn't it?"

"I'll buy you a new one, Carter. Thank you."

Carter didn't turn around. "You shouldn't have tricked me like that, Helma. This could have ended a lot worse."

"I know that," Helma said, suddenly dizzy and laying her head on Syndi's lap again. In the distance she heard the welcome approach of sirens.

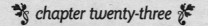

chapter twenty-three

NEARLY THERE

Two weeks later

"I'm still uncertain why I said 'Two Knights,' " Wayne Gallant told Helma.

He sat on the sofa in Helma's apartment, his cane on the floor, one arm in a cast and sling, one leg in a walking cast held straight out in front of him and resting on a footstool. He'd ridden the elevator up to the third floor. Helma had been about to take the staircase and meet the elevator at the top, when he asked, "Ride with me, would you?"

And without a moment's hesitation, she had.

They'd eaten a light meal of salad and broiled chicken and now sat in Helma's living room drinking wine. Her drapes were open onto the bay even though it was dark and there was no view. A persistent dull rain pounded on the roof of the Bayside Arms, and inside, she'd turned off a Bach CD in favor of listening to the weather. On the dining room table two candles burned down in silver holders in the midst of the remains of dinner. Dishes still sat on the table. Boy Cat Zukas lay curled in his basket, occasionally opening his golden eyes to cast bored glances at Helma and Wayne.

"It makes sense that's what you said," Helma told him.

He laughed. "No, *you're* the one who made sense out of it. I still don't remember the fall. It's a blank."

"I believe that when you saw the book, *Behind the Looking Glass*, your unconscious mind parlayed your confrontation with Skip into one of your favorite segments of the book: the battle of the Red Knight and the White Knight."

"Maybe," Wayne said, "but you translated my mumbling into a full-blown theory."

"There *was* a Knights Fight Club and you *did* spar with Skip and Lewis and TNT," Helma reminded him.

He smiled at her. "I definitely can't claim I was referring to *that*, not even unconsciously. If Skip hadn't panicked, if he'd come up with a legitimate-sounding excuse as to why he was on that old trail, he might have gotten away with it. I would have believed it was a coincidence. But when he tried to escape . . . I knew."

"He was looking for the book on the oyster farm road, wasn't he?" Helma asked.

Wayne frowned and took a sip of wine. "I almost recall him holding a book in his hand."

"He must have been reading it Sunday morning while he was waiting for Lewis to appear." She shuddered. "So cold-blooded."

Wayne nodded. "How's Mary Lynn?"

"Better. It was a terrible blow on top of her husband's death to learn that Skip was the killer; she'd thought he was her friend. TNT is letting her stay in his apartment for the present but I think she disrupts his lifestyle."

"Kids do that to you," Wayne said. "And then when they leave, it's like a hole in your heart."

"One more week," Helma said. "I'll miss them, too. They're interesting young people."

He grinned the grin that lifted only one side of his mouth. *"Interesting?"*

Helma nodded. "If I'd known children were that interesting, I'd—" Helma stopped, wondering what in the world she'd been about to say.

"You'd what?" he teased. "You're blushing."

"Nothing."

"Can I ask you something?"

"Of course," she agreed warily.

"Skip swears he didn't check out *Behind the Looking Glass*. Who did?"

"I'd never betray the privacy of a library patron," Helma told him. "Not under any circumstances."

Wayne sighed. "That's why you're a heroine in the library world, I guess."

The wire services had picked up the article in the *Bellehaven Daily News*, and word had leaked out that Helma was the librarian who, under pressure, refused to give up a borrower's name. Librarians across the country had rushed forward to offer support; she'd received a commendation from the Librarians for Freedom Association, and *Library Journal* was sending a photographer next week to take her picture. Ms. Moon had been forced to bow with the circumstances and had even written a laudatory statement about how Helma "personified the virtues of the profession."

"That's healing nicely," Wayne said, setting down his glass and touching Helma's cheek with his left hand. She was always amazed by the size of his hands. Ruth claimed she could tell what was most important about a man from the size of his hands, but had never explained her theory.

"Dr. McGowan said he can smooth out the scars from the stitches, but I don't feel they're unattractive. I may keep them."

"Good. You earned them. Any word from Ruth?"

Ruth had climbed the steps of the shuttle plane to Sea-Tac, dressed in khaki, her face pale beneath her makeup. "I'm scared to death," she'd confessed to Helma. "I'd rather face a cadre of art critics."

"One postcard. She sounded happy but no word yet when she's returning."

Wayne reached for his glass of wine on the coffee

table, but because of his injuries he grazed the glass with his hand and knocked it over. Wine spilled across the magazines and puddled on the table.

Both Wayne and Helma lunged for the glass, bumping shoulders, and Helma's own glass flew out of her hands onto the carpeted floor. Wayne gasped in pain and began to topple, his leg twisting off the footstool. Boy Cat Zukas hissed in his basket. Helma reached for Wayne, trying to prop him up without hurting his shoulder worse, but he was too heavy and he fell across her, pushing her flat on the sofa. They lay there nose-to-nose.

"I think I need a couple of burly orderlies to get me up," he said, and laughed.

As big a man as Wayne Gallant was, Helma was surprised how perfectly comfortable she was with his weight on top of her. "Or a hoist," she said, and in a second they were both laughing, but neither moved.

His laughter ended first. He smiled at her, and Helma felt Chief of Police Wayne Gallant's lips lightly touch her scarred cheek and then brush across her chin to her throat and back up to her lips. She sighed.

And now the reader must quietly leave this scene. Slip past Boy Cat Zukas who has closed his eyes and curled into a tighter ball, and through the sliding glass doors onto the balcony of apartment 3F. Despite the rain, which will end soon, it is a lovely evening, fragrant with the season's late blooming flowers and the salt of the sea.